In the Wind

Out of the Box, Book 2

Robert J. Crane

In the Wind
Out of the Box, Book 2

Robert J. Crane
Copyright © 2014 Midian Press
All Rights Reserved.

1st Edition

Author's Note: This book takes place roughly six months after the events of *Power: The Girl in the Box, Book 10* and two years prior to those of *Limitless: Out of the Box, Book*

Prologue

I remember the day my dad left for the last time.

He ruffles my hair with his wind, this power he has to control the currents of air. It blows right through my thick, wavy locks like a good wind should. It doesn't make me smile like it usually does, though, because I've got that sour look of a kid who's five and doesn't want his dad to leave.

"It's gonna be okay," he tells me, bending down to look me in the eye. The world around us is dark because it's like four in the morning, the tick of an old pendulum-powered clock the only thing that breaks the silence of the early morning. I can see his eyes in the dim light. We're in my room; his face is inches from mine. I can smell that strong scent he has, sweet and musky, something I'll forever associate with him. My hands are woven tight across my chest. He's left before, many times, to do "important work," in his words.

I don't care.

I'm five.

I want my dad.

"It's just for a few weeks," he says, and even at my young age I can hear the strain in his voice. I know I'm not making it easy on him, and there's a rough satisfaction in that. "Then I'll be back. Maybe I'll bring Sierra with me."

This drives me further into my shell. Sierra is my new stepmother, whom I've met exactly once. It was not a happy meeting. I can feel my face; there are no tears running their course down my cheeks. I say nothing, in preparation for my sullen, resentful teenage years.

"I left you my watch." He gestures vaguely to the cherrywood dresser behind him. I can barely see it in the dark. The only light source is from outside my room, somewhere down the hall. "I'll be back when the little numbers on the side of the face read twenty-two, okay? Count the days for me?"

He tries to get me to look him in the eye, but fails. I'm not a quiet kid, but I'm holding it all in right now. Like a master.

"It'll be okay," he says and forces a hug. I go limp in his arms, refusing to wrap mine around him. All I can feel is that hot, blistering resentment, my emotions boiling over in ways I lack the vocabulary to express. I pretend I'm asleep, a lump in the bed that he has to hold up with all his strength. "I love you," he says, and he gently lowers my boned-fish carcass back to the sheets, which are hot and scratchy and uncomfortable.

He ruffles my hair with his power one last time, playfully, but I close my eyes and continue to pretend I'm asleep. It's a fiction, and we both know it. "See you later, kiddo," he says as he stands.

I feel the bed move as he does, the seismic shift of my world rocking as he removes his weight from the mattress. I lie as still as I can, eyes squeezed tight. I see his silhouette blurred through my squint as he pauses at the door. "I'm proud of you, Reed," he says, and I shut my eyes tight, blotting out the last hint of light. "You're growing up so fast." I know even at this age that I'm not acting like it right now, but he doesn't push it and I don't say a word.

When I open my eyes again five minutes, five hours, five years later, he's already gone. I hear faint voices in the distance, and then the shutting of a door. The silence creeps into the room, the light in the hall turns off, and I'm left alone in the dark.

It's the last time I see my father alive.

1.

The wind is a tricky thing; if it blows hard enough, it can destroy. If it blows lightly, it can help sow a field, give you sweet, cool relief on a hot day, or even move a little topsoil around. However it blows, the wind is an instrument of change, a herald and an enforcer.

But as for how hard it blows?

Well, that's kind of on me.

My name is Reed Treston, in case you didn't know. I'm an Aeolus, which … well, it's … kind of hard to explain. I have the power of wind at my disposal. Okay, that wasn't so hard to explain. But it's not like I can summon a hurricane. No, that's a little much. I can do a gust, though, a good one, a solid one that can break down a wall. If it's not, y'know, concrete or something. I can blow down a hut. Knock over a person. Lift them up in the air for a little while. I'm getting pretty good at that.

Actually, it's what I'm doing right now.

I point my hands at the ground, let the power of the wind run through me, and a little tornado a couple inches across blows out of each hand, keeping me about six feet off the ground. Not gonna lie, I look a little like Tony Stark trying out his armor thrusters for the first time. Gentle sway, back and forth over the blue mats that cover the training room floor. Because that's where I am, the training room. It's the only place on campus for this sort of regimented mayhem, with its aroma of sweat and crushed dreams. Not mine, of course. That's from all the poor bastards my sister has absolutely crushed in this place. Yeah, that's a good idea, I tell the agents: take on the most powerful person in the friggin' world in a martial arts contest. It's always worth a good laugh. Except for that one time she broke that guy's arm. He was not laughing much.

I'm just hovering. Holding position. Because that's what I do, like a weight lifter holding his bench press as long as he can. Maybe this builds muscles of a different sort, I dunno. Maybe it's all a placebo, a thing that happens in my head that makes me think I'm getting stronger. I don't care. I need to be stronger. Need to be able to hover longer.

Because, dammit, my sister can fly.

And I'm a windkeeper, and I friggin' can't. It's not right.

My arms ache, all up and down, like I've been lifting weights all day. I haven't. This is all I've done, this little bit of wind-aided levitation. Sitting here, gliding above the surface of the earth for … oh, I dunno … my eyes scan over to the big clock on the wall … fifteen minutes?

Shit.

Fifteen freaking minutes?

I realize a little late I've been holding my breath and let it out. I fall to the earth in a barely controlled descent, flaring a gust of wind just before I crash down. It slows my impact, keeping me from taking it full on like I'm a ton of bricks. I'm not; I'm in reasonably good shape. But my ankle disagrees. It makes a little noise firing off the nerves in pain, telling me I'm a fat ass, and I grunt as I regain my footing.

"Nice dismount, Mary Lou Retton." There's enough sarcasm in the comment to poison a more sincere and earnest person than me. It flies over my shoulder as if fired from a slingshot, but I don't need to turn my head to know who's speaking.

Sienna Nealon. Hero of the whole damned world. Queen of the Metahuman Policing and Threat Response. Whatever—we call it the agency. Pain in my ass.

Also my little sister. Half-sister, technically.

I let out another one of those sighs. It's genuine. The clock is telling me I only lasted fifteen minutes, and I was pretty sure—while I was fighting to keep my eyes off of it—that I'd been in the air for at least sixteen years, maybe more. It's a disappointment. Not crushing, like a kick to the groin with a steel-toed boot, but it hurts the ol' ego.

Kind of like having your little sister as your boss. Maybe you don't say anything about it, but it's not really good for the self-esteem.

"If I wanted annoying commentary," I say, steadying myself after my awkward landing, "I'd put on a Gilbert Gottfried Blu-ray and turn on the track."

"Oh God," she says, "Has Gilbert Gottfried ever done a film commentary? Have we reached that cultural nadir?"

"The Kardashians," I say simply, wiping the copious beads of sweat from my forehead with the sleeve of my sweatshirt. It's a little chilly in the training room. Snow still blankets the ground outside, the gift of Minnesota to her residents. It's a special gift, too, something the rest of the U.S. isn't dealing with right now. They get spring; we get the hard, frigid shaft of winter.

Note to self: do not use the phrase "Hard, frigid shaft of winter" ever again. It has unpleasant connotations around here.

"Right," Sienna says, acknowledging my obvious point. "Clearly, it's all downhill from here. Gilbert Gottfried commentaries on everything."

I crack a smile. Working for little sis has its pluses, the big one being that she's as snarky as I am. "Did you come here solely to mock and deride me?" I ask.

She emerges into view in front of me, wearing a winter coat that's kind of … fluffy. It's cold outside, so I suppose this is forgivable, but still … fluffy. She looks soft, and if you know Sienna Nealon, "soft" is not a word that springs to mind when thinking about her. Not ever. "It's Ariadne's," she says, catching my look. "I left my winter coat at my dorm and didn't want to—never mind."

She looks flustered for a second, which does happen from time to time with her. I suspect she's got a really fast-moving internal monologue, with rip currents that could just about snap your neck. I can see it sometimes on her face, that she's holding something back. It makes me wish I could pull a Zollers because I know she's thinking something good, but whenever I ask her about it later, she begs off. "Anyway, no. I did not come merely to mock and deride you." She makes a face. "And we really shouldn't use the word 'deride you' anymore. Too phonetically close to – well, it lands us in the neighborhood of that whole step-sibling erotica thing that seems to be proliferating nowadays." Pretty sure my face explodes with an unpleasant expression on that one, because she looks tentative for a second. "It's this whole thing," she goes on, "like a genre unto itself, and it kinda makes me shudder—"

"Okay," I say, "back on point, please, before I get totally squicked out." She has a tendency to digress sometimes. Maybe it's better I don't have the power to read her internal monologue.

She gets serious. "Rocha picked up an NSA intercept this morning from a known bad guy in Rome."

I raise an eyebrow. "Known bad guy?"

"It's a technical term," she says. "It mentioned 'Alpha' in the scramble, and somehow I don't think they're talking about werewolves."

I feel myself squint at her. "What do you know about werewolves?"

"Only what those lovely, smutty books involving—" She cuts herself off, and I can see her pale cheeks redden. "You know what? Never mind. Point is, Alpha. Rome. Not

7

werewolves." Her expression softens, her cheeks return to their normal, all snowy and freckled, and her voice lowers to a hush. "Thought you'd want to know."

"Got any context for it?" I ask. I had worked for a group called Alpha pretty much my entire adult life. They were based out of Rome, at least up until they'd gotten wiped out in the war.

"Not much," she says, and pulls a folded piece of paper out of her fluffy coat. She hands it over tentatively, like she's afraid it'll blow away in the non-existent wind. Which ... I guess is kind of a hazard around me. I unfold it and start reading to find it's ... pretty much in Italian. As an email from Rome might be, I suppose. "It reads like a letter of introduction," she says helpfully, "two guys, using codenames that translate into," she scrunched her slightly pointed nose up in recall, "'Wrench' and 'Axis,' I think. Google was not super helpful on this."

"If only there was someone on campus who spoke fluent Italian," I say, giving her the sidelong look.

"I'm not asking Dr. Perugini," she says, returning my look with one of her own. "She hates me. And is possibly also crazy." *Crazy hot,* I think. "Anyway, it just sort of hints at past good times and suggests that they might find it profitable or fun to work together again on something that 'Wrench,'" she makes air quotes, "is doing. Salutations, hope to hear from you soon, end of email." She shrugs. "It's not much."

I give it a moment's thought. Sienna and I are the only ones with powers left at the agency at this point. We've been hanging out here since the war ended six months ago, watching our little team dissolve until it was just her and me. Winds of change, blowing right through, altering the landscape a day at a time. I've seen enough change by this point—for example, my entire organization getting blown away in the war—that I'm used to it. Sort of.

She's not. This has been hitting her hard, but she's buttoned up enough she'll never admit it. Even watching her boyfriend leave quietly in the night hasn't undone my sis.

But she's watching me now like I'm gonna bolt. Not with suspicion, exactly; just that little hint of fear.

Meanwhile, I'm swimming in a river of curiosity, no lie. Which makes it harder to say this. "You think you can spare me for a few days?" I ask.

It's barely visible, this little flinch she does. "Sure." Like it's no big deal. But it is. She's not being passive aggressive or anything, so this won't bite me in the ass later, but I can tell she's feeling the losses.

"I want to check it out," I say, honestly, "maybe get to the bottom of this. Could be there's some survivors from Alpha, kept their heads down during the war." *During the extermination of our people,* I don't say. She still feels the guilt on that one, too, even though there's nothing she could have done differently.

"Sure," she says. "I wouldn't have brought it to you if I thought it was nothing." She laughs nervously. "Or if I couldn't make do without you for a few days here." But there's a seriousness behind her eyes when the laugh fades. It says, *Don't leave.* Or at least, *Don't be gone long.*

I wipe my sweaty forehead on my sleeve again, a fresh round of droplets coursing their way down. Damn, that fifteen minutes was terrible. "You sure you can make do without me?" I ask, giving her one last chance to dodge loneliness. She's not so good at dealing. Repression, thy name is Sienna.

"It may surprise you to know this," she says with some bravado, "but I survived for quite a few years before you showed up at my door, bro." She calls me bro all the time. Like it's ironic. She's kind of a hipster, I think, making obscure references and wearing kind of dowdy clothes. I would never tell her this, though, because I want to live. She gets serious again. "This isn't much to go on, though. Like …

little bitty pieces, scattered to the four winds. Sure you want to try and pick them up?"

I gently blow a gust of air out of my index finger as I point it at her like a gun, and it whips her hair for just a second, stirring it—and a smile. "I have some small experience with that," I say. And I give her a smile of my own on my way to go pack, surprisingly eager to go somewhere for the first time in months.

2.

To my complete and utter lack of surprise, there are no direct flights between Rome, Italy, and Minneapolis, Minnesota. This leaves me sitting in a Mexican cantina in the Detroit airport for about three hours on a layover. Not a big deal, really; the margaritas are fricking fantastic, the best I can recall having in recent memory, and the food is spot on, too. I hate flying, especially on long trips. Back when I had an employer with deep pockets, we did things like flying first class everywhere. Even when the agency was still secret and generated its own money—ahem—off the books (insider trading, *cough cough*) we could occasionally charter a jet. Which came in handy for things like prisoner transport.

Ever since we metas—people with powers—got outed on national television by the president, the agency has had a much tighter rein around it. We can't do squat nowadays in terms of spending money. We're dependent on the incredibly screwed-up budgetary process, which is a real let down after being able to basically do whatever the hell we wanted without oversight. It's not like we were grossly irresponsible or anything, but when you're as big as me—over six feet, with the long legs to match—bitching about sitting in coach comes as naturally as the urge to find a restroom when you've got a full bladder.

Oh, how I miss the days of money.

The pay cut hurt, too. I'm getting paid like a brand-new government worker, not a single ounce of seniority. If my room and board weren't covered, I'm pretty sure I'd be making minimum wage.

Anyway, I'm sitting in this cantina, buying my own drinks on my government credit card, when—surprise, surprise—my sister's interview with Gail Roth, that witch from the National News Channel comes up on a soundbite while they're interviewing a congressman about the 'meta problem.' That's what they call it when they're being sensitive. It was not a good interview. Sienna, as hard as she tried—and there's some doubt in my mind that she tried very hard, honestly—came off kind of … snide. Snarky. Sarcastic.

So, basically, like herself.

Anyway, that did not go over well in the media, where it was felt that she was perhaps being a little obnoxious to Gail Roth, a well-established, well-liked mama badger and proxy for every reporter out there. The news panel shows turned pretty ugly for the next few days, and the Department of Homeland Security made some bullshit excuse and canceled every other appearance they'd had Sienna scheduled for. It looked bad, but sending her out to do more interviews probably would have been worse. A lot worse.

But oh, how they loved to trot out clips from the interview for entertainment value. They always seem to cut them just right, too, to make Sienna look even more petulant.

Thankfully, the bar's TV is on mute. I carefully avert my eyes from the scrolling black box of text running across the bottom of the screen with its frequent misspellings. I have a margarita in front of me, the remains of a quesadilla staring up from my plate, and I decide I ain't got time for this shit. I'm about two seconds from speaking up to get the bartender to change it when loud, obnoxious voices—probably cable news anchors—reach my ears.

"I'd like to show her my power," one guy down the bar says to his buddy next to him. They're both wearing suits, their ties loosened, a full beer mug in front of each of them. Sitting their fat, middle-aged asses on the blue bar stools, a barely sober mess in the middle of the cantina. The cantina is an explosion of color. These two assclowns are a black hole in the middle of the place, all serious business. Except for what they're saying. It's serious bullshit.

The second guy chuckles, waiting to hear the joke. "You're not one of them, are you? You ain't got a power, do ya?"

"My power," the first guy says, and he's just barely slurring, any good judgment he has washed away in the river of beer he's taken down, "is to rock her bed all—night—long." He emphasizes each syllable of the last three words with perverted glee, and his companion is beset by a wicked case of the giggles.

A gust of wind—sudden, violent, and strangely out of nowhere—blasts the stools from beneath both of their asses and they topple to the floor. There's a clatter as other furniture is disturbed by this mysterious atmospheric phenomenon, this strange wind that blows from down the bar, originating … well, gosh, just about from my seat. How about that. Weird, huh?

Their landings are spectacular. Both are doused with beer, unprepared for the sudden meeting of their asses and the cold tile floor. I take a drink of my lovely margarita to hide my pride in making the introduction. There are protestations of surprise, bewildered confusion from both the drunks as well as the bartender and the wait staff. During the commotion I finish my margarita and order another one. I nibble on the quesadilla, even though it's gone cold, and find it surprisingly satisfying.

I stay a while longer, through a few more margaritas, but stop short of getting completely tanked. When the moment arrives, I shuffle past the drunkards, now sipping a complimentary beer, mumbling to each other about that oh-so-strange experience they had. They're buffoons at best, assholes at worst, and I feel no remorse for what I did. It feels good, in fact, albeit petty. Don't mess with my family.

I almost make it to the door, and then I send them another little gift of wind. They hit the floor sputtering, their fancy suits drenched from top to bottom in their fresh beers. I try to keep from laughing as I stagger toward my gate, hoping I'll be able to sleep on the plane.

3.

Rome is quite a town. If you've never been, you should go. I will caution you about a few things, though:

1. You will see many feats of driving excellence in Rome. Many will involve the moped, which seems to be the preferred national mode of transportation. Moped drivers are exempt from the laws of all logic and reason, and drive like those Ministry of Magic cars in Harry Potter, finding gaps in traffic and slipping through even the most improbably small holes like they're greased. Okay, it's mostly because they're as crazy as cab drivers, but still. Which brings me to point two:

2. The cabbies in Rome are nuts. This is in addition to piling multiple people in a cab at the airport. It's like a commuter van, except you all have to pay a cab rate, and they drop you off in sequence. Hope you're first, not last, because it's a real shit-fest when you're stuck going an hour out of your way to drop off some German tourist who can make lame puns in English. Cabbies in Rome make New York cab drivers look like rank amateurs in the crazy-as-hell department.

3. The city is organized, but in kind of a nutty way. Not quite as narrow of alley and passage as, say, London, but

it's still a mess of building and rebuilding that goes back to ancient times and probably before.

Also, odds are good that you're going to have a hell of a time finding a decent-sized bed. Just fair warning.

I spend an hour in the cab, no shit, before I get dropped off at my hotel, which is paid for by my sister's agency and my Uncle Sam. The hotel has the words "Five Stars" in the name, but is not anywhere close to a five-star hotel otherwise, the lying bastards. I get my little narrow bed, with another lonely one just beside it, a plank of wood nailed to the wall that's maybe supposed to be a desk, and I have to be happy about it, because let's face it—I wouldn't be here on my own. Rome is also a pretty expensive city, and at twenty-five, I'm probably a little old to stay in a youth hostel. Possibly also a little too clean-shaven.

I bounce around my room long enough to unpack the basics, and then I'm out the door again. There's a café near the Piazza Navona that I'm bound for, and I hop a taxi. Once again, I see many feats of driving excellence. I get the feeling it's like a battle to the cabbies, like they're fighting a lonely war against every other car on the road. I don't know Italian well enough to tell if this lady is swearing under her breath or not, but my euros would be on yes.

She lets me out in front of a door after driving me in a long-ass circle around a block. I can't read the name of the place, and it wouldn't make much sense to me even if I could. On my earlier trips it always seemed like everyone in Rome spoke English, and I doubt everyone has forgotten the language in the last few months.

I breeze into the café, past a cooler full of panini sandwiches prepared for tourists wandering the cobbled streets with sore feet and rumbling stomachs. My stomach rumbles, too, but I'm busy. I nod at the guy behind the counter, and he nods back, even though he has no idea who I am. I get the feeling that happens a lot in this particular café.

I make my way past all the battered tables and chairs, ignoring the smells that tempt me to stop and get a sandwich of my own—one that's bursting with mushrooms catches my eye—and enter a portal in the back. Bathrooms wait to my left, and their smell is projected into the hallway in which I stand. To my right is a white door, flecks of paint falling off. It looks like it hasn't felt the touch of a fresh brush since the days when Mussolini was giving speeches.

I push at the door, let it crack open. It squeals, makes a little noise to let me know it doesn't appreciate me touching it, but swings open even so. My eyes start to adjust to the dim.

Before I can see, though, I feel something sharp against my belly, and I hold my breath. There's not so much as a threat, a warning, nothing—before I feel it poke me, hard, telling me everything I need to know about the intentions of the person standing just inside the door.

4.

This isn't the first time I've had a knife on me, but it's certainly more novel nowadays than what I'm used to, which is guns. Guns are scary. I can't dodge a bullet, can't blast it out of the way. I hold my hands up in the air, reaching for the sky like it's something I can touch. Well, maybe I sort of could touch it, being an Aeolus.

Words of Italian are breathed in the dark, and I feel the pinch of frustration. I don't speak Italian. I know, ugly American, working in Rome, doesn't speak the language. This is the sort of thing the French want to murder their tourists for. But in my defense, a) I wasn't in Rome THAT MUCH, and b) almost all the Italians I've met speak enough English to make conversation possible. They're amazing in that regard. Friendly, warm, wonderful people.

Except for this bastard holding a knife to my gut. If he were a pro, he'd hold it to my neck.

Another burst of rapid-fire Italian fills my ears, florid and completely incomprehensible. I ponder being a dick and muttering, *"No comprendo,"* but it feels too stereotypical. "I don't understand," I say instead.

There is a pause in the dark, and I hear the click of a lamp. "Reed Treston," says a deep Italian voice, with all the rolling syllables that come with it. It's an old voice, filled with years and wisdom, and hints at hundreds of thousands of cigarettes smoked.

"Giuseppe," I say in reply, nodding my head. He notices for the first time that while my hands are in the air, my palms are pointed directly at him, ready to send him into a wall with a gust of wind at the first hint of applied pressure on the knife's edge.

Giuseppe hastily throws the knife upon a nearby desk with a clatter. He's lit a desk lamp, one of those kind that bend so you can study papers up close with blinding light. I watch his face for reaction, but he doesn't give much. Tossing the knife was a good start.

Giuseppe is probably in his sixties, with dark, olive skin and a shock of white hair that crowns him. He looks like a mafioso, like something out of *The Godfather*, but his humble surroundings reveal that he's no Michael Corleone. We're standing in a storage room that he's made into his office, and the cot in the corner tells me a lot about how he's living, too.

If this were a movie, this would be the point where he claps me on the back, embracing me like a lost son or a favorite nephew, demonstrating our long, deep history. You know what I'm talking about? Where the cool main character shows he's beloved by everybody, everywhere, because he has friends in places you can't imagine?

Yeah, that doesn't happen here. Giuseppe tosses the knife; that's about the only concession he'll make on my behalf. "It has been a long time, my friend," he says. But he's just being Italian in calling me his friend, and I know it and he knows it.

"Alpha fell," I say, lowering my hands. He knows I've got power. Giuseppe's an information broker, trading in details and dealing in nuggets. I'm sure he sells other stuff, too, but I don't want to know about it. "I've been working out of town."

"The sound they made when falling did not escape even my diminishing hearing," Giuseppe says with a wave. He's being modest about the hearing part. Giuseppe could hear a dollar fluttering to the ground in the breeze. Or maybe he's being really literal, and he's going actually deaf. He settles his slightly rotund figure upon the desk. "I miss them."

I feel my eye twinge. "You miss their money."

"Which is why I am so glad to see you, *my friend*," he says, his wolfish grin widening. "Roma is the town of *amore*, but love does not come cheap."

"Still chasing the vino, women and song, huh, Giuseppe?" I take a glance at his desk; it's covered with papers sliding in every damned direction.

"As I said before, I am not hearing as well anymore, so I have had to lay off the music," Giuseppe says.

"But not the wine or the women?" I ask.

He's still smiling, but it gets deeper. "Some sacrifices are not worth the making."

"Uh huh," I say, deciding to cut to the point. "I'm here for info."

He makes a gesture with both hands that is totally Italian, that takes in the whole shabby setting around us, and it says, *Obviously*. Because no one comes back here for the ambiance.

"Friends of mine," I say, being cagey, "picked up word about a couple former operatives of Alpha that are still in town."

Giuseppe picks up a pen and a pad that's barely big enough to take a drink order on. He clicks the ballpoint down and looks like he's ready for transcription. "Do these people have a name?"

I'm blushing. "Uh … 'Wrench' and 'Axis.'" He gives me the skeptical look and I feel compelled to add to that. "Probably not the names their mothers gave them. It comes from an email."

He sets a wary eye upon me. "This thing … will take some doing."

"How much … doing?" I ask, cutting to the chase.

He shrugs, very continental, very inscrutable. "Some."

Fortunately, this I'm prepared for. "I've got a thousand euros for you to start with, possibly more depending on what you end with."

He arches a long, white eyebrow. "I would prefer no end. In fact, if we could come to an accommodation as I had with your previous employers …"

I'm definitely not authorized for that; the agency Sienna runs doesn't interface well with CIA, and I am fairly certain they run the spies in the government. If we were still in charge of ourselves, I might have been able to do something. "Start with this," I tell him, focusing on maintaining my poker face, "then we'll talk."

He brightens, just a hint. "Is there anything else?"

I blink. "What else would there be?"

He's got a smug sort of smile, a small one, very contained, very much an enticement. "I could include some other things of interest at the right price—such as other movements in Rome, and the area, of your kind …" He widens the smile, knows he's set the bait and left the hook dangling oh-so-perfectly … "Perhaps an introduction to others in the area?"

It's not my money, so I toss a few euros on the hook. "Sure. Give me what you've got."

He bows his head, his smile satisfied. "I will need a few hours." He sounds really official, and I get the sense that Giuseppe's wine and women are a very expensive habit. "Come back tonight? Say around … nine?"

I think in Italy that "nine" means more like "ten or later," but I nod. I'll still be here at nine; it's not like I have anything else to do, and I've still got my very American sense of timing. "See you then," I say and leave back the way I came, out through the café and into the sun-kissed alleyways of Rome.

5.

Anselmo

Anselmo Serafini looks out upon the valley below his hilltop villa, taking in the whole of Firenze—the Americans call it Florence, but this version of the name, so very feminine, bothers him—and he lets a small, satisfied sound escape his lips.

Everything moves according to plan. His plan. Months of effort, of putting in the time, of building the alliances.

He has a cigar in his hand, and its smoke gently wafts off the overlook. Trees surround him, the greenery a beautiful oasis in the heart of Italy. He stands and sniffs the fresh air, far removed from the hustle and bustle that chokes the streets of Firenze itself. He has a great disdain for them, these tourists. But he likes their money, likes the way it flows into the hands of local business …and how he reaches his own hands out and takes a little here—a small fee to insure that those business do not come to misfortune.

"*Capo*," he hears softly from behind him, and he turns, taking a puff from his cigar. It is a rich, heavy flavor, and it would mingle well with the drink he should have in his hand. But there is no drink, and he thinks that this is a great shame, and makes a note to summon a servant to bring him one as soon as this young man has his say.

Anselmo has known Lorenzo Benedetti for most of the young man's life. He has rugged good looks, with a hint of a scar across his nose. His hair is long, tucked back behind him in a ponytail, as many of the youth do these days. It does not bother Anselmo, though he keeps his own hair quite a bit shorter. Lorenzo's sleeves are also short, even in the slightly brisk air, and Anselmo can see the hints of tattoos peeking out from the muscled, darkened biceps. A snake head is barely visible—

"*Capo?*" Lorenzo calls again, and Anselmo is stirred out of his reverie.

"*Sì?*" Anselmo says. "What is it?" He has patience, all the patience in the world for this young man. So valuable. So precious.

So rare.

"One of our contacts in Rome," Lorenzo says. He has a tightness in his face that bespeaks his concern. Lorenzo worries too much, Anselmo thinks, he frets over the slightest things. Lorenzo is a details man—or boy, sometimes— though, and it is good to have a details man on the payroll; Anselmo knows this through long experience. Lorenzo frets so Anselmo does not have to, and this is fine. Anselmo is nearly one hundred years the senior of Lorenzo, after all, and has quite enough on his mind without the additional cares. "He has been … approached … by a long-time information broker. He has mentioned …" Lorenzo's face twists, "… my code name."

Anselmo lets out a hearty, belly laugh that he cannot help. His sense of absurdity is the only thing that keeps him from seizing Lorenzo by the cheeks—those strong, masculine cheekbones—and forcing him into a chair, pushing a drink into his hand and lighting a cigar in his mouth. The boy worries, always, and about the most absurd things. "Your *code name?*" Anselmo says, not bothering with a straight face.

Lorenzo clearly does not find this funny. He darts past Anselmo, and Anselmo watches this furtive, jerky movement with great amusement. A glass of vino or brandy could only make this better. Lorenzo speaks. "Someone has read my emails."

Anselmo smiles around the cigar, keeping it tight in his lips. "Yes, even I, in my backward ways, hear this is possible these days. Is why I try to keep our business … how do you say it? Offline?" He shrugs. "You never know when the Carabinieri are listening."

"This is serious, *Capo*," Lorenzo says. The young man is flustered, reeks of a teenager's cologne, sharp and far too sweet for Anselmo's nose. He can almost taste it, and it affects the flavor of his cigar for a moment. "No one should know this! They could know about my … dealings. For the plan." He says the last word furtively, as though there is a Carabinieri operative in the bushes listening to them at this very moment.

Anselmo stifles a laugh. Lorenzo is a young man, and his ego is that of a young man. Fragile, easily damaged. The boy puffs himself up and tries to look strong, but he does not yet have the true confidence of a true man. "So someone has been reading your emails." He humors the boy. Why not? "What do you wish to do about it?"

"I need to deal with this, *Capo*," Lorenzo says. He is asking permission, his tone is hushed and supplicatory. "I will take a few men to Rome, and dispense with this … Giuseppe."

Anselmo needs only a moment to ponder this. His plan is moving, always moving, and now clattering toward fruition like a train on the last mile to the station. Lorenzo is a part of it, a part of his future. An important part. So is his little friend in Rome. The boy is distressed, fretting. What is one more body on the pile, after all? Anselmo waves at him, imagines the gesture sending him forth like a servant. "Go deal with your problems, then. You have your *Capo's* blessing."

"Grazie, Capo," Lorenzo says, and bows his head sharply. The respect is obvious, and the young man retreats as soon as he has what he wants. He is a good boy, Anselmo thinks, still clamping his lips around his cigar and taking a puff. Young. Headstrong. Concerned about some of the wrong things. But good. A very good boy.

Anselmo dismisses the thought as soon as Lorenzo is gone. It is a detail, and not worth fretting over. He pays others to do this for him, after all. The sun is sinking lower in a deep blue sky, and Anselmo has a craving for a drink of wine. This Giuseppe, whoever he is, is fast approaching his last sundown, Anselmo thinks as he motions for a servant lurking in the shadows to come forth. Anselmo smacks his lips together as he anticipates the flavor of the wine, and any further thought of what he has just casually ordered is stricken from his mind as he turns back to matters of real interest.

6.

Reed

There's an energy in a city like Rome that you don't find in a rural campus like we have at the agency. I've tried to explain this to Sienna, but she doesn't get it. She doesn't like crowds, though. She's claustrophobic about people, if that's a thing. That's a thing, right? There's a name for it, like agoraphobia, but it's not the wide-open spaces that bother her, it's the people. We've been to cities; I've taken her to downtown Minneapolis, although it hasn't been very crowded when we've been. Uptown is worse on a Saturday night in the summer, with its slickly dressed women and hipster men. Younger, edgier, busier. Yeah, that's uptown, and she doesn't like it. I can't get her to New York City, either. She fears it.

I love it.

The streets of Rome can be crowded. It's got bustle, and I thrive in that. People walk to and fro, pass you on the street. Smoke wafts because cigarette smoking is like the national pastime here, right up there with driving mopeds like you just had your sense of fear surgically removed. Shopkeepers and random beggars come out at you, accosting the pedestrians. One of them I throw some euros at, the other I studiously avoid. You decide which is which, but my hands are empty as I walk.

I like the energy of Rome. It fills me up, makes me feel like I'm part of something bigger than myself. I get a sense of electricity in a crowd, carried along on the currents. I walk most of the way back to the hotel, and the layout of the streets is coming back to me now. It takes a while, sure, walking through old Rome. I see what they call the "Wedding Cake," which is really a World War 1 monument to someone or another. It's a white building on a hill that has a lot of tiers. I use it as my guide to find the Via Nazionale then start heading east toward the Piazza della Repubblica. It's a bit of a walk, but I manage.

My hotel is off a side street not too far from the train station. I make the jaunt in less than an hour, careful to not get run over crossing the street. It feels like a danger here. Rogue mopeds and all that.

The clock reads 4:18 when I close the door to the room, and I sigh, knowing I've got time to kill and little to kill it with. My fancy government cell phone has no internet connection in Rome, but I can make calls or text if I'm of a mind to. I'm not, though; pretty much every friend I have is … well, Sienna.

I watched the drawdown of the agency after we beat Sovereign, and it was a slow bleed to death. Janus and Kat left first, giving it a respectable few weeks before they took off. Zollers went next, quiet and serious, off to seek his fortunes—or whatever—elsewhere. I sensed that he had some skepticism about how the government would handle a telepath in its employ and decided to get lost before they figured out what they had their hands on. I couldn't blame him; I consider myself fortunate that they haven't figured out a military application for a strong breeze yet.

From a distance, I watched the dance that Sienna and Scott did, and it kind of put me off love for a while. I mean, I saw what happened between her and Zack, too, but this was different. The touch of death was apparently no longer an issue (I didn't want any details, so I never asked), but I have meta ears and I sleep one apartment away from them. Intimacy was not the problem this time. This time, it was something simpler.

Change.

I could feel it in the wind. I'm conditioned to by this point, but Sienna? She's still new to this world, really. Raised as a shutaway until seventeen, the girl's still got a lot to learn, even with everything on her shoulders. She picks it up quickly, but this whole relationship thing is complex. It's a twist. I don't think it's something you can pick up in a book. Though if they made a practical "Art of War" type guide for love, she'd probably read it.

I watched them drift. Scott got disillusioned by the war, and no matter much he protested otherwise, he couldn't see himself doing this law enforcement and policing thing forever. So first he left the agency, went to work for his dad. Making money, building a life, but still hanging around with his girlfriend whenever he could.

But Sienna and I? We work a lot.

This job doesn't come with normal hours. It comes with a mad desire to consume every waking one and the ones where you're sleeping, too, when possible. Since the news about metas came out, we've had like a bajillion reports of meta activity. Most of them are false. Guess who's in a good position to sift the true from the false? Not the FBI. Not local law enforcement. They don't deal with metas or meta crimes on anything approaching a regular basis; how would they even know?

I watched Scott get distant. Watched him get irritable about the time demands. He was working a job, a nine to five that gave him plenty of opportunity to hang with his buddies and drink beer on the weekends. Even as fast-paced as his dad's company was, it wasn't as demanding as what Sienna and I were up to. I watched it eat at him. He tried to be supportive at first, I think, but it just dragged him down a little at a time.

At some point, I guess, after three weeks in which you haven't seen your girlfriend, things get ... awkward? Annoying? Resentment builds. What's the point of being with someone if you're on a catch-as-can basis? Scott was looking for someone to share his life with. Sienna didn't have a life to share.

I sympathized. I watched it all dissolve. After Sienna's disastrous interview with Gail Roth, it was over.

I pretty much took notes on the whole thing. Looked at it as a cautionary tale: people in our position, they don't really get a chance at love in the traditional style. Spouse, kids, house in the 'burbs? Nah. For us, the demands are everything. I pour myself into my work, pour myself into training.

Sienna lapsed after Scott left, just drove herself into the job, and I've gone along for the ride.

No love.

No life.

Just work.

I can get behind that.

I guess we're alike in that regard.

I stumble around my hotel room staring at the walls. Time passes like that fossilized amber in Jurassic Park; which is to say it doesn't really move at all. It's like stasis, like liquid almost gone solid, the minutes passing like hours. I connect to wifi and dull the pain by reading websites. Trolling Reddit. I'd eat, but I'm not hungry. I'd drink, but I've got work to do later.

The hours go like death. This is the way it is between jobs, between investigations, and I hate it. Sienna hates it. This is why I stick with her, because she and I are alike. And because there's no one else on the planet who would put up with our crazy, all-work-no-play asses.

7.

Hallelujah, it turns seven o'clock as my stomach lets off its first rumble of hunger. I eat a dinner in a café on the corner, Pollo alla Romana, which tastes like chicken saltimbocca to me, but whatever. It's good. I pick at it for longer than is probably necessary, but I don't want to have time to go back to my room before my nine o'clock—oh, heavens, Giuseppe, please be okay with me showing up at nine—meeting.

I stroll down the Via Nazionale as the sun fades in the sky. The city darkens, lights pop on. Cigarette smoke still hangs in the air, but the volume turns down a little. Stores are closing, they're rolling up the sidewalks of Rome, Italy, like it's a small town. It's not tourist season, I guess, so why would they stay open late?

I mosey and meander, and I hate every minute of it. If this is stopping to smell the roses, all I'm getting is a whiff of the fertilizer. I'm bored and cranky, and the walk takes even longer because I'm dragging it out. I stop and look at architecture I'm not really interested in, and wish that I'd brought my iPad on the trip because at least if I had it, I could read through my comic collection to kill time. It's more fun than trolling Reddit, which is kind of like fishing with dynamite in a barrel.

I skirt the edge of the Piazza Navona, which is pretty quiet compared to how I've seen it in the past. I dip down the alleyway toward Giuseppe's place of business. When I used to visit him, he wasn't living in his office. No cot, less clutter. He almost looked respectable. Times are tough, though, I suppose. I don't exactly read economic forecasts, but I get the sense that although tourists probably still swarm this town in the summer, it's probably not all sunshine and roses for the Italians, either. Mostly fertilizer in their case, too, I guess.

It's easy to lose track of yourself on a city street, especially if you're distracted. As I'm walking, I'm not so distracted, though. The alleys are tight, the quarters are close, and I'm acutely aware of every moment of it. I don't love confined conditions, and I certainly don't mind crowds, but on a night like this, in an alley in Rome, you'd be hard pressed to find a crowd.

I find one anyway.

They're malingering outside Giuseppe's shop front. I say malingering because it's obvious that they're not up to any good. Oh, they're dressed casually enough. To the untrained eye, they probably look like they belong. Hell, on a summer day, when the alleys are booming and burgeoning, and people have set up those little cloths and laid out their wares so they can run from the cops in five seconds flat, these guys would maybe—just maybe—blend in.

On a near-winter night, when everything's closing early and it's almost nine o'clock? Not so much.

I become aware that a couple have fallen in behind me. They're all cautious, not giving much of anything away. It's their body language that tips me almost as much as the sudden crowd. Ten guys all bunched in an alley is suspicious. When they're all holding themselves stiff and straight, heads swiveling to look in every direction, even the most head-up-his-ass tourist is gonna notice something's afoot.

I consider glancing back to confirm what my ears are telling me—that there are two of them easing along behind me, cutting off my retreat. Giuseppe's shop is closed, no doubt, even though the storefront is very open and the lights are on. The guy who was behind the counter earlier is missing as surely as good taste from a Nickelback listener. In his place are a couple of these mooks, standing in the aisle between the tables and the counter, blocking the path. The message is clear: *move along.*

Getting into a ten-against-one fight in an alley in Rome is the kind of stupid that I pride myself on not being. I keep it casual, drifting along, pretending to ignore these guys. I can see their skepticism, every one of their studious eyeballs on me. They're thinking about it, trying to figure out who I am.

I try to make it easier on them. "Hey, how's it going?" I ask, putting casual emphasis on my English as I nod at one of the guys and keep moving. I like a good fight, but I'm not exactly a heavyweight like my sis. My mind is racing, and I'm trying to figure out if there's a way I can help Giuseppe without getting myself killed. These guys look like they could be armed, and I'm very definitely not. I'm not the hugest fan of guns (also unlike my sis), but right now I'm wishing the Italians would have let me come into the country with a gun. Instead I'm pretty well down to a pen and my powers. It's not nothing, but these guys have coats on that suggest they're concealing.

The lead one acknowledges me with a nod, and I can see him put at ease by speaking English. I'm a tourist, clearly, here in the off-season. I keep walking, threading through their little crowd like it's no big deal, I'm just wandering through. They're relaxed now, put off their guard by what they've seen of me.

Then a heavy shout of something in Italian that I don't understand cracks from somewhere in Giuseppe's storefront, and I can feel the mood change in an instant. Burly Italian men at instant attention, ramrods driven down into their slouching spines, hands fumbling in their coats as they go for their weapons.

Panic seizes me as I stand there, in the middle of a pack of enemies who are reaching for their guns, tight in a Roman alleyway, and oh shit, do I feel really damned far from the safety of home; just a lonely man in the middle of danger in a foreign land, without a friend to call my own.

8.

I see guns emerge from coats like they're drawing in slow motion, a John Woo-style vision of gunplay granted me by my meta abilities. It's not that slow, though, and I don't have a ton of time to respond, so I let my panic give me a little strength, and I twist as I thrust my arms out in both directions, forward and back.

A gust of wind tears loose from each hand, creating a short-duration wind tunnel effect. I catch four guys in the sweep, and for a moment it's a scene out of a Weather Channel wet-dream hurricane report; full-grown men are ripped from the ground and tossed in the air. I feel it down my arms, the power draining from me. It's a quick exertion, a sudden, high-weight, low-rep workout for my abilities. I throw everything into it, send those guys tumbling, and I feel my head rush as I let off the power.

I don't even have time to assess what happens to those four, though, because I've got others whose weapons have nearly cleared their holster. A quick assessment tells me that I'm very lucky; only half of the six remaining actually have guns. Whoopee.

I throw a hand behind me, pointing at a wall of the alley, and trigger a gust. It launches me forward, straight into two of my quickdraw opponents. I'm still panicking a little, the sheer weight of the numbers daunting me. I'm solo, after all, no one to watch my back, and this is not what I was expecting when I hopped the plane. I launch into the two gunmen with a shoulder check. They're grouped tight enough that I bowl them over like ten pins, hitting one in the sensitive belly so hard he goes, "OOOOF!" Another commonality shared by all mankind. Knock the wind out of us, do we not make the same noises?

I barely have time to punch the other in the face before he raises his gun to shoot me. Fortunately, my punches are somewhat harder than a normal human's, and his head rockets into the cobblestone street, knocking him stupid. I fumble for his gun, figuring this might be the moment to put all that practice sis has forced me to do, to work, and I roll, coming up ready to shoot.

But the last gunman? He's got a damned arrow sticking out of his head.

It looks a little like one of those comic props, where you wear it like a headband, but there's blood dripping down on his coat, and the angle is off, like it came in above his ear and is sticking out of his lower jaw. His eyes are registering shock, but his brain hasn't quite figured out what happened yet.

Judging from the wound, it never will.

There are still three guys in play by my count, and they're wielding clubs and blunt instruments. I want to know how an arrow came to be sticking out of that guy's head, but I want to live through the next five seconds a lot more, so I focus on the matters at hand.

I know a thing or two about fighting. When you've got strength beyond that of a normal human's, it makes a street fight kind of a trivial thing. There was a time when Sienna would have killed these clowns, probably, and without much thought. She didn't used to be that way, but she got to a point where she realized that some people are just bad. People who want to kill others are generally not easily redeemed. Those with super powers that want to kill others are usually not easy to contain, either.

But these are garden-variety human idiots, so I just beat the living hell out of them in three moves and leave them drooling blood on the cobblestones.

I'm not Sienna. I still have some mercy left in me.

I'm just about to look up to see where that arrow came from when I hear a slow, clapping sound coming from the storefront. It's really dramatic, and I get the feeling I'm about the meet the leader of this little expedition. Why are they always dramatic? Why can't there just be a low-key villain, for once, someone who's clearly read the Evil Overlord List and is just going quietly about their malicious business?

On second thought, that would probably be really bad. Scratch that.

"Reed Treston," the man says, and I realize he's wearing a frigging ski mask. It's not quite cold enough to justify this, and none of his thugs are wearing one, which gives me pause. His voice is accented, Italian, and I am suddenly sure he's the one who shouted the warning to the men in the alley that set this whole shitstorm to flying.

"Overly dramatic villain," I say, acknowledging him for what he is. I catch a flicker of confusion in the eyes as he steps into the alley to face me. A hunch occurs to me. "Or should I call you … 'Axis'?"

I make two assumptions here that could go badly wrong—one, this guy could very well not be related to my inquiries of Giuseppe at all. Two, even if he is related to them, he might not be either one of them. Also, it's fifty-fifty whether he's Axis or Wrench. Though my money would be on Axis, because Wrench is a dumb nickname, bereft of drama, and this guy plainly has the drama thing in spades.

His eyes flare, and I'm feeling pretty good about my conclusion jumping for about a second. Then he flips three throwing knives out of his pockets and they come rocketing at me in a gust of wind, and suddenly I'm not so enthused about my intelligence because I'm an idiot for provoking this guy.

I barely throw up a wind blast of defense in time. He's strong, plainly an Aeolus, like me, and the knives come driving at me hard enough to bury themselves in a telephone pole up to the handle. I turn sideways to shrink my profile, and one of them cuts a line in my jacket as it passes. I can still see the rage in his eyes and I just know he's coming back with another handful of blades when he throws a hand up to ward off something I haven't even seen.

It's an arrow. Another one. And it misses him by about a foot because he throws a gust hard and broad enough that I almost fall down. The arrow plunks into a cooler to his left, spearing its way through a bottle of water. The sound of trickling liquid fills the air as the wind dies down.

My back is against the wall of the alley and I catch his eyes again. There's enough uncertainty behind the rage that I know if he wants to make a fight of it, I'm gonna be in serious trouble. The arrow is affecting his calculations, though, and the flicker gives me enough time to regain my footing and put on my game face. It's all bluster, though, and I hope he doesn't know it.

He doesn't. He throws another broad-based gust as an arrow streaks at him, and this time it's blown off course in the other direction, shattering a glass deli display and lodging itself in a panini.

Dramatic villain guy decides to live to fight another day, and my head is spinning a little too hard to want to pursue. He dodges into the dark of Giuseppe's storefront, and I see him crash through a back door and disappear into the night.

I stand there, hand out, thinking about the threat that just ran off in front of me when I hear the sound of feet landing lightly on the cobblestones next to me. I'm about to turn and thank Oliver Queen for his help when I get a glimpse of the bow pointed straight at me, the sharp head of a hunter's arrow about six inches from my cheek, and I hold my thanks.

Murderous eyes stare at me, half-lidded, squinting, dark, fingers drawing the string of the bow back with grace and restraint, and I realize—like that old joke says—that this person who has just gotten me out of the deep shit is not even remotely my friend.

9.

It takes about a second for me to realize that past the elegant lines of the bow are equally elegant lines of a woman's face. The male brain is designed to rapidly search for two things: threats and sex partners. In her I see the potential for both, though the arrow pointed at my eye indicates which one is more likely at the moment.

"Uh, hi," I say, nearly at a loss for words.

She says something unintelligible, something presumably Italian, and for the umpteenth time that night I realize that when you're a tourist in Rome, speaking English is okay. When you're up to your hip waders in dealing with real Italian problems, failure to grasp the language is a real detriment.

"I'm sorry, I don't understand," I say, hoping that in and of itself is not grounds for her to fill me full of arrows. The one I'm staring at looks … pointy.

She twitches, the bow moving just a centimeter. Beyond the death that's aimed right at me, I can sense hesitation. I can also sense that part of her wants to do it, that she's remorselessly done this to other men before. My eyes flick past her and the thug with the arrow through his head puts the truth to my thinking. She's a killer. But she's not with them.

"Who are you?" I ask, figuring that if she's going to kill me, she's going to do it whether I ask her a question or not.

She draws back harder and I almost flinch. I keep from it, though I'm sure my poker face suffers a little. The broad head of her arrow isn't like the little training pokes that I've used when I've played with a bow. This thing is sharp, wicked, looks about a mile wide on three sides that come to a point. If it enters my eye socket, I'm brain damaged for sure, best case scenario. Meta healing powers don't make me invulnerable.

She mutters something else, something I can't understand even though I hear it. She could be asking for cold water for all I know.

Wait, no, I know that one: *agua freddo*. She doesn't say that.

I keep my hands in the air until she finally—thank the heavens—lowers the bow and releases the tension on the drawn arrow. I get the feeling she could get it back up and release before I could do much more than draw a breath, though, so I keep my hands in the air in a very clear posture of surrender. All I'm missing is a white flag.

She doesn't take her eyes off me as she circles toward the entry to Giuseppe's storefront. She delivers a sharp, lightning-fast kick to the side of the head of one of the thugs I'd knocked out with my opening gambit, and I can hear him die. She doesn't even blink, just keeps walking. She's dressed in black and tan, and has what looks like a miniature golf bag on her shoulder. It's open with a dozen or more arrow shafts sticking out. I focus on it for a second and realize that it could pretty much pass for a backpack or a purse on the street.

She leaves me in the alley as she goes into Giuseppe's store, and I debate whether to push my luck by following her. Obviously I'm thinking Giuseppe's dead, because the evil villain has fled the scene without so much as a look back and he'd be a lot less likely to do that if he'd left a trail. Curiosity killed the cat, though, and I'm not so keen on being next.

Still, I follow her, wondering exactly how stupid I am every step of the way.

There are a few groaning guys on the floor of the alley as I walk into the store. I can see a body behind the deli counter; it's the guy who I'd gotten the grudging nod from earlier. He's good and dead, neck open, and I don't feel a need to get any closer to confirm it. I tread slowly and a little loudly toward the back room, half expecting an arrow to come whizzing out at me.

I stick my hands around the corner first. "Hello?" I call out. "*Buongiorno?*" I hear silence, so I peek an eye around.

She's favoring me with a look that tells me she currently estimates my IQ is in the minus points column. I step out from behind the wall, hands still in the air as she stands before Giuseppe's desk. He's dead on the floor—big surprise—in a puddle of blood that I avoid as I step into his office. I cringe a little at the smell, which is equal parts the tang of the blood and the odor of someone soiling themselves.

This woman—this avatar of death itself—stands there, rifling through the papers on his desk. She's playing it cool, but I can see her keeping an eye on me in case I'm not actually an idiot. I feel like an idiot, though, no doubt about it. You can't stand in the middle of a murder scene at someone else's mercy with your hands in the air and feel competent and in control.

I step inside but keep my distance, treating her the way you'd treat a dog that's growling. No sudden moves, and I use an overabundance of caution. She stops as she reaches a piece of paper, and I recognize it's from the pad Giuseppe wrote on earlier when he "took my order." It looks like he's added to it, though, put some other stuff down.

Her eyes flash as she looks at me, and I see a hint of anger. She grabs the paper and slips it into a jacket pocket. As dangerous as she is, I feel like she should be wearing all black leather, but she's not. She's wearing jeans and a blouse.

I'm not someone who notices shoes, but hers are running shoes, very sensible.

"Can I ask what that says?" I keep my stance non-confrontational, sensing the current of irritation from her.

She hesitates, and I wonder why. She mumbles something, and I feel like I almost understand it.

"Sorry?" I ask.

She sighs, grudgingly, reluctantly, two thousand pounds of pressure seeping out of a metal container with a hiss. "It says … Father Emmanuel, the Vatican … you stupid American." She's got an accent, of course. She takes the paper out and tosses it on the ground between us. It misses the blood by inches and I stoop to pick it up, never taking my eyes off her. There's a long number written on it, and I suspect it's an Italian phone number.

"Who are you?" I ask again, but this time it doesn't make her angrier. Surprisingly.

"I am no one," she says, and her discomfort is palpable. She's a caged animal, submitting to my question while she plans her next move. "And you would do well to remember that." She moves to look at the desk and I catch a perfect profile—sculpted features on a tall woman. She's not super thin and not over-the-top voluptuous with the curves, either. She's athletic, and it shows, someone who's put her running shoes to good use.

"Okay, No One," I say, and this draws a sour look from her, "did you know Giuseppe?"

"Everyone knew Giuseppe," she says, her voice tinged with bitterness.

"I was going to meet him tonight," I say, giving this up as a peace offering. "He was supposed to … help me with something."

She looks at me, weighing her options. Her body is tense with the fight or flight instinct. I'm not sure if she's thinking about fighting me or someone else, fleeing from me or from the situation. I see it pass, though, and by the way she starts for the door I know the decision isn't good. "He won't be helping you now," she says, like it's the end of the conversation.

"I … see that," I say, clearly Captain Obvious-o (or however they say it in Italian). "Why were you here?"

"Because he asked me to meet you," she says simply, and I know it's because she's made the decision that she's done. She's on her way out the door, literally and figuratively. She moves her head and her dark hair whips behind her as she freezes, lit by the lights of the shop. "But I cannot help you."

"Uh, you did help me, though," I say. "The arrows through those guys' heads? That was a big help."

"I cannot help you any further," she clarifies and darts out into the shop and around the corner.

"What do you want?" I ask, trailing after her. I clear the corner and she's waiting, not quite in ambush, but in warning. She's just lurking there, in fatal distance, and I can see her whole body coiled to strike. She wouldn't need the bow to kill me, not at this range; she makes it clear to me without words, without motion, with almost nothing but her eyes. I sense old power here, metahuman power that transcends the modern age.

"I want to be left alone," she says, and I almost believe her. Her eyes flash, a vibrant green, and she turns. I'm left with the impression that I should by no means approach her from behind or do anything but speak to her retreating back.

"I'm not sure that's an option anymore," I call after her. "That guy, the one who flung the knives? If he's dramatic enough to wear a mask and do all this, he's probably enough of a villain to want revenge."

She doesn't even stop, just makes her way out through the bodies of the henchmen, the living still stirring back to wakefulness. In a ballet of death worthy of my own sister, she stomps five of them into corpses in less than three seconds. It's like something out of a video game, fast-twitch muscles deployed more quickly than my eye can keep up with the motions, unerring death strikes delivered like a pro killer. "Let him come if he wants!" she calls out, and I see her leap up, straight up the wall, and onto the rooftop from whence she came. The voice calls out in the night, "I do not fear him."

I almost believe her. Almost. But there's just a hint of doubt, and it's enough to tell me that whatever I'm up against, it's a lot bigger than me. It's enough to make this badass woman—who kills men as easily as some of us eat and drink—scared.

10.

Anselmo

Anselmo hears the phone ring as he is about to lie down for the night. His mistress is with him, her young skin so enticing, so enthralling. He is tired, he has eaten well and had much to drink, but he is still considering whether to take his liberties with her when he hears the ringing. He has left strict instructions not to be disturbed, for just this reason; at his age, the mood strikes only half as often—or less—than it used to, and he is most cognizant and jealous of this fact.

He somehow knows, instinctively, that it is Lorenzo. The boy frets, so of course he would want to communicate—even over-communicate—these worries that are on his mind. Anselmo knows, knows and is prepared to instruct the servant who will knock on his door to hold the call, to warn Lorenzo away.

But when the knock comes, it has more urgency than a simple report. It thumps quickly against the wood, and Anselmo feels himself sigh against those Egyptian cotton sheets, feels his interest wane as his annoyance rises in its place. He considers shouting his disapproval, but to what end? "Come in," he says instead, and the door opens as his mistress rustles the covers to hide her nakedness. Anselmo does not bother.

"Sir," the servant says. She is young, plump. Something Anselmo will taste at some point, perhaps, if he feels the urge. "It is Lorenzo."

"Yes, I know," Anselmo says. He rolls to give the servant girl a look. "Can it not wait?"

She avoids his gaze, turning her attention to the wall behind him. This brings a smile to Anselmo's face. "He says it cannot wait until tomorrow."

Anselmo sighs and feels his body heave to sit upright. He is still in fine condition, really, far younger looking than his years would seem to indicate. He doesn't have a belly that juts outward like so many older men, and though his chest hair is grey, not all his hair has turned, as the servant can now see. He takes the phone from her outstretched hand, staring at her face even as she tries to hide from his gaze. It is a game to him, a pleasant one. Yes, he wants to taste her now. Some afternoon perhaps, when his mistress is out shopping … "Lorenzo?"

"Capo," Lorenzo says, and it is urgent. "I ran into … a problem."

Anselmo remains unimpressed. "What sort of problem?"

"Two of our kind," Lorenzo says. "Reed Treston, formerly of Alpha. He was the one who hired Giuseppe."

Anselmo lets another sigh, failing to see the problem. "And?"

"He works for the government of the United States," Lorenzo says. "You remember his sister? She was on the news, Sienna—"

"Ahhh," Anselmo says. This is interesting. The servant girl lingers, eyes averted, making a study of the painting above his bed. "Yes, I recall her. You ran across her brother?"

"And another woman," Lorenzo says, "with a bow and arrow. It could be her, perhaps—"

Anselmo frowns at the mere mention. "A woman with a bow? And arrows?"

"*Sì, Capo,*" Lorenzo says, and he sounds like a man two steps from panic, "if she is in town with him, this brother and sister—"

"This is not your Sienna," Anselmo says, frowning. The thought of sex has left him in an instant, cold annoyance replacing what had been rising desire. "This is someone else. Someone slightly troublesome."

"But if the brother is here—"

"Does this succubus use a bow and arrow that you have heard of?" Anselmo asks. "No? It is not her. I know who this is. She is a pain in my ass, but it is not your American girl."

"But her brother is here," Lorenzo says. "He is asking questions. If you say this woman with the bow is not her, I trust your judgment. But she could still come—"

"Mmm," Anselmo says, deep in thought. "This is a vexation. You had a run-in with this Reed?"

"Yes," Lorenzo says. "I almost killed him but for the woman—"

"Remember yourself," Anselmo says, almost impatiently; to say such a thing on an open line is foolishness, and that Lorenzo would risk it is a measure of how rattled he is. "Whatever problems you are having can be dealt with." He clears his throat, thinking about it, measuring the situation. "Come back home. We need to … consult … in order to find the best way to deal with this situation you have created." He waits, and hearing no argument, knows that Lorenzo does not dare argue, that he has caught hold of himself. "We will discuss it and find something mutually agreeable."

With that, Anselmo hangs up the phone, not another word said. The meaning is clear enough, after all. He glances at the servant girl and smiles, tightly. Not tonight, he knows. Now the tension is upon him, his mind is in motion. He watches her retreat with a lack of interest and leans against the padded headboard of his bed. His mistress is already asleep, or feigning it, but he does not care.

He lies awake for three hours, staring at the far wall, and musing dark thoughts. Killing is the first resort, this he knows; now he merely needs an idea for how to make it happen without dragging the sister into it until the wheels of his plan are finished turning … and there are only a few days left until it is done …

11.

Reed

I make it back to the hotel in a haze. The walk feels like it takes forever, and not in the boring way that the journey to Giuseppe's shop did. This one's tinged with panic and other bad feelings. Every honking horn on the Via Nazionale sends me looking over my shoulder; every siren I hear makes me wonder if they're coming for me. I've got the piece of paper from Giuseppe's desk crumpled in my pocket, and I check to make sure it's still there every few minutes, as if it would simply vanish should I leave it alone for too long.

I barely notice the splendor of Rome at night. I spare a thought for the idea of tossing coins into Trevi fountain, wishing I could do this whole day over again. Except that fountain's for love or something, isn't it? I can't even remember, and I just end up thinking about Veronica Mars in a bad romance movie fishing coins out of it, as if that makes any sense at all in the circumstances.

My mind spins along at a thousand miles per second. I'm not a leader; I'm a follower. I've been in a few tight situations, I'm not ashamed to say, and I managed my way out of them through careful thinking and a cool head. That's all gone now. I just had a woman with a bow and arrow nearly click my lights out, and that's after ten thugs and a meta jumped me. My sole contact in Rome is dead, and all I have left is—

I fish the paper out of my pocket and stare at it again. There is a long string of numerals that I recognize as a phone number. Most Americans would probably think of it as a random sequence of digits, but it's all there—country code and number. I go to the hotel telephone and dial it. It honks at me like one of those store alarms when you walk through it with stolen merchandise. I try again and it still doesn't like it. I use my cell phone and get an error message.

My frustration rises, but I call the front desk. *"Pronto!"* A male voice answers, making me wonder what the hell that's about.

"Uh, hello?" I ask. Does *pronto* mean fast? Or now? Hell if I know.

"Yes, sir?" the voice at the other end of the line asks.

"I need help making a call," I say. He talks me through it. I hang up and try again, and get the honking noise again that tells me I've failed at this most basic of exercises.

The clock tells me it's now after ten at night. I've got a number for a Father Emmanuel at the Vatican, but I know nothing about him. Not who he is, nor why Giuseppe wanted me to have his number. Hell, maybe Giuseppe didn't even mean for me to have his number; maybe he was going to confession after he talked with me, to exchange his wine and women for a plethora of Hail Marys. In which case he was a little late.

I lie down on the bed without bothering to undress. I stare at the slender bed opposite and wonder what the hell I should be doing. The answer is obvious—call Sienna.

I sigh.

I take a long, hot shower in the old, scraped white tub. It looks like a remnant from World War II. I don't care. I sink down into the tub and let the hot water wash over me, trying to swallow my pride.

It doesn't go down easy.

I think this is what younger siblings probably feel like. You're always in someone else's shadow, always in competition with them. Our parents aren't even alive anymore—and our mothers were different people, in any case—but she's still my fricking sister.

My younger sister.

I come out of the bathroom and eye the phone like it's my oldest enemy. I taste bitterness in my mouth and curse this day, curse this moment, curse the fact that I even came to this damned country again. Then I pick up my phone and dial Sienna's number. It goes straight to voicemail.

I hesitate a moment then dial the agency campus. I get the switchboard operator and give her my identification number, at which point she loosens up a little. I ask for Sienna and get routed to her assistant. She's out of town, the guy tells me. I don't really like him all that much, to be honest. He tells me she'll be back in a few days; she's on assignment for some other government department. Probably a boondoggle, I know. He tells me to try her cell, and rather than shove a lot of heated words across the phone lines, I just thank him and hang up.

I fall down on the bed, my bare ass sitting on a threadbare comforter. I feel suddenly uncomfortable wondering how many people have had sex on this exact spot, so I stand up and eye the comforter. I think of those black light investigations of hotel rooms and get nauseous—

I shake that thought out of my head and get back on point.

As near as I can tell, I'm screwed.

I'm standing in the capital of Italy, and I clearly don't know what I'm doing. Little sister is out of reach, and the bad guy has killed my only lead and then run off into the night. A mystery woman has pulled some mystery shit and then vanished, and I'm left with a phone number my tiny fricking brain can't figure out how to dial.

Talk about a stranger in a strange land.

I pull the comforter down and sit directly on the sheet. Somehow this makes me feel better, thoughts of a black light aside. Besides, it's a single bed. How could anyone—never mind. Lust will find a way.

I'm reliving that memory of the villain at Guiseppe's shop shouting something to his cohorts in Italian when a little bitty seed of an idea gets planted. I reject it as stupid and go on thinking for another hour, beating myself up all the while. But that idea keeps growing until I start to think maybe—just maybe—it's a viable idea. And after another thirty minutes or so, when the clock almost reads midnight, I give up and dial the agency again, figuring I'll at least ask. I get the operator again and make my request, having her transfer me to another number entirely.

12.

I open my hotel room door the next day to find Dr. Isabella Perugini looking at me over those wide-eyed, extra-dark sunglasses of the style that seems to be popular in America at the moment. Dr. Perugini would look good in those military birth control glasses, though, so this is not exactly a bold statement. She has that long-suffering look that I've come to expect from her, the one that drives my sister batty, but she shoulders her way into the room without so much as a *"Buongiorno."*

I am okay with all this for one reason: Isabella Perugini is, without a doubt, the hottest woman on the agency campus. Bar none.

Not one of the guys has the balls to say it to her face—she's pretty scary when angry—but we all talk about her behind her back. She is the perfect storm of fury when she's mad, balancing on those heels that she wears, hiding her assets pretty poorly under that ever-present white lab coat and scrubs when she's been at work for a long day. She can't hide them that well, though, because she has what I heard one of the teens call—this was in the Directorate days, before the school got blown up —"a bangin' body."

She sits down on the comforter of the bed I didn't sleep in, apparently without concern that it would glow under a black light. She's wearing a black dress so short I'm a little worried that the comforter will impregnate her, and she crosses her legs as she leans back, as casually as though I had walked into the medical unit and announced I had a rash. Which I would not do. Because ... hello, embarrassing. Minneapolis has clinics for that sort of thing.

"So here I am," she announces, as though I might have missed her entrance.

"I really appreciate you coming," I say, both nervous and a little ill from all that's happened in the last day or so. "And so quickly. Thank you again." I feel like I'm laying it on thick, but I'm grateful both because she took a ten-hour flight to get here on short notice and also because I've maybe kinda got a massive crush on her. So gratitude seems apropos.

She waves me off. "So what is this that is going on?" she asks. Her Italian accent and off-kilter syntax are ridiculously sexy.

I explain what's happened. She nods along, looking concerned. She doesn't really smile. Like ... ever. I haven't seen it, anyway. Her dark hair is straight and totally in place, which I find interesting considering she's been on a plane as long as she has.

I get to the end of my story and she leans back, pondering. "The Vatican?" she asks.

I nod. "No idea who this Father Emmanuel is, though."

She looks thoughtful. I let the doctor ponder it while I watch her in as non-creepy a way as I can. "So we should go to the Vatican, yes?" she asks.

I freeze. I've considered this, but honestly, I was waiting on her to get here ... and possibly to do my thinking for me.

When did that happen? I used to work on my own, all the time. Sure, I'd take directives from Alpha HQ, but they left me alone with the run of most of the United States, and I was left to manage my own time. I took the initiative on things, dammit. I *was* Alpha in middle America; recruiting, keeping an eye on Omega, living the good life on the road and maybe having a one-night stand or two here and there—

Okay. Yes. Okay, that was me at one point. I was like the James Bond of metahumans, but more sensitive. And without a British accent. Now I find myself as the right hand man of my little sister, playing *CHiPs* or something with her. What was that cop show with William Shatner? *TJ Hooker?* I'm like TJ Hooker's partner. Did TJ Hooker have a partner? Whatever. I might as well be riding in the sidecar.

I blink as all this crosses through my mind, and I fear for the first time that I've become a beta male, a supporting character in a cast that's headed by my younger sibling.

How have I not noticed this? She at least had a boyfriend—two of them. Why have I been content to do nothing?

I vanquish these wussified thoughts and nod sharply. "Yeah, let's go the Vatican," I say. I'm ready to charge the gates or storm the walls or something, anything to prove my manhood in front of Dr. Perugini. I know it sounds foolish, but I don't care.

"It will be faster if we join a tour group," she says to me, and I frown. Alpha Male—that's my new nickname for myself—SHUT UP I KNOW IT'S LAME—is not a tour group joiner. She bats her eyelashes at me. Seriously, she does this. I know she's doing it. She knows I know she's doing it.

"Okay," I say.

And Alpha Male gets blown away by the winds of reason as I nod along with her plan.

13.

Alpha Male may not like to admit it, but the cab ride proves that Dr. Perugini is right. When we reach Vatican City, we pass by an insanely long line that stretches in front of massive fortress walls. A few times I consider asking her exactly who they're preparing to fend off siege from, and then I remember that this city is old enough that they actually have been besieged. Then I wonder if maybe they were besieged during World War II. I can't imagine anyone really wanting to go along with Hitler and il Douche (or however you spell Mussolini's nickname; I think I nailed it, personally).

The taxi makes several winding turns, and there's still a fricking line. It's long, like thousands of people long, and this isn't even really tourist season. I'm not Catholic or even one of the faithful, so I don't really understand the spiritual significance of this place. Historical, I sort of see, and cultural, even, given how much of Western Civ is driven by Biblical art and inspiration. But so far it just looks like a fortress, one of more than I can count in Europe. Though admittedly much bigger than the others I've seen.

We pull out in front of an entrance that looks a lot more modern than the wall it's built into, and I step out. The words MUSEI VATICANI are written on top of a stylized arch capped with statuary, and I admire the artistry for a moment. We booked the tour group at the last second, knowing we'd missed the bus and would have to meet them here. It was a case of split second timing, and the unfortunate thing about it was that it gave Dr. Perugini a chance to change into a more sensible—and less senselessness-inducing—dress. While I mourn the loss of that particular distraction—holy shit, her legs are asdfghjkl;—it allows me to focus a little better because I'm left with fewer parts of her body to surreptitiously check out.

Elvis's "Hound Dog" plays in my head, but "Hound" is replaced with "Horn." Alpha Male is having some problems, y'all. He ain't nothin' but a horn dog.

I can't help but feeling that if Giuseppe had been a little more than just a mercenary information broker, I'd be more motivated to take my eyes off the good doctor. I mean, if he'd been one of those close friends like in the movies—if we'd embraced in the bro hug like the tropes say we should—I'd totally have motivation beyond horn dog ones.

Okay, I still have motivation. But I'm suddenly acutely—and cutely—aware that I've somehow managed to get the most beautiful woman in the agency to come with me, alone, on a mission. If Scott could see me now he'd be like, *"Dude."* And I'd be like, *"Dude."* And nod my head, wide-eyed and surreptitiously, at Perugini.

I kinda miss Scott. I should have called him after he and Sienna broke up, but I didn't, because of Sienna. But he would totally get this.

When it comes to motivation, this is the thing that's on my mind. I comfort myself by thinking that if Giuseppe could see me now, he'd be pleased at the thought of me trying to impress the good doctor. Yes, let's bring this back to him somehow. That should make me feel less guilty.

We get sorted with our tour group, but it takes a while, during which Dr. Perugini stands there coolly with her oversized sunglasses, her arms folded across her chest as though the entire world can just revolve around her. It probably does.

It takes our tour guide a while to wrangle twenty middle-aged and old folks—and us, because Dr. Perugini is probably like, late thirties or so? And I'm in my twenties. It takes a while to get us all moving in the same direction. I pity this guy on days when he has a full bus. He carries an umbrella as the maypole for us to all rally to, and with long, shuffling steps our group enters a modern-looking—well, circa 1960's/70's with giant concrete supports—lobby to begin the tour.

This takes a while, too, because once we pass security everyone needs to use the bathroom. By "everyone," I mean everyone but me and Dr. Perugini. She doesn't take off the sunglasses, and I wonder if it's because she's using them as cover to look at everyone without them knowing it or if it's because she wants to look cool.

"So," I say, dipping into my great font of conversational skills. She looks at me, waiting for me to say something else, and I falter. I run through possible responses, come up with nil that doesn't make me look like an 'idiot, and shrug my shoulders.

She looks at me for a second and then turns back to watching the lobby. As soon as she's not looking, I grimace at my stupidity. Way to go, Alpha Moron.

Once I've had enough time to transition through the five stages and come to acceptance of the fact that I'm a maroon, we start moving again. We go up an escalator that runs past a spiraling ramp into a sunlit room that's covered by a geodesic dome type structure. Except it's more of a glass ceiling.

"Hm," she says, the first words she's come out with in a while. "Pretty."

"You know the geodesic dome was invented by Buckminster Fuller," I say, and suddenly wonder why the Vatican doesn't have like ten thousand Bibles within easy reach, just in case visitors decide to convert. Because right now I would take one and jam it down my piehole to keep myself from speaking. Praise Jesus, hallelujah. The word of

God jutting out of my gullet could not be any more damaging to my cred with Perugini than my last few efforts in any case.

If she has an opinion on my idiocy, I miss it while trying to dig a hole in the earth to bury myself in. It's actually less that and more a hot flush that crawls up my cheeks and blots out my memory of the following crucial seconds. Probably a defense mechanism for Alpha Male's pride. Because he needs one.

The tour guide goes on a bit, leading us out into an expansive and sprawling courtyard. There's something globe-like in the middle that brings to mind an *Assassin's Creed* game. The day is brisk but not cold. There's a wind, but it's not frigid. Minnesota and Wisconsin have acclimated me to freezing my ass off at a much lower temperature than the balance of humanity would find acceptable. I don't even have a jacket to offer Dr. Perugini, not that she'd take it at this point. Probably worried that my idiocy is contagious.

No, of course she wouldn't think that; she's a doctor. She just knows it's genetic and that she wouldn't want to have children with me.

See how my mind leaps, all wild and fancy free? This is how I end up on verbal cliffs.

We step into the building that encloses the courtyard, and I listen to the guide doing his thing. I'm on hyper alert now, eyes off Dr. Perugini, because I just know I'll look like an even bigger moron if I get caught looking at the way her posterior causes the fabric of her dress to shimmer as she walks. I think I've made enough of a fool of myself for today, so I focus. If only I could have achieved this state of Zen some twenty minutes and innumerable embarrassments ago.

Part of this increased focus is because the tour guide is talking about some interesting stuff. We pass through a sculpture gallery, and he talks about how all those white marble statues from Ancient Greece and Rome probably had colored paint on them at some point. I try to imagine them with purple, yellow and red hues on them and it breaks my fricking brain. (Arguments could be made in light of my missteps with Dr. Perugini that my brain is already broken, and I see the reason in them.)

This place is art and architecture, everywhere. I'm not even that much of a fan of this stuff, and my senses are overwhelmed. There's more statuary than in a sculptor's shop, more frescoed or painted and gilded ceilings and crown-molding-ish trim on hallways than I imagine you'd find in the most ornate palaces of Europe. I start to make a sarcastic remark about it all to Perugini, but I remember to shut up just in time, because it's the sort of thing that would probably be offensive to the majority of the population.

I wish, not for the first time, that Sienna was here. Now, though, it's just so I'd have someone I could snark freely with.

We work our way quietly through countless displays. I see a statue by Michaelangelo that's some of the finest work I can imagine. I keep my mouth shut, taking it all in. I pass security guards, every single one of whom is playing on a cell phone. I consider taking a sculpture off a stand just to see if they'll notice, but ultimately decide not to commit a criminal act with my crush standing only feet away from me.

Perugini is expressionless throughout the whole thing. She's about the coolest customer I can imagine, outside of the bow and arrow lady last night. I try to decide whether this has something to do with her medical training or if she's just an impassive person. I do not come up with an answer.

We file down a hallway into a miniature recreation of the Pantheon that sits in the heart of Rome, and I wonder at how the Vatican, symbol of Christianity, accumulated such a crazy amount of pagan art. Perugini's interest begins to show as the tour guide turns us loose to wander around the circle of the Pantheon, the Greek gods standing on pedestals before us.

"Hmm," she says as we pause before a pretty amazing statue of Ceres. I can't really see behind the sunglasses, but Perugini angles her head to read the display.

"It's Demeter," I say, wondering if she'll recognize the more commonly known Greek name.

She looks up at me. Sunlight streams in from an eye-like portal directly overhead in the dome. "Oh?" she asks and nods to the next statue in line. "And that one?"

"Apollo," I say. He carries a mighty staff—not that kind; get your mind out of the gutter—and his robes are flowing and exquisitely carved.

"You seem like an expert on this," she says, still cool. We meander to the next statue, and I admire her grace instead of looking at the carved marble. She nods at it and I glance up. I feel a little sick. "Which is this one?"

I angle my head down, looking intently at the floor, which is composed of white tiles interspersed with the occasional black one in some pattern my brain doesn't want to put together right now. "It's Hera," I say, but I can't look at the statue. It actually looks like her, too, which is why I don't want to look it in the eye. Look *her* in the eye.

I was there when Hera died. But more than that, I was there when Hera lived. She was the head of Alpha; she was my boss. She was more than that, though; she was a guide, a mentor, a voice of authority in a world where the craziness of what we were up against was enough to make me question the cause sometimes. She was my north star—my Sienna before there was Sienna. I followed her, believed in her. I kept doing what she would have wanted me to long after she was dead.

I still am. She believed in Sienna.

I believe in Sienna.

I keep walking, pausing in front of the next statue. If Perugini senses my despondency—which let's face it, she probably doesn't, because why would she be studying me intently?—she doesn't say anything. "Who is this?" she asks, testing me again, and I look up.

I don't recognize this one, at least not at first. Then I do, and probably do a double take right there in the middle of the fricking room, like I've seen something I can't believe. Which I totally have. I cannot believe what I'm seeing.

My eyes fall to the placard at the base of the statue, seeking out the knowledge I need. There's the name, that's the goddess. She even has a frigging bow in her hand, just like she did when I saw her last night.

"Diana," I whisper, and the name is full of significance to me in a way that is probably lost on Dr. Perugini. It all makes a crazy amount of sense now, and yet not a damned bit. Why would she have been there last night? Why would Giuseppe try to introduce me to her, of all people? What does she have to do with all this? And then my eyes fall on her title, and I wonder if it's a clue all by itself.

"Goddess of the Hunt."

14.

I'm blown away by this revelation for at least the next thirty minutes. Maybe even an hour. I stumble along like one of the old tourists, just thinking it through. I shouldn't be surprised that the Goddess of the frigging Hunt would survive an extermination of our species, should I? She knows hunters, so she knows how to avoid being prey, right?

She dropped off that rooftop like some character out of a superhero movie. Like a female Hawkeye. Or like that Japanese Hawkeye in the last Wolverine movie. Arrows a flyin', my ass being saved—yeah, it was hero-type stuff. And she was clearly a total badass, too.

So Giuseppe wanted to introduce me to one of "my kind," as he put it, here in Rome. So he plans an intro to a— she's gotta be like a hired killer or something with that skillset. She can't just be carrying a bow around Rome for shits and giggles, can she?

She's the Goddess of the Hunt. I suppose she can do just about whatever she damned well pleases.

But the intro goes wrong, and Giuseppe's inquiries get him killed by … someone. Someone scary enough that the huntress doesn't want to get involved. She whacks like seven-eight of their guys, but she doesn't want to get into this.

Stupidly, Alpha Male charges ahead where the Goddess of the Hunt fears to tread. Because my rallying cry is "MORONS FORWARD!" or something of that sort. Mercy.

I say none of this to Dr. Perugini, because a) she's not going to believe me, and b) none of this makes me look cool, especially the part where I'm not the Big Damn Hero doing the saving. Also, there are a lot of tourists around us and most of them speak English. Call me self-conscious, but I don't want anyone thinking I'm crazy. There is still a widely accepted cult of skepticism about the existence of metahumans, even after the Minneapolis incident.

We go through a corridor of tapestries, and one of them has a Jesus that the tour guide swears is watching. I picture someone behind the wall like in the old movies, eyeballs staring out, then dismiss that thought as utter nonsense. Then I move, and I swear the tapestry's eyes move with me. No, I am not a fan of the "Jesus is watching" tapestry. It's like he can sense my impure thoughts about Dr. Perugini and he is not pleased. Come on, man, your dad supposedly intelligently designed her. Like this wasn't predictable.

I manage to center my thinking back on the search for this priest, Father Emmanuel, just about the time we get to the Sistine Chapel. They get pretty serious about keeping out people in shorts and short skirts, and I glance at Dr. Perugini. She raises her eyebrows almost imperceptibly at me, and I suddenly realize why she changed her clothes before she came here; they wouldn't have let her in wearing what she'd had on before. I watch a couple of American northerners get culled from the pack for non-regulation clothing, and we pass on through into the Chapel.

It's about this time I realize I need to talk to Perugini about what to do regarding this priest. The problem is, you're not really supposed to talk in the Sistine Chapel. This doesn't seem to stop most people, though, and I'm kind of embarrassed for them. There's a security guard whose primary function seems to be to loudly shush people every thirty seconds or so, as the crowd within the Chapel goes from a buzz to a roar in between his invocations. I'm not a huge rule-nazi, but this is just pathetic, and it makes me despair for the species.

The guide gives us ten minutes, and Perugini sits on a bench on the far end of the main room. She leaves space for me to join her, so I do, sitting down as I stare up at the frescoes. There's a lot going on up there, some pretty impressive stuff. I note the rule that you're not supposed to take pictures, but people are disregarding that left and right as well. Jeez, people. Is nothing sacred anymore? Uhh … literally, I guess, given the location.

Perugini speaks as we're leaving the Chapel, and now I see a conversion station for those who have been moved by the frescoes to join Christianity. No Bibles on the table, though, which is totally a deal breaker since I suspect I'm not done saying stupid stuff in her presence. "What about this priest?" she asks, probably reminded of our situation by the fact that there's a black priest sitting at the conversion table. And because this is the Vatican, he is also playing on a cell phone. Seriously.

"Well, I have a number for him," I say, "but I don't know if his phone's turned off or what, because I can't get through to him."

I see her eyebrow arch, barely, under the expansive sunglasses. She holds out a hand, palm up, and it takes a second for my slow-ass brain to interpret this as her asking for the number. I hand her the slip of paper and she continues to look at me, palm still outstretched, until I hand over my phone as well. With both in hand, she looks down and dials, her sunglasses still hiding any emotion her eyes might reveal.

A sharp, surprisingly loud rendition of Pharrell's "Happy" echo through the corridor and almost makes me snatch my phone out of Dr. Perugini's hand in embarrassment. Then I realize it's not my phone that's making the sound.

It's the African priest's.

It takes a few seconds for it all to register with me—he apologizes to everyone around, profusely, embarrassed, in a low, sonorous voice with an accent that tells me he probably is from somewhere in Africa. He then puts his head down again, and I look back to Perugini.

"Went to voicemail," she says, and we both look at the priest. He's fooling with the phone, but he's plainly refused the call.

"Dial it again," I say, and pass by her to make my way—slowly—toward the table. I see her comply, and this time the air is filled with a low buzz before he rejects the call again and I feel a smile creep onto my face at the blind, beautiful luck that has finally—somehow—swept in on the winds.

15.

"Father Emmanuel?" I ask, and he blinks twice in surprise and looks up.

"Yes?" he asks, and I smile at this stroke of luck.

"My name is Reed Treston," I say, and pause. What the hell am I supposed to say next? I go for the crazy. "I got your name from a man named Giuseppe—"

I don't get any more out before a shadow falls down his features. "Not here," he says quietly. "Not now."

"Uh, okay," I say, and look around the hallway. There are tourists everywhere. "Where, then? And when?"

He looks a few degrees down from panic, even as he remains seated with the cell phone clenched in his hands. "Two hours. There's a café just down the Via della Conciliazione. A block from the Castel Sant'Angel." He mentions the name of the café and then clams up. His expression is furtive, and I wonder what a priest in the middle of the Vatican has to be nervous about.

Also, I dig his ringtone choice. I've been rocking the Pharrell ringtone for a while myself.

"Two hours," I say, nodding at him, and then head back down the hall. Dr. Perugini falls in beside me, and I can tell by her expression she overheard everything. "What do you think his deal is?" I ask, more rhetorically than anything.

"He looked like he needed a change of undergarments after you spoke to him," she observes. Her wry humor is the first hint of emotion I've caught from her.

We finish the tour, meander around St. Peter's square, but don't go into the basilica. It's a little crowded, but not too bad. I try to imagine the place on a day when the pope is doing something here, and I envision a crowd so intense that Sienna would lose her shit just from the sheer volume of people.

Perugini leads the way and we walk from the square down the big damned street, the Via della Conciliazione. We make it almost to the end before I realize that the Castel Sant'Angelo is hiding behind some trees, directly ahead. It's a fortress, a massive circular structure that towers over Rome. I saw it when we crossed the Tiber to get here, but I hadn't realized how close it was to the Vatican.

We stop in the nearest café and wait. I watch the clock for the first five minutes. Perugini says nothing, just orders a Coke Light and sits there, sipping. I squelch my fantasy about being that Coke within seconds.

"Why did you come here?" I suddenly blurt out.

She cocks her head at me, and finally she takes off her sunglasses. I've seen her eyes many a time. They're a lovely, lovely shade of brown. "Because you asked," she says. And that kind of warms me for a moment, until she goes on. "And because it's a free trip to Italy, of course." She sips the Coke. "This is a paid vacation, you know this, yes? All funded by the agency. How can I refuse a chance to go home for free?"

My brief moment of hope at "Because you asked," dies in a fire. "Okay, then," I manage to get out, hopefully without squeaking. "You deserve a vacation." She probably does, too. The last year or two haven't exactly been kind to any of us, and if I recall correctly, she ended up locked in a car trunk because of Kat at some point.

She nods in agreement—basically with herself, since I was already agreeing with her—and sips some more Coke. We sit in a companionable silence, and the minutes drag by.

I'm groping for another (probably idiotic) icebreaker when I see Father Emmanuel appear in the entry to the café.

I have never been so happy to see a holy man in my life. I would even confess right now—in private, of course—if that would save me from saying something else stupid to Dr. Perugini. His Lord may move in mysterious ways, but my mouth moves in pretty knuckleheaded ones.

"Thank you for coming," Father Emmanuel says as he takes a seat next to me, as though I'm doing him some sort of favor. I blink at this, but for once I shut I mouth and let him go on. "When I reached out to Giuseppe after receiving his name, I was concerned that no one would be able to help me."

I raise an eyebrow at Perugini. She raises one back at me. We both keep listening.

"I hate to …" Emmanuel lowers his head, and it's clear that what's on his mind is something with weight. "… I hate to … squeal? Is that the word you use? To complain outside the organization?" He looks up and I can see he's a little tortured. English is plainly not his first language, but he does a pretty good job considering that he probably also speaks Latin and whatever his native tongue is.

"That's right," I say. Now I'm just mystified. He wants to talk about internal Vatican matters? What does this have to do with me? With Giuseppe? I'm just smart enough to know that revealing my ignorance while he's pouring his soul out on the table is one sure path to shutting him up, so I stop talking. Again. If only I had similar control around Perugini, alas.

"They are simply not set up to deal with this level of treachery," Emmanuel says, shaking his head. "This level of … deceit and indecency." I stifle a completely unproductive joke about the history of the church. Even in the few moments that I've known him, Emmanuel seems like a good guy.

"Go on," I say. Helpful. Super helpful. "Maybe just getting it out there will help you work through the solutions." And vague. Alpha Male is nothing if not vague.

"I do not even know where to start," Emmanuel says, and his desperation is thick in the air.

"The beginning," Perugini says, and I realize that I don't have the market cornered on vague. She's inscrutable again, even with the sunglasses off.

"I came here from Mombasa over a year ago," Emmanuel says, and his head is still down. He won't meet my eyes, and I wonder if he's ashamed. "I needed sanctuary, and the church knew this."

"Sanctuary from what?" I ask, and then the answer comes to me before he can answer. "From the extinction. From Century wiping out metakind."

He nods, but still won't raise his head to look at us. "There are other priests and nuns, of course, that are like myself. The church knows us." He finally looks up. "There is no shame; we are all children of God, all loved. But when Sovereign began to move—" I shouldn't be surprised that a priest can knowledgeably discuss events I was intimately involved in, but somehow I am, "—they reacted differently than almost any other country. They gathered us together and protected us here in Vatican City. They isolated us from exposure to the outside world, limited access, used the intelligence they accumulated about Century's methods to keep us hidden and safe." He opens his hands and I can see the sweat glistening on his palms. "They managed to do what no other country could."

"They protected their meta population," I say in a low voice.

He nods. "But not only theirs, I found out."

This elicits a frown from me. "Did they take in others?"

He looks away and nods again. "Some. Where they could, and where they were certain that these people were not Century spies." He purses his lips. "This is where the problem lies." He folds his hands. "Where *my* problem lies."

I lean in, very serious. "So what is your problem?" I ask, now unconcerned about dispelling the image that I'm totally informed. He's in the boat; there's no reason to be coy now. (Because we're not in a koi pond, har har.)

"One of the outsiders that they gave sanctuary to," Emmanuel says, still looking down. "*He* is the problem. He is using us—the church. He's hiding now. He got in because his brother is a priest, and now we continue to shield him while he—while he—" Emmanuel makes a noise of utter frustration, something a holy man trying to avoid the sin of wrath might make, and I suspect his next confession will be interesting if he doesn't keep this to himself. "He's still using us to hide."

I narrow my eyes as I realize that this is moral outrage. It's as serious as can be for him; whatever this situation is, it offends him on a deeply personal level. "What's this guy doing?" I ask.

Emmanuel looks up, and his dark eyes flash. "It's not just what he's doing, but who he is. He is a criminal," Emmanuel says, "and I think he's still committing crimes—while using our sanctuary to keep himself hidden."

16.

Father Emmanuel doesn't give us much more than that. He's jumpy, and he leaves a few minutes later, promising that if he can find more—proof of his claims, for instance—he'll be in touch. I get the sense he's carrying a bit of a load, but I also get the sense he's not telling me everything.

Like how he figured out this guy is still active as a criminal. Did Emmanuel witness something? Or is he a telepath?

Dr. Perugini and I head back to the hotel. I spring for a cab, because her gait is showing the first signs that she might be developing a blister and I'm sensitive like that.

On the ride back to the hotel, we're pretty quiet. The windows are cracked, letting cool air drift in on the stretches where the cabbie revs the engine up to redline. Then he slams on the brakes as we come to a traffic light and audibly protests in muted Italian. I decide he must be related to the last swearing cab driver I had.

Dr. Perugini says nothing, hiding behind her sunglasses, eyes fixed straight ahead. She's lost in thought, I can tell even through the lenses, and I don't want to be the one to disturb her.

The threads of my little Italian tapestry (not the "Jesus is watching you" one, but the one I'm spinning from all the different things I'm dealing with here) are getting more and more complicated. I've got an info broker's murder. One of the old goddesses. A guy with powers like mine. A priest who's a meta and says that there's a criminal meta hiding in the Vatican. And a villain who's dropping the name of my old organization in a letter to a former colleague.

I'm gonna need some help tying these strands off, I decide, so I whip out my phone and make a call. When Dr. Perugini glances at me, I give her an apologetic look. I hate when people start fiddling with their phones or take phone calls in my presence without excusing themselves first. And from the look on her face, Perugini feels the same way.

"Helloooooo?" the voice at the other end of the phone says, pretty chipper. But then, it's like ten in the morning there.

"J.J., my man," I say, "it's Reed."

"Reed for speed!" J.J. says. "How's the crazy race going?" I know what he's trying to say with that. He and I have some geekhood in common. He might be stretching it a little with that metaphor, but J.J. is good people.

"Not bad, not bad," I say breezily. "Hey, I'm in Rome chasing some stuff down. Running into some walls here."

"And you want me to come in LIKE A WRECKING BALL?" He delivers the last bit with gusto, and I imagine the people in the cubicles around him turning their heads to stare as if they can see his weirdness through the grey plastic.

"Nailed it," I say, a little singsongy. Perugini gives me a look, and I calm down eight notches to be all serious business on the phone. "Yeah, if you can help me get a lead on some things, I'd appreciate it."

"What's the what?" he says. No, he did not misspeak. "What's the what?" is an actual sentence. It means, roughly translated from the geek, "What's up?" or "What do you need help with in this instance?" He and I speak the same language.

"Did Sienna or Rocha fill you in about these email intercepts that sent me over here?" I pause, hear a snicker, and go on. "Right. Of course not."

"You know I'm a mushroom over here, bro. In the dark, 24/7. I'm growing fungus—"

"Okay, so," I interrupt, "Rocha and the NSA picked something up referencing Alpha, my old organization. Kind of an introduction letter from a former member to someone else. They go by code names, and I met one of them last night, but with a mask on."

"Whoa, whoa, whoa," J.J. says. "Slow it down. Did NSA not give you a suspected identity on the email sender?"

"They did not," I say. "I assumed it's because they didn't have it. All I got was the tag 'Known Bad Guy.' Highly technical term, I am assured."

"Bad assumption, thinking they don't have it," he says. "It could be classified. We've run across that before. Or it could be coded as 'need to know,' and you have to ask."

I frown. I assumed when Sienna handed off the info that she'd given me everything she had. She probably did; but we're still pretty new to this whole thing where we're actively networking with other agencies, so it's possible she didn't think to dig deeper than what Rocha sent. It's also highly probable she didn't think this thing would blow up in my face the way it did, so there's that. "Can you dig?" I ask him.

"I'm already in the dark and in the dirt anyway," he says, almost chirping. "I'll get right on it, bro. Anything for you. So, hey … when are you coming back? Because the new *Captain America* movie is coming out next week in Italy, a full week earlier than we get it stateside—"

I see Perugini staring at me through those dark sunglasses, and I'm suddenly aware that she can hear every word he's saying. "Gotta go," I say and hang up before J.J. has a chance to embarrass me further. I shoot Perugini a muted smile, a tight one, and wave my phone. "J.J. He's … helpful."

She gives me barely more than an "Mmm," before nodding slightly and turning to look back out the window.

When we get to the hotel, she follows me to the elevator and we head up. I realize for the first time I don't even know where her room is, so I ask. "Down the hall from yours," she answers. "Two doors."

"Ah," I say, nodding. We get out on the same floor and I follow her awkwardly, fumbling for my key—because I actually have a key, a giant oversized one. My five-star hotel has yet to upgrade to the card key system embraced by even the cheesiest off-ramp motels in America.

She stops two doors down, cool, still hiding behind her sunglasses, and favors me with a look. "Dinner in an hour, say?" she asks, and it hits me like two by four to the back of the head—she wants me to go to dinner with her.

Then it strikes me like a bucket of cold water poured down the back of my shirt: we're here on business, and we'll be eating dinner together as colleagues. "Sure," I mumble, still managing a smile. Then I fumble open my door and shut it, clicking the lock and putting my back against it like I'm a teenager in an overly dramatic high-school movie.

I'm about to take a moment to wallow in self-pity when I realize that the air currents in the room are all wrong. There's a smell, a hint of something, and the shades are open, giving me a view of the rooftop across the way. The window is shut, though, so at least there's that. The maid service at work, I guess, getting my heart back down off the ledge.

I take a few steps in and glance in the bathroom as I pass. Everything seems to be in order, there—

Then I clear the corner and get whacked from behind, and it's not like a two by four or a bucket of cold water. It's like a train running me over and then shoving itself into my ear. I hit the floor and feel my world start to spin, darkness rising out of the floor to drown me in its choking embrace.

17.

I am hauled off the ground, still pretty out of it, but awake enough to know this is happening. I can see the room around me, dimly, and it takes a few seconds to get my bearings, to realize that this is my room with the single beds, with the downturned, pregnancy-inducing comforters. I feel sick. And not because of the comforters.

Someone has seriously whacked the shit out of me. I've had my lights turned out a few times, and it's not the gentle stuff of movies. I can feel blood trailing down the back of my skull, can barely keep my eyes open. I suspect a concussion. At least, that's the thought that rises above the others, shouting like it's delivering some astounding news. Hark! What is there, upon the horizon? A concussion, and my already scrambled brain, prone to speaking stupidity in front of the beautiful doctor, rendered still more mushy!

There's a face in front of me, and I recognize it, and I kick myself for not making the connection earlier. "Lorenzo Benedetti," I say.

"Reed," the villain says in return. I know he's the villain even without the mask he was wearing at Giuseppe's shop, because now that I'm not busy running around in circles or trying to not look like an ass in front of Perugini, I remember him from Alpha. Of course, I hadn't known he was an Aeolus then, or I might have made the connection sooner. "Do you remember Fintan O'Niall?"

I turn my head back to see a guy, and I know without a doubt that he's "Wrench." He's got the look, and—yeah, okay, I remember Fintan now. What a jackass he was. "Hard to forget a face like his." This is true. He's got a flat nose that looks like it's been broken so many times that he just gave up on ever setting it right again. He's got a grin, and it's not pretty at all. His smile is missing teeth.

I'm hanging off the ground, completely at his mercy, and it occurs to me what he is, because I faced off with him in Alpha training one time: he's a Firbolg. Gets a battle fury on that lets him fight like a drunken, ragey Irishman. Which he also is. "It's like a reunion," I say. "If only Hera or the others were with us now." I'm woozy, but I wish that much was true. Because I know they're planning to kill me and dammit, I could use some help. "So …" I barely get out, "… social call?"

"What did you tell Giuseppe?" Lorenzo asks me. He's hanging out next to the bed, a little too nervous to sit down. Which is annoying, because if he's going to kill me, I want him to at least have his pants be unwittingly soiled by some other dude's genetic material.

"Oh, well," I say, my brain not giving me much to work with in my bid to forestall my fast-approaching death, "the real question is what he told me, and who I told." I don't smile, because I'm trying to raise doubts, not piss him off until he tortures me. Though it occurs to me a second later that the two might not be mutually exclusive.

"We'll get to that," Lorenzo says, just a hair too calmly for my taste. He doesn't smile, but that's Lorenzo. Dude always had a bug up his ass about stuff. Micro-manager. He had my job, but for Italy, which kept him busy since Omega had this whole area shot through with organized crime that they got a piece of. Out the wazoo, actually, if Italy had a wazoo. I might place it around Sicily, personally.

"When did you cross the field?" I ask him, and hope I'm speaking clearly enough that he gets my meaning. "Go to the dark side?"

He scoffs with a little laugh. "I don't see much of the light side left standing."

"Maybe not here," I say, "but across the pond they're still kicking." I see him blanch just a little, a hint of something. It occurs to me that Lorenzo is not much of a leader. He's a flunky at heart, a remora looking to attach himself to someone stronger. Then it occurs to me that I've just taken a rather significant blow to the head, but not quickly enough to keep me from saying something stupid first: "You're worried about my sister showing up."

I sting his pride and hit him right in his insecurities all in one, and it's blatantly obvious to me even in my completely staggered state. His calm facade disintegrates, and now I know for a fact I'm about to be tortured. Unfortunately I'm still aware enough that this is a serious concern, because I have enough time to imagine them mangling my man-parts and making me even more useless to Dr. Perugini—like I wasn't useless enough already—before Lorenzo takes his first step forward in menace. He's furious, and I feel Fintan's arms tighten around me. He's strong enough that this would be a problem even if I wasn't trying to regain control of my muscles. He's got me in a full nelson and my arms are locked upward where they couldn't do a bit of damage—

I see motion outside the window just before the first arrow breaks the glass. Fintan panics and his grasp loosens; I hit him with an elbow and twist down so I can get a hand to point against the wall. I trigger a gust with everything I have—mostly shitting-myself levels of panic—and we both crash through the bathroom wall and land in the tub in a storm of plaster and wood splinters. I can feel the impact of his broad shoulders against studs and crossbeams, and I bet they hurt. When his neck crashes against that shitty bathtub, I feel his grip loosen enough to allow me to throw my hands down and use my powers to blast up while thumping his body against the thick tub. I see his eyes flash in anger, and I know I need to get out of his range as quickly as possible.

I throw both hands at him and trigger my powers again. The force of air slams him down again and vaults me back through the destroyed wall. I hear Lorenzo fending off arrows, glass continually tinkling as he clears the remaining shards out of the window while trying to keep Diana—I presume—from using him for target practice. He's damned strong; I wouldn't be able to do half of what he's doing, and that's really frustrating to Alpha Male. I see him look back at me with furious eyes, and then he lashes out with a full gusting burst from his hands, clearing the air in front of him, and then he lifts off the ground by directing a gust through his feet.

His feet!

I didn't even know you could do that.

It's a takeoff, and he shoots right through the window then drops to the alley below. I see Diana now. She's on the opposite rooftop, taking cool and precise aim, but she leans over the ledge to shoot at him and gets blown back. She recovers nicely, but it spoils her shot. She looks over again a moment later, and I conclude he's gone because she's right back to paying attention to me a moment later.

There's a shattering noise behind me and Fintan bursts right through the wall of my bathroom and into the hotel hallway. Not exactly five-star construction either, apparently, because the dude is gone. I hear his footsteps fading down the hall, followed by a crash as he goes out a window. I turn back to my own destroyed window to find Diana standing there, leering at me, inside my actual room now. I didn't even hear her jump.

"Fool," she says, like that's not completely obvious to all of us by now.

"Yeah," I say, "you're not exactly catching me at my best, here."

"Do you know who they are?" she asks.

"Former Alpha," I say, going right to the truth. I could have been a little cagey about it, but she's saved my life twice in two days. I figure I owe her this much.

Also, head still hurts. Owch.

"Do you know why they're here?" she asks me, still seething, like she's resentful that she had to lurk on a rooftop and save my life. Jeez, just stay home next time. This is like the lifesaving equivalent of a woman telling you, "Fine."

"Something something criminal something," I say, blinking my eyes to ward off the impending coma. That happens after a concussion, right? "I dunno. Conquering the world? That's big with the evil types, right?" She doesn't react visibly, the contempt radiating off her at least twenty degrees cooler than the outside air now flooding my room. "Weather domination? Tickets for a live taping of *The X Factor*? Throw me a bone here."

She raises a fist and I think she's about to hit me, but she stops herself at the last moment. "You are an idiot."

I'm just tired by this point, and I've just had the crap kicked out of me. "Yeah, okay." Why fight it? Oh, right, it's what Alpha Male would do. I just don't have the energy. "Why'd you come save my life, then?"

This seems to enrage her further. Her nose flares, she bares her teeth, and a bonfire starts in her eyes (not literally—feel like I should say that, though, since some metas could maybe really do that). She doesn't strike me, but I can see her knuckles whitening as she clenches her fist. She stands that way for a second, then seems to think the better of it and casually turns and jumps out to the next roof. She's gone even as I hear the sirens of the Carabinieri coming down the street.

I look at my stuff, my little lonely suitcase of crap, and I shove all my things inside in thirty seconds flat. I'm turning to leave when I see Perugini through the massive hole in my bathroom wall. She's got her little roller suitcase out as well, sunglasses on, and she's ready to move. "Check out time?" she quips, but she's not smiling.

"Something like that," I say, but my words are kind of sprawling, like I'd like to do at the moment. I want to fall down on a non-dirty bed and sleep for a while. I blink, thinking I should probably have the doctor examine me first. Heh. Examine me, Doctor.

I sigh and thread my way down the little hallway and unlock the door. I pull the bolt and then shut the door carefully behind me, then toss the overlarge room key back through the hole in the bathroom wall. "What do you bet they charge the company card for that?" I ask her as we make for the staircase.

"You are as bad as your sister," she says, and it sounds like she's scolding me. Whatever. I wasn't going to get examined in the good way anyhow. I take the lead as we get the hell out of there, and we're already halfway down the street when the first police car pulls up in front of the hotel.

18.

I'm not quite shaking as I stroll the streets of Rome with Dr. Perugini at my side, but only because I'm holding it in for her. Nobody wants to look weak and vulnerable, right? I can usually play pretty cool when I need to. I mean, I've faced death more times than I can count. But I just got overpowered in a hotel room and made it out by the very skin of my teeth. It was only good luck or stupidity that kept O'Niall and Benedetti from figuring out Perugini was with me and dragging her into this situation. After all, if they could track me down, they could probably figure out I had someone else along for the ride.

I have no idea where I'm going, but I pull my roller suitcase behind with a determined rattle as if I know what I'm doing. Perugini is calmer, cooler, her eyes still hidden behind the dark, oversized glasses that keep her emotions out of view. She says nothing, apparently content to let me lead us in a pointless path along the Via Nazionale. I want to scream, cry, and lose my shit in the nearest alleyway.

It's like the night my father said goodbye all over again, and just like last time, I manage to stave off emotion and keep it together.

I should have seen it coming. Benedetti knew me when we met at Giuseppe's shop. He called me out by name. How hard would it be to track me down after that? Stupid, Reed, stupid. Alpha male; Omega brain.

"How did he do it?" I murmur to myself. There was certainly no shortage of ways. Call every hotel in town, ask for Mr. Treston. Hack the systems, maybe? J.J. would know better than I if that was possible. Good old-fashioned bribery and investigation were also a possibility. "However they did it, they could do it again," I say under my breath.

"So no more hotels," Dr. Perugini says, and I snap around to look at her, slightly surprised. I have almost forgotten she was there.

"Well," I say, "I'm not sure I love the idea of sleeping on the streets."

"There are other places," she says.

"Such as?"

"Friends," she says simply.

I feel the burn of that one. "I think the closest thing to friends I had left in Rome just tried to kill me." Not that that's saying much. The realization hits that I don't really have any friends anywhere. Not anymore.

She makes an annoyed sound. "I was talking about *my* friends. I have many of them."

I blink at her. "Do you, now?"

"I do." She cocks her head at me in a self-assured way. "Including one that is almost certainly in Barcelona on business and would happily let us use her apartment."

"I, uh …" I stumble over my words. "Well, that would certainly be helpful." Slick recovery. Not.

"Mm," she says. Pulling a cell phone from her pocket, she begins to dial. She walks on, suitcase in hand, a picture of calm and elegance as she strolls the street. Someone answers and she starts to speak Italian so fast that I couldn't catch up at a run.

I mentally flog myself for being so fricking useless. I used to be able to handle anything that came my way. Now I'm reliant on other people and my sister and … I feel my head slump forward and I stare at the sidewalk as I go along. Where did it all go wrong? When did I get in over my head?

Not just this particular time. When did I get to the point where I became an official lackey, like Fintan O'Niall? Like Lorenzo Benedetti, if I had to guess? Because they were not the sort of guys who stepped out on their own.

Maybe I wasn't either, though. I followed Hera, then I followed my sister. Before that, I was pretty much in the care of my family. Maybe I was really a follower who had convinced himself he was a leader because I could operate at a distance. But I was still following the whole time, really. Did that make me a weak person?

I look at the doctor, who is leading the way ahead of me. That fact—and my reaction to this entire situation—certainly doesn't suggest that I'm a strong person.

How long have I just been following, content to do that, not caring that I wasn't even in charge of my own fate? Years. Years and years. I tell myself I do it for the cause, because the cause was—is—good, but I don't believe it for more than a second.

I just got saved by an old-school goddess, and now I'm being saved by Dr. Perugini. Women keep saving me. Which I'm egalitarian enough to not let bother me on a gender level. What bothers me is that somewhere along the line I've become a damsel in distress, incapable of solving my own problems.

Not good, Alpha Male. Kinda makes you Beta Male.

Perugini hangs up and tosses a look back at me. "Okay, I know where we can go."

"Thank you," I mutter, and I mean it. I'm not stupid enough to discard help offered at this point, especially because if I let Alpha Male run rampant and start swinging his cod around, it would do precisely dick to get me closer to my goal.

But it is at this point that I ask myself—for the first time, really—what is my goal?

Then it becomes clear in an instant: I have to stop Lorenzo, Fintan, and whoever is behind them from pulling off whatever they're trying to do. Why?

Because I'm the good guy. And they've proven they're not.

As far as answers go, it feels simplistic, but right. Who comes to a person's hotel to kill them for no reason? They're into something, up to something, and whatever it is, it isn't a conspiracy to increase the sales of Girl Scout cookies. Although that would be delicious.

"Okay," I say, still following Perugini, and she looks back at me curiously. "Let's go get settled, and then we need to figure some things out."

She stares back at me, her pace slowing slightly. She waits for me to say something more for a minute then speaks. "Such as?"

"I need to talk to Father Emmanuel again," I say. "He's got something more to tell. Maybe his guy is tied into this—whatever—scheme that's going on. And I need to talk to Diana again." I feel my jaw tighten. "She knows more than she's telling, too."

Her eyebrow lifts visibly over her glasses. "You seem more certain now than you were before."

I almost stop in the middle of the sidewalk. "Really?"

"*Sì,*" she says, but she keeps walking and turns her head to look straight ahead. "It looks good on you, this certainty." She moves along, same stride as she'd had moments before. Same stride she'd had as we were escaping the hotel, actually.

Me? I guess that for the next few miles, my chest is puffed out and maybe I'm strutting a little. Maybe. Just a little.

19.

Anselmo lies still, enjoying the relaxed torpor of the greatly relieved. All his stress has been bled out, all his ill feelings are now gone. He thinks he can hear faint crying from the bathroom, the sound of a girl turned to a woman, but it does not intrude on his calm. He feels a sense of great release, considers getting a cigar and a brandy, and then he hears a door slam in the distance and a commotion rises down the hall.

He sighs once more, pulling the sheet from his form. He can hear the yelling voice of Lorenzo, and the tranquility that had settled upon him rises with his blood pressure. The boy is simply too wound up. He needs a release, Anselmo thinks, something to allow the coil that is pinched up his ass to let loose.

Anselmo reaches the door just before the first hammering knock heralds Lorenzo's arrival. He pauses to allow the loud, thundering sound to conclude, and then opens it without so much as a robe on.

Lorenzo takes a step back, as well he should. Anselmo stands proudly, fully naked, and swings the door wide. "Yes?" Anselmo asks, as though the boy's interruption were of no consequence.

Lorenzo looks vaguely horrified as he gives Anselmo an almost imperceptible look up and down. "You're—" He cuts himself off before saying whatever is on his mind.

"I am what?" Anselmo almost smiles at this. He is aware of how this must look, and it brings him some small amusement, consolation for the nap he has undoubtedly lost with all this hubbub.

"Are you … well?" Lorenzo asks, keeping his eyes anchored upon Anselmo's.

"Quite well," Anselmo says with a sly smile. "You, on the other hand, my young friend, do not look nearly so well."

"The attempt on Reed Treston, it did not … go well," Lorenzo falters. "The woman with the bow and arrow, she interfered again."

Anselmo can feel his brow pucker at this news. The smell in the room is decidedly unpleasant, he realizes now that fresh air is coming in from the hallway, and it stews in his nostrils. "Was anyone injured?"

Lorenzo shakes his head. "No. Fintan and I both made it out alive, but only barely."

Anselmo presses his lips together at this, shaking his head. He is not accustomed to his orders failing to be carried out. "I have clearly sent a boy to do a man's job."

Lorenzo goes scarlet at the goad, as Anselmo knew he would. "I can do it, but I need—"

"What?" Anselmo asks, feeling an unreasonable rush of good humor, possibly driven by his recent release. "A rocket launcher? You have been thwarted twice by a woman with a bow and arrow. Apparently you are incapable of carrying out this modest task appointed you." Anselmo shrugs his shoulders. "We do what we can, but you—you are showing me very clearly what you cannot do."

"I can do it," Lorenzo protests. "I can handle him. I have proven I can handle him—"

"You have proven nothing," Anselmo says with a sigh. His afternoon is in tatters, but the fog of release is still mellowing him somewhat. "You have wasted days now upon this, and have nothing to show for it. I think it is time that I take a hand and show you how business is conducted." He rolls his shoulders around once, limbering up, shaking off the torpor. "You have exposed our colleague, Mr. O'Niall, who was to remain in secret where he was, to this boy you have yet to kill. This is unacceptable, especially with the plan so very close to fruition." Anselmo feels his face darken. "You have identified this Treston as a threat, yet have failed to kill him. Now, whether he was actually a threat or not, he has become one. I need days. Days to complete this business, to conquer and unify—" Anselmo feels the goodwill burning off, feels the rage rising. "No. We conclude this now. We take the train back to Rome, find this prick and end him."

Lorenzo's face is still slightly red. "And the woman? The archer?"

Anselmo waves at him, then turns, exposing his backside to his employee. "I have dealt with her before. Perhaps we will even kill her first. Nothing is allowed to stand in the way of what I have in mind." He ignores the sounds from the bathroom and makes his way to his closet. Lorenzo does not dare to enter, as well he should not. "I will teach you, boy, how to handle a woman who gets in your way."

He pulls a suit off the rack and begins to dress. He ignores the mess that coats his lower body, and steps into his five-thousand-euro suit. After all, the blood that currently coats his skin will be nothing compared to what he'll have upon him once done with this business.

He ponders—just for a moment—wearing his cheapest suit instead. Then he remembers what will happen in only a few days, and decides that five thousand euros to prove a point is an inconsequential amount, and he continues to dress without giving it another thought.

20.

Reed

I call Father Emmanuel about five times in a row before he picks up. Dial, listen to it ring, imagine "Happy" blaring in his chambers at the Vatican, hear it go to voicemail, and repeat. When he picks up, it's with a voice that's worn, tired, and hushed, and I feel more than a little empathy for him. "Hello?"

"Father Emmanuel," I say, pacing the wood floor of Dr. Perugini's friend's apartment. It's a sweeping sort of place, high ceilinged and sophisticated, the sort of thing they'd charge you ten billion dollars for in New York. "It's Reed Treston."

"I know who it is," Emmanuel says, still whispering. "What do you want?"

"I need a name," I say. "Of the guy who's being sheltered."

I can almost hear him shake his head over the phone. "I can't ... I mean ..."

"Fine," I say. I anticipated this. I got the sense from Emmanuel that in his previous life, squealers were not looked upon favorably. "I guess I'll just have to expose Fintan O'Niall on my own, then."

There's a predictable moment of shocked silence. "How did you know?" he asks at last.

I take it easy on him and spare him the whole truth that he'd just confirmed it for me. "I ran across him earlier today. Nasty guy. He's definitely doing some criminal stuff." Yes, I tricked a priest. At least I knew his power wasn't telepathy.

"I find no relief in this," Emmanuel says. "I would rather have been proven wrong."

"What made you suspect him to begin with?" I ask.

There's a moment of silence on the phone. "I caught him coming in one night over the wall, and his hands were red with blood."

I think about it for a beat. "Are the metas not allowed to come and go as they please?"

"No," Emmanuel answers. "Sanctuary comes with the price of secrecy. Once they leave, they are out for good."

I chew that one over for a second. "You could just tell on him."

"He has … connections," Emmanuel says wearily. "I just don't want to …" His voice trails off.

"Yeah," I say, and somehow I know what he means, even though it's a pretty vague statement. "Blowback and all that. Well, he's definitely into something outside your walls. He's teaming up with some unsavory folks."

"How unsavory?" Emmanuel asks. Now I've piqued his curiosity. "Like mafia?"

That one triggers a thought that I hadn't really considered before. "Maybe," I say. "I don't know how organized they are, but it seems like they've got a plan and a purpose to what they're doing." I kick myself for not thinking it earlier. This is the country where La Cosa Nostra came from, after all. Italy has a mafia. It has a _huge_ damned mafia. Which would probably love to have a super-powered enforcer on hand. God knows they were up to their eyebrows in meta help with Omega before that organization got snuffed. That left humans in charge of organized crime in Italy again, and Lorenzo—

That bastard.

"I'll look into it and get back to you," I say abruptly, hanging up on Emmanuel before he can say anything else. I want to crawl inside my own head—or at least the internet—and start figuring this out. It's all supposition, sure, but what the hell job connects Lorenzo to Fintan, who's hiding in the Vatican? Why is he still hiding? Who are they working for? Could it be related to organized crime?

My gaze swivels to Dr. Perugini, who is watching me from the couch, one eyebrow cocked. She's not got her sunglasses on anymore, but I'm still wondering what she's thinking. "Tell me everything you know about the mafia in Italy," I say, and pocket my phone.

Her eyebrow climbs even higher. "You might want to take a seat," she says and makes a faint gesture to the sofa across from her, "because this subject? This could take all night."

21.

She runs me through a laundry list of organized crime families so long I can barely keep up. It's detailed, and yet it's still pretty surface level. I stop her after ten minutes, holding up my hand as my head swims. Names like, "Sacra Corona Unita," "Camorra," and "'Ndrangheta" stick in my head like parsley in teeth. "Okay," I say to her, "so there really is a pretty big mob tradition in Italy. The movies didn't get that wrong."

She shrugs. "It's not all bad, but they are certainly here, as they are everywhere. Things have gotten better since the new prime minister made opposing them part of his platform."

I rub my hands over my face. "This is the sort of thing Omega was so good at. Sliding into places and corrupting officials through fear and bribery. Taking over rackets, or at least demanding a percentage to allow them to operate without interference."

She gives me a squint. "Omega? The group that Kat and Janus were part of?"

"Yeah," I say, "Crime was their raison d'être. It was what they did, using their meta powers to put fear and terror into everyone they could squeeze a buck out of." I run a hand through my hair, brushing it out of my eyes. "Hera broke from them, founded Alpha after they started down that path. She opposed them all the way up until we had a bigger threat."

Perugini's face is stony, masklike. "Why?"

I blink in surprise. "Why, what? Why did she oppose them?" The doctor gives me a slight nod. "Because she believed in a higher duty. That we weren't just given power so we could prey on people, control them, make money from their vices and weaknesses." I felt my voice get soft. "I thought everyone who was in Alpha believed in that." I think of Lorenzo and Fintan, and I taste bile in the back of my throat. Their betrayal stings, which is funny, since I didn't even really know them all that well. I picture Hera and imagine her reaction to this. It's not pretty.

I think about Diana—Artemis—whatever—Goddess of the Hunt, and I try again to fit this puzzle piece in. She's an assassin? Some sort of hired killer? But she's helping me. In all my time with Alpha, I had never heard of anyone like her. That doesn't preclude the possibility she was secretly part of the group, but somehow I doubt it. Alpha didn't tend to tread in the killing realm unless we had to, anyway. She kills like it's nothing.

I put my head against the back of the couch. It's leather, it's comfortable, and I think—not for the first time—about just going to sleep for a while. My head is spinning, though, and I wonder if I'll be able to calm down enough to even rest.

I rub my eyes and turn my gaze back to Dr. Perugini. There's a balcony that overlooks the street below, and I realize the curtains are open. Fortunately, there's no one on the roof opposite, but it tumbles to mind exactly how much worse I am at operational security than my sister is, and I kick myself again.

"What is this?" Dr. Perugini asks, and I glance at her.

"What is what?" I ask, a little confused.

"This thing you do with your face," she says, and scrunches up her nose in what I assume is an impersonation of me. It's not flattering to me, but it looks kind of cute on her.

"I dunno," I say, "probably frustration."

"It is not a good look," she says, shaking her head. She stands and walks toward the only bedroom before I have a chance to recover enough to ask her about sleeping arrangements. She shuts the door, and I'm left staring at it.

I want to jump right to the idea that this is a metaphor for my life, but it feels too easy. There are doors in my face, sure, but if my sister were here, she wouldn't be despairing. Hell, she's probably off on an adventure of her own at this very moment. Craziness is abounding, souls are being drained, enemies are mounting an attack on her, old friends are betraying—

Okay, I'm projecting.

Even I'm aware of my inner monologue gaining a disproportionate amount of angst. We won the battle against the worst enemy metakind had ever seen, and now I'm left to deal with the fallout of some slackers who have betrayed everything I stood for when I joined this fight. I may have navigated a long path since the day I first started working for Alpha, but it stings, even without a bro-close relationship with Fintan or Lorenzo. They've pissed on everything I believed in, and I'm taking it personally. Ever have someone say something that just goes against everything you believe? It feels even worse when it's not on the internet.

I'm stewing in my own juices when the bedroom door opens again. I start to say something to Perugini and then shut up when I realize she's not wearing a stitch. Nothing. Nada.

She stares at me coolly, long fingers against the door frame, and one leg crossed over the other, arms positioned just so in order to leave an aura of mystery that is not lost on me even as my brain defaults to teenage-boy mode. "Well," I say, articulating the first and only thought that comes to mind, "you're not getting into the Sistine Chapel like *that*."

She smiles and makes a sound in the back of her throat that feels almost like the beginnings of a laugh. Then she makes a beckoning gesture with her forefinger, and I realize I'm standing at attention. Then the rest of me stands a moment later, and then my brain shows up to ruin the day.

"Wait," I say, shaking my head. "This is … it's … I mean, look," and I'm trying not to—look, I mean, "it's not that I couldn't use—"

She sighs, exasperated. "Who said anything about you?" This might qualify as pouty, but she has way too much gravitas for it to come off as anything other than commanding and sexy. "I am on vacation. This is what I want to do on vacation. You are here, you are clearly of a mind to participate," she gestures vaguely at my lower body—which, yes, is still at attention— "and I am going to use you since you have dragged me here and continue to take advantage of my help."

I blink a few times. "So, really, I'd be repaying you for your assistance." I take a couple tentative steps toward her, almost running my shin into a coffee table and my thigh into the arm of the couch. "I'd be failing to—uh—fulfill my end of the bargain if I don't—uh—assist you with—"

I wander close enough to her for her to spare an arm—giving me a hell of a view of her upper body—to put a finger across my lips. "Let's not spoil the moment by talking," she says.

She kisses me, and I return her kiss wholeheartedly, feeling her warm flesh press against me. I put all thoughts of organized crime, of betrayal, of all this maddening stuff out of my head as she runs fingers through my hair and clutches, pulling my lips to hers. Her kisses are hungry, enticing, and she practically rips my shirt off. I press against her, skin to skin, as we stumble backward toward the bed. My questions about sleeping arrangements are irrelevant, I realize, and my worries are all dissolved and forgotten in the moments that follow, as I remember how much fun it can be to just go along with the wind as it blows.

21.

I awaken to sunlight streaming through the edges of the curtains. Perugini is on her side of the bed, I'm on mine. She's facing away from me, her dark hair against the white sheets a pleasant change from the empty space I usually wake to. I realize with surprise I've slept the sleep of the dead. With the exception of one middle-of-the-night awakening in which she tempted me once more, I don't recall waking even once.

I tiptoe to the bathroom to find a marble-appointed monstrosity that has mirrors everywhere, including just above the toilet. I stare at myself as I pee, feeling a little awkward and self-conscious about it all. If I really were Alpha Male, I'd probably be congratulating my junk on a successful night. *Way to go, champ, you were a real clinch player,* I refrain from saying.

This sparks some guilty feelings that remind me—yet again—that I am apparently not the most confident dude in the world. I mean, what if Dr. Perugini was just feeling sorry for me? That's a nasty little thought, and it makes me feel more than a little sick as I stare at myself in about twenty different mirrors. Who the hell owns this place, and how much do they like looking at themselves naked?

I open the bathroom door to find Dr. Perugini stirring. Her hair is as messy as I've ever seen it, because she's usually totally put together. Her sleepy eyes find me as she rolls over in bed and kicks the sheets off as she sits up. She looks damned lovely, but I hold back, standing against the bathroom door. Naked. Yeah. Still.

"Good morning," she says, and it just sounds sexy.

"Morning," I say. I do not sound sexy so much as hideously unsure of myself.

She catches my insecurity, and there's a subtle waver in her eyes as she straightens her posture. "What?"

"I just … I don't want to feel like I'm using you," I say, and I realize that every man at the agency would probably be ready to drag me out back and put a bullet in my head right now to put me out of my misery. This is sad. I slept with a beautiful woman last night and I feel guilty. WHY? What is wrong with me?

She doesn't seem to be as affected as I am. "You aren't. I told you, I was using you." She shrugs lightly. "If you were using me in return, this seems fair." Like it's no big deal.

"I just …"

She sighs. "Listen. You are a grown man. You act like a boy sometimes, but men do this. This is understood." She smiles, just slightly. "I am a grown woman. I do what I want. Did you not want to do what we did?" She sweeps a hand down her body, and I'm keenly aware that indeed, I do want to do … that. Her. Because she's a person, not a thing. The act is a thing. Ah, hell. Whatever.

"No, I did," I say. "Still do." I gulp a little. "I just … ugh." I let my head fall down. "I just …"

"You don't like my Brazilian wax?" she asks, and I blush for no good reason.

"I think the Brazilians do a great many things very well," I say, "including steakhouses and waxing." I catch a glimmer of amusement in her eye at this. "I feel guilty, like I dragged you into this and I'm exposing you to danger and … I just feel completely lost." I throw my arms up a little. "How sad is that? I feel completely out of control, like I don't know what the hell I'm doing."

She stares at me and nods subtly. "I know one area in which you appear to know what you're doing."

"Heh." That elicits a muted laugh from me. "Well, that's a relief, because it's been a while."

She shrugs lightly again. "Not so long." She slips out of bed and starts toward me. "You worry too much."

"I usually don't," I say, a little troubled by this. When someone else is in charge, I kinda just go with the flow. I'm a great lieutenant, able to take charge and get things done when the final responsibility lies elsewhere.

So why do I suddenly feel like I'm a kid in my bedroom, trying not to feel completely lost as my father says goodbye?

"Come back to bed," she says and takes my hand. I don't really resist, and she pulls me closer to her, back to the bed. We fall upon the sheets, silken and cool, welcoming. She runs fingers through my hair again, and lays my head upon her chest. I lie there, feeling the rise and fall of her breathing, listening to her heart beating.

I lie there for a while longer, just listening, just feeling her against me, until my eyes close and I drift back to sleep.

22.

It has been a while since Anselmo has taken the train to Rome, he realizes as he sits in the first-class car with his drink in hand. The rattle of the tracks, the tunnels that pass in the blink of an eye, the sprawling countryside, these are all things that he vaguely recalls from countless cross-country journeys. He barely notices them anymore, though, even when he travels, he thinks as he swirls the cognac in his glass while the green fields streak by.

"*Capo,*" Lorenzo says, causing him to turn his head. Lorenzo sits across the aisle from him, the little treats the cabin attendant has brought resting on the tray before him. "*Capo,* what do we do?"

"I told you," Anselmo says with the patient air of one who is used to giving instruction. "We will settle your problems."

"Yes, but how?" Lorenzo says, and the nerves are obvious on the boy's face. The smell of the cognac is strong in Anselmo's nose, the weight of the glass in his hand feels insignificant, and the flash of another tunnel passing by outside the window is irritating. They have the cabin to themselves, the attendant having already moved back to the next car. "We do not know where Reed Treston is."

"You think like a boy," Anselmo says, taking a sip of the cognac. It is weak, weak like Lorenzo. Given time, perhaps, it would become stronger. Like Lorenzo. "I must teach you to think like a man."

Anselmo sees the flush. The insult hits home, the pride flares. He buries the smile, knowing he has hit Lorenzo where any man would feel it, as surely as if he'd slapped the boy in his groin. "What do you mean, *Capo*?" Lorenzo squeezes out, voice an octave lower, like his balls just dropped. Good. Anselmo hopes they will, and soon.

"There are many ways to compel a man to do that which you wish," Anselmo says, taking another sip of his cognac. "You can bribe him. A flash of euros, an offer of smuggled cigarettes, drugs, women. Men have weaknesses. Failing that, there is threatening. Every man responds to threats, though in different ways." Anselmo ponders his glass. "You have threatened this boy twice—"

"I did not threaten him," Lorenzo says, and there is a hue on his skin that suggests rage. Anselmo finds some great joy in this. "I was ready to kill him."

"But you failed," Anselmo says with a shrug. "And so it is all threat. And he responds, running, hiding, instead of facing his problems as a man." Anselmo grabs his own balls with his free hand, shaking his arm. "Threats, they fail. He runs, he hides. I presume that if your contacts in the airports and train stations knew he was leaving town, you would already be aware of this, yes?" He waits for the nod, and continues. "So he hides. He hides in Rome."

"He could have taken a car—"

"He has no car," Anselmo dismisses this foolishness. "He hides, as boys do, like a child from his father, to avoid the fearsome anger." He makes a wave to take in the countryside. "He hides. But he cannot escape the anger. Threats, bribery … the last solution is the simplest." Anselmo snaps his fingers. "Now you must find something to threaten him with. A weak point. Something that he fears. Some loyalty that can be exploited." He grabs his own crotch again. "You get him by the balls, and you drag him out of his little hiding hole."

Lorenzo's face is all practiced skepticism. "But how, *Capo*? How do you find this man when he is hiding? He was alone, he has no friends left in the town now that—"

Anselmo takes a sip of the cognac. "He is hiding somewhere. This should tell you that he is with friends." He turned to look Lorenzo right in the eye. "Or allies, perhaps?"

"But who?" Lorenzo asks. "The woman archer?"

Anselmo nods. "Diana." He thinks back to their last meeting, those stunning green eyes, so full of anger. "Yes … I think she is just the place to start."

23.

Reed

I awake to an empty room and an empty bed, and I feel better than I have in some time. I can hear movement in the next room, and the bedroom door is drawn closed so that only a crack of light is visible. I yawn and stretch, feeling a clarity and certainty that doesn't just come from getting laid last night. It comes from knowing what I need to do next.

I find my phone next to the bed and dial J.J. I glance at the clock as it's ringing. I'm hoping he's awake and moving around by now, because it's like afternoon here. There's a faint roar of a crowd somewhere outside my window, but it's background noise under the static of the phone.

"Reed Indeed," J.J. answers, a little sleepy. "What's the haps, dude?"

"Sorry if I woke you up, man," I say by way of apology. "Things are moving here, and I need some knowledge."

"You called the right guy," he says, and I can hear him puffing up over the miles between us. "What can I do for you?"

"Did you get anything else on what I asked you about last night?" I ask.

"Mmmm." I hear him moving, then the faint click of a computer. "Nada so far, but the NSA's gears tend to move a little slow sometimes when it comes to granting other agencies' requests."

"Damn," I mutter. "I need details on a guy named Lorenzo Benedetti. He was with me in Alpha back in the day, but he looks like he's crossed over to the dark side."

There is a moment's pause before he replies. "Not to mix your movie metaphor, but do you guys have like a Sean Bean-Pierce Brosnan thing going on?"

"Huh?" My mind sprints to catch up, making the connection a few seconds later. "Oh, *GoldenEye.* Yeah, kinda, I guess." I pause as something occurs to me. "Except I only wish I had Bond's level of self-confidence. Also, I wouldn't say no to an Aston-Martin right now."

"You should try morning affirmations," J.J. says, and I can hear a cat purring in the background.

"For the self-confidence?"

"And the Aston Martin," he says. "You never get what you don't ask the universe for."

"Right," I say. Now is not the time to argue about the law of attraction. "Can you get back to me once you have something?"

"Can do," he says. "I suspect the NSA will come back with something on those emails first—"

"Oh," I say, "I think Lorenzo is 'Axis,' and a guy named Fintan O'Niall is 'Wrench.' Just FYI."

"That's helpful," J.J. says. "I might be able to do something with that in other areas of the intelligence community. I'll give you a call in a few hours. Peace out." He hangs up, saving me the trouble of finding an excuse to do the same.

I wander out into the living area to find Dr. Perugini in the kitchen. The smell of something cooking fills the air, and it looks like eggs. I wonder where she got them, and then I realize it's a TV dinner of some kind. A breakfast dinner? A TV breakfast? Whatever the case, she's stirring the meal and the microwave door is open. The TV is playing softly in the background, the volume down presumably so that she doesn't disturb me. Crowds are moving around on the screen, brandishing signs in Italian. "What's that?" I ask.

She sighs. "Another strike. This is normal in Italy." She turns to me. "You want something to eat?"

I smother the smartass reply that comes to mind, something about being in the mood for Brazilian. "Sure," I say instead, but the way her eyes glitter, I think she knows I just stifled myself.

24.

Anselmo

"Everything is for sale," Anselmo whispers as he walks down the poorly lit hall of an apartment building, which might have been built during the post-war construction period of the 1950s. There are protests just outside, and for once he is gratified rather than annoyed by them. The noise of the crowd is audible throughout the old building, a low roar that masks the sound of his movements. Lorenzo follows close behind him, a stiff look of discomfort and annoyance plastered upon his face.

"How did you find her?" Lorenzo interrupts to ask the question Anselmo was about to answer, unbidden.

"As I said," Anselmo says, squashing his impatience with the boy, "everything is for sale. When you know who to look for, then all you need to know is who to ask, who will know the details." Anselmo straightens his tie and suit as he halts in front of a wooden door. "And there is no shortage of people in Rome who will gladly pay attention to details in exchange for money."

Anselmo delivers a sharp kick to the door, shattering it off its frame and sending into the apartment. As it falls he sees movement behind it, across a dimly lit room that has every curtain drawn.

It takes only a moment for him to confirm that yes, it is Diana, by both the speed of her motion and the precision of her movements. He begins to dart into the apartment after her, but a rush of wind blasts past him.

It sweeps hard into the small apartment, knocking over a sofa and striking the dark-haired woman. He sees her bow and quiver propped against the wall. It is plain to him that she is going for them when the wind strikes. It rips her feet from beneath her, but she curls into a ball as the blast hits her.

Anselmo watches as the strength of the wind and her reaction carry her through a window, shattering it. Light floods the darkened apartment as his quarry is hurled into the sunlit street below. The roar of the protesting crowds enters the room, louder now through the broken window, and Anselmo feels his patience dissolve as Diana disappears from view, falling onto the avenue below.

"You imbecile!" he spits at Lorenzo, and then sprints for the stairs without caring if his protegé follows.

25.

The change of tone on the TV is immediate. Even though I don't understand much Italian, the difference in the way they are speaking is enough to turn my head. I look in time to see a woman with long, dark hair come cannonballing out of a window to land in a stunned crowd. I estimate she fell two or three floors, thrown out of a window in a nearby building.

The commentators go into a shocked silence, but only for a second. Her fallen form is stretched out on the pavement, and then she staggers back to her feet with meta speed, and I catch a glimpse of her face.

It's the Goddess of the Hunt, and she's bleeding from cuts on her back and forehead. She looks like hell—wary and pissed, with a tinge of fear. She's lacking any weapons, and she looks staggered, which is not a good sign.

I can hear Perugini take a sharp breath behind me, as dumbstruck as I am by what's happening on the TV. "Where is this?" I ask, turning to look at her.

Wordlessly, she points at the wall behind me, and I remember the dull roar of the strike in progress. "Three blocks," she says when she regains her power of speech.

I run for the balcony, thankful that I took a moment to get dressed before joining her for breakfast. I burst out the double doors and use my power to leap up onto a rooftop, not really thinking as I spring into action.

26.

She is still in the street when Anselmo comes out of the building, and this is all good news as far as he in concerned. She looks unsure, the huntress turned into prey. Her doubt is exquisite, and he knows that while this is not the first time she has suffered this reversal of roles, it is very probably the last.

"Stay back," he says to Lorenzo as they step onto the sidewalk. Anselmo is ready for this, sees the news cameras, and knows how to play it. The young buck, though, has already proven that he is too busy swinging his balls around to be trusted with the most basic of decisions. Anselmo throws up a hand to halt the boy, to keep him from charging in and making even more of a spectacle. This is a delicate maneuver, and made all the simpler by the roles dictated.

Anselmo is the hunter.

Diana is the prey.

Prey runs.

The hunter follows.

She does not disappoint him, catching sight of the two of them from her place in the center of the crowd, a ring of concerned onlookers gathered in a knot around her. There is no hesitation; she flees, knocking over pedestrians with all

109

the force she commands. Bodies fall, screams fill the air, and the huntress is on the run.

"Carefully," Anselmo says, breaking into a sprint of his own. He parallels Diana's path down the middle of the road, mirroring it on the sidewalk, careful to avoid the breathless, mad sprint that she employs without care for the humans she runs over. Anselmo has patience and follows, knowing she will cross into an alley soon. It is inevitable, the hare diving into the rushes to avoid the hawk.

But Anselmo will not be lost so easily. For he is a hunter, and she is the prey, and no matter how long it takes, his pride will force him to wear her down. He can smell her fear, can sense her helplessness without her weapons. He will pursue her from one end of the city to the other, will keep her from doubling back to familiar territory. Will wait for her to move somewhere secluded, somewhere quiet.

And then he will show her just how weak she truly is as he ends her long life once and for all.

27.

I blast across rooftop gaps without much in the way of thought. I'm sprinting, charging in the direction I can hear the crowd. At the apex of my next jump I see the mob scene, the countless people gathered to protest whatever they're protesting. I've been in crowds like that before and the energy is incredible. Even from this distance I can tell things are off, though. There's an aura of uncertainty that makes its way through the crowd noise, faint screams that indicate something has gone awry.

I burst onto the edge of a major street and the full glory of the scene is laid out before me. There's a gash in the crowd like someone has taken a razor and run it through, removing everything in the path. I follow it to its conclusion, about two hundred yards down the way, and I see Diana playing fullback and charging through the heart of the protest. My eyes catch movement across the street and I see why she's running.

Lorenzo. That bastard.

He's following behind an older guy, and I know I've found the boss. The guy looks like he's in his forties or fifties. If he's meta, that could mean he's a few hundred years old or it could mean thousands. I don't like the possibilities in either case, but I see them following her down the street, taking the slightly less crowded sidewalks, threading through people instead of plowing them down. I know their intentions are ill even if their methods are surprisingly gentle.

I take off after them, the sentry above, and try to keep a low profile as I leap from roof to roof in pursuit.

28.

Anselmo

She takes the path of most resistance, and this pleases Anselmo. Panicked, fearful—it means she is reacting rather than thinking. A fine state for her to be in. She has fought her way through some three hundred meters of crowd by this point and has yet to look back or make a move to run down an alley. Anselmo can predict it, though, especially as she turns to look at him for the first time since she took off. He sees the wild eyes, the instinctive terror. All good. All very good.

She elbow checks a young man and sends him flying ten feet into the air, and the crowd gasps as one. It is the hardest, most panicked hit she has made yet, and it fully reveals to everyone what she is. Anselmo picks his way through a gap as people scream and start to run in the opposite direction. The herd is spooked and is trying to escape now that they've recognized a true threat rather than a simple novelty.

Cutting through a crowd with precise motions comes easily to Anselmo. It does not require brute strength or any of the fearsome charging that Diana has employed. No, it is a simple matter to easily redirect the people flowing around him with concentrated strikes, gentle shoves that compel them out of his path without harming them or sending them flying. The struggle has slowed her down; his calm allows

113

him to pursue easily. A sharp knife through soft meat; that is Anselmo. Lorenzo follows silently in his wake.

She makes the mouth of the alley but is not alone. Others are running from her in a panic now, running with her, a living mass of panic snaking its way into a space far too small for them. Diana goes into this place with none of the grace that might have allowed her to calmly move away. She writhes, she panics, she strikes, and the humans shriek and struggle back. The alley becomes a tight-knit crowd, a panic turned to riot in the confined space.

The strike of hand against bone, of flesh against weaker flesh echoes. The crowd on the street adapts, responds, sees the mayhem in the alley and runs the other way. Anselmo drives into the heart of the chaos, calmly redirecting the screaming strikers out of his path and to their own safety.

He smiles as he sees her at the heart of a bloody mass of people. They shrink from her in fear even as she freezes to look at him. It is a second where she knows exactly where she stands. The alley before her is crammed with people fleeing, crying, falling, stumbling, desperate to get away and blocking her easy retreat in the process. It is a solid wall of bodies between her and freedom, and an easy corridor between her and death.

Her flight instinct falters, and he can see her panic recede under her resolve.

She knows there is no escape.

He knows that she knows. And while this is hardly the private place he had hoped for, a quick conclusion to the business at hand is in the offing. "Hello, Diana," he says, as amiably as the snake to the varmint it is wrapped around. Victory is assured; now there is no cause to be rude. "It would appear you are—"

The tornado hits Anselmo with the force of a bomb, bouncing him hard against the cobblestone alley. He goes airborne for a full second before crashing back to land on his face, nose smacking against the ground. It is a stunning sensation, weightlessness followed by the sense of power driving him to the earth.

"Howdy," the man says as Anselmo raises his eyes to see Diana still standing there, a companion now at her side. The flare of wind around his legs tells Anselmo who the interloper is, why he is here, and that his own plan has gone just slightly wrong. The man holds a hand pointed at Anselmo as if making a threat. "I saw you guys picking on this woman, and thought I'd—"

There comes the sound of tearing, of something ripping, and Anselmo watches the light enter the man's eyes in realization. It is a sweet one.

Anselmo rips a chunk of pavement five feet square off the road and has it in his hands, above his head, before the boy—Reed, he remembers the name—can do anything to react. It is heavy, perhaps a ton, but it holds together well, a perfect projectile, which he heaves at the two of them with something approaching irritation.

"Oh, shit," Reed says simply, staring at his impending death. And Anselmo watches with satisfaction as Reed and Diana disappear behind a ton of thrown debris.

29.

Reed

I see it coming and want to kick myself for the lame response. It's half the alley, the cobblestone all in a clump. I can taste the dry dust the guy raised when he pulled it up, billowing ahead in a cloud propelled by the force of his action. When he lifts it and I see he's going to toss it at us, my customary response pops out without thought.

Metas who can lift heavy objects are a dime a dozen. Metas who can rip up a street and throw it through the air like they're tossing a tennis ball are not, and it's always cause for concern when you run across someone with that much power.

The adrenaline is already pumping through me, and I feel flush. The world slows down a little as the bricks come toward us in a low arc. If they hit, I have no doubt they'll mash my upper body into a lovely jam that would nicely spread on whatever bread they serve in the nearest café.

I summon all my power, and I mean all of it. I throw up my hands, palms out, and gather my energy. It's like sprinting, or lifting more weight than I've ever put up in my life, and I can feel it all down my arms. I set my feet without thinking about it much, lock myself as much into place as I can.

I propel all that force, every bit of it I can muster, down my arms, through my wrists, and out my hands. Taking a page out of Lorenzo's book, I try something new and try to throw some wind using my head as a focusing channel. I can feel it working, adding a little to the gust that sweeps before me like the start of a tornado.

The flying stones catch in midair, hover for just a brief moment, and then I pour it on. Everything I've got, from the toes up, I put into this. I throw power I don't even know I have into this. I see my efforts rewarded. A few bricks fall to earth, but the majority reverse their course and go flying back at that asshole who threw them at me.

I can see the surprise as the first cobblestones hit. He's buried in a second, before he has a chance to respond. Dust fills the air, a cloud like a sandstorm has moved in, and I can tell by the dispersion that Lorenzo hasn't even had time to think about volleying back. The street lands on my attacker, burying him under a ton of debris and hoisting the bastard on his own petard. Drink up on that irony, pal.

I can feel a smile creep onto my face even as the weariness hits, and I turn to look at Diana. I'm exhausted but celebratory, because I've just pulled off a miracle of the sort that really shouldn't be possible. I feel like a king, like a badass, like Sienna, and I kind of want someone to acknowledge my triumph.

She's not much into acknowledging though, because her face is still plastered with horror. Her lip quivers, and her eyes are still fixed on the alley behind me. The triumph flees in half a heartbeat and I turn, watching the last of the dust clear as somehow—*somehow*—this guy emerges from it, his expensive suit in tatters but looking none the worse for wear otherwise. His bronzed skin looks like iron, even with his slightly saggy man-tits, and I get the feeling that this is not going to go well for me.

I want to collapse but I don't, instead letting my stomach sink as those same two lame words come back to me again.

"Oh, shit."

30.

I hope for a monologue, for a chance to think. How does someone take a ton of bricks to the upper body and walk away? He doesn't even look mad, though his face is a little pinched. He's got the look of a man who moves with power, with confidence, and I kinda want to wilt away. The bastard just ripped the road right off the ground and hurled it at me, and didn't even blanch when I sent it back at him.

This is so not good.

"So you are Reed Treston," he says with a thick Italian accent, and I don't even like the sound of my name coming from him. I'm standing there, a hand held protectively in front of Diana—as if it'd do a damned thing—and he's just staring at us, slightly covered in the dust from a pile of rubble hitting him. Lorenzo is a few steps behind him, looking cautiously at us. Okay, he looks a little pissed, actually, but I'm ten steps past caring.

"And I here I don't even know your name," I say, at a loss for what else to say.

"My name is not something you should worry about." He gives me that look, like he's about to land on me like a ton of bricks, that whole "angry father" thing, and I'm just wondering how I'm going to get out of this. I give Diana what I assume is a panicked glance, and she returns it with one of her own. But there's something else I catch, too, a slight motion of her right hand that's obscured from that guy's view by my body.

She rolls her finger, like she's suggesting I stall him.

"What should I worry about?" I say as I turn back around. I can stall for time; this is not an issue. He's not advancing very quickly, and he takes a moment to look back at the mouth of the alley, where the strike on the street beyond has cleared a little. Police sirens are audible as the Carabinieri make their approach known. I make a gesture to indicate his toplessness. "Because it looks like maybe you oughta worry about skin cancer, based on that tan. Did you know the risk factors—"

His eyes widen slightly at my stupidity, and I hear movement behind me. I glance back just in time to see Diana kick a chunk of fallen cobblestone straight up, directly into her hand. In a flash she throws it with unerring accuracy right into shirtless guy's eyes, where it shatters into dust as he flinches, his eyes closed.

"Come on!" Diana shouts as she rabbits. She turns, taking off down the now-clear alley behind her without waiting to see if I'm smart enough to come along. I'm smart enough, though, dammit. I spare a glance to see our enemy brushing the crumbs of the broken stone out of his eyes, Lorenzo at his side like a concerned son, and then I'm behind a branch in the alley two seconds later, following Diana's shapely form as we sprint away.

31.

To say a metahuman is fleet of foot is like saying a sports car can go kinda fast. Diana is one of the old gods, and she tears along like she's a Ferrari on an open freeway. I'm hauling ass to keep up, the tan walls of the alleyway whizzing by at high speed, sweat from my earlier exertion dripping off my forehead. Thankfully, running exerts a different kind of power than hurling wind at people, but I'm still not as fast as she is, even on my best day. She's got a lead of half the alley on me, bursting out onto a major road as I look back to see Lorenzo and the iron man coming after us. The older guy looks pissed, and I'm not so eager to get caught, so I put all thoughts of fatigue behind me and run faster.

I dodge past a street vendor set up on a white sheet, a ton of knock-off—or maybe stolen—purses spread out in front of him. He sees me coming and scoops them up in the sheet, just one giant bundle. I hate to be a dick, but I snatch it out of his hand before he can even react and toss the whole thing right at my pursuers.

Pretty much like I'd planned, Lorenzo strikes out at the sheet and it explodes into a rain of leather handbags that get blown right out of his defensive funnel. Net result on their pursuit? Pretty much nothing. But it makes Lorenzo blanch a couple of times as purses smack him about the face and neck, slowing him down.

His boss doesn't slow down at all.

I make the mouth of the alley and see Diana has left me behind. She's down the street now, disappearing into another alley, and I'm reminded about that old joke with the two hikers that run into an ornery bear in the woods. One of them stops to lace up his tennis shoes, and the other asks him why he'd bother; he can't possibly outrun the bear. "I don't have to outrun the bear," he says. "I just have to outrun you."

Well, Diana has damned sure outrun me. *Way to go, hero*, my mind tells me. Now it's two-on-one, and not in my favor.

I'm halfway across the street when it occurs to me that this doesn't have to remain two-on-one. Whoever this guy is, he's a tough sonofabitch, but he looks pretty earthbound.

And even though I'm tired, I'm definitely not.

I look for the building of lowest height that I can see, and my eyes alight on a two-story apartment building about a block down the way. Unless the man of iron is also a jumping-bean-type meta, he's not gonna be able to scale it easily. He's fast—I confirm as I look behind me—but I'm guessing he can't leap tall buildings in a single bound.

Lorenzo can, of course, but I'm going to have to deal with him whether I stay on the ground or not.

I make it to just below the short building and leap, hoping that I've got enough juice to do this. I send out a blast of air just as I'm about to pancake on the side of the roof, and manage to get a few more feet of height before my jet stream falters. I throw up a hand and land four fingers on the side of the building's crest. I'm left hanging there with one hand for a good two seconds before I manage to pull myself up.

A shadow sails over my head onto the rooftop just as I'm rolling to my feet, and I know I'm screwed even before I see Lorenzo there, blocking my way forward.

He's got his hands up, ready to blast me—probably off the building—and a wicked smile that has about zero room for mercy. I start to brace myself but don't even get a half a chance before the gust comes, strong like a hurricane, and I feel myself go tumbling backward into oblivion, the world spinning around me as I fall back to the earth.

32.

Joy pervades Anselmo as the Treston boy hits the ground and bounces once, hard. It's that same kind of pleasure he felt the first time he beat a man to death. That relentless happiness that came from hammering his flesh with fist, listening to the bones break and the hard slap of his knuckles as his victim cried out in pain. There was begging, and it was sweet. Pleading, and it was sweeter still.

The Treston boy hits the ground with a sound like knuckles against tenderized skin, and it is a sweet remembrance for Anselmo. He approaches the fallen form with no trepidation, even as he sees the lad stirring. He reaches in and grabs him around the neck in a chokehold, feeling his forearm lock into place around a soft throat. There is a choking sound, and Anselmo applies pressure, ripping the boy's feet from underneath him, folding him over with superior strength, pushing him into a ball and dragging him toward the nearest alley.

The streets are filled with activity, with people rushing to and fro. A murder here, in public, might go unsolved simply from so many conflicting witness accounts. On the other hand, although it seems no one is paying attention to too much of anything in the chaos, it is also entirely possible that someone could be wielding one of those cell phone cameras

123

that are now everywhere. Anselmo makes a face, pained and disdainful. The world has changed, and not always for the better. There had been a time when public murder was the easiest thing to get away with.

But this is Rome, not home, and the tourists and politicians find this sort of thing eminently objectionable.

And for now, they still rule the streets.

For a few days more, in any case.

Anselmo drags the Treston boy into the alley. It is dark, the sun hidden behind one of the nearby buildings. Anselmo looks up to see Lorenzo staring down at him, his own sense of satisfaction well in place. "Did I not tell you?" Anselmo calls up to him. "Find a weak point, did I not say?" Anselmo grins. "We have him by the balls now, yes?"

He has Treston. Of that, there is no doubt. His arms are locked around the boy's neck, and the snap is mere moments away. With that single move, it will be over. He can even see it in Lorenzo's eyes, the respect. It was always there, of course, but he has proven once more why he is the *Capo*, the one to lead.

The one to lead them all.

He pushes just a little harder, savors the grunt from the boy. Anselmo feels the smile stretching his features as he prepares to snap the boy's neck once and for all ...

33.

I'm screwed. And not in the good way that Dr. Perugini did last night, either, but the way that means my journey ends facedown in an Italian alley, neck at a horribly unwieldy angle. I can feel the man of iron's lock around my throat, and I know I'm seconds away from feeling the crack that signifies that I'm dead. My hands flail wildly, unable to reach, unable to touch, unable to stop him.

A shadow descends in a flying arc from above as a warning shout fills the air. I feel the weight of something slam into the guy and he grunts. I can't tell if he's startled or what, but his grip loosens and I yank my hands down and pour my desperation into a burst of wind that kicks both my shoes off even as it blows me into the air.

I can see Diana propelled alongside me, eyes wide, as I rise upward. We make it to the rooftop and I glance back to see the bastard she just saved me from leaning against the wall, shaking his head with utter fury on his face.

It's not a good look on him, and I'm possessed of a desire to run.

Diana is already ahead of me as usual, taking off along a gravel rooftop, once again without concern to see if I'm following. I follow, though, and realize after a minute or two that she's not going as fast this time. She's letting me keep up. I glance back and see Lorenzo on our trail. No hint of the real threat, though, and I wonder if maybe—just maybe—at a two to one advantage, we might be able to turn the tables on him this round.

Then a knife goes flying past me, propelled by Lorenzo's gust, missing me by inches, and I decide to keep running.

Diana, though, she stops as she hears the *thunk*. I wonder what she's up to, looping around a small shed-like structure on the roof we're traversing. She disappears behind it, and I wonder if she's about to make another attempt to leave me behind. Bear bait once more, that's me.

I see her out of the corner of my eye as she swings around to grab the knife that's buried in a wooden support. She takes hold of it and then meets my eyes, her green ones flaring. "Hit him!" she shouts.

"With what?" I ask, and then realize that's a dumb question. I turn to see Lorenzo making the leap onto our rooftop. He doesn't even need a gust to assist. Diana is still moving, heading straight for him.

I summon up a pretty piss-poor gust. Lorenzo sees it coming and tries to counter, but he's in mid air and doesn't really have the ability to alter his direction to go anywhere but up or back. He flares a blast of wind at mine, but they basically cancel each other out, and he arcs slightly slower toward the ground.

Diana doesn't stop running, though. She makes it to the edge of our rooftop just as he's about ten feet from landing. His arms are still outstretched and pointing at me, trying to fend off my sorry attack. He sees her, but maybe disregards her as a threat.

Big mistake.

She twirls the knife in her fingers like she's a pro juggler, and then hurls it at him faster than anything I've seen thrown. It catches him in the side, just below the ribcage, and he grunts in pain. His gust stops immediately, and I throw the last little remainder of my power at him. It's not much, but it blows him back about twelve inches.

Which is just enough to cause him to miss the rooftop.

I can hear him land in the alley below. It's not exactly a pretty sound; something like flesh on cobblestone never is. He screams some, then whimpers, makes a few crying noises. Diana spares a look over the side, but only for a second. She runs back across the rooftop toward me, not even bothering to stop and see if I'm okay. I'm not, by the way. I'm down on one knee, breathing hard from the exertion. I feel like I've not only gone ten rounds with a boxer, but I'm more than a little lightheaded.

"Come on!" she says, and I feel like my only choice is to comply. I pick myself up and follow her off the rooftop as she leaps to the next one, still on the run.

34.

Anselmo finds Lorenzo a few alleys over. The landing looks as though it would be painful for the average person, or even the average meta. Anselmo has little ability to empathize, and instead nudges Lorenzo with a toe. It is restraint, though, because his first instinct is to kick the boy, to let his rage flow out in a series of blows that will vent all the irritation he is experiencing at this setback.

There is blood running down Lorenzo's side from the knife that remains rooted somewhere near his kidney. Anselmo shakes his head and grasps at the blade, tugging it out without ceremony or mercy. Lorenzo screams, and it's a slightly sweet tonic to Anselmo's ears. It's curiously unsatisfying, though. It leaves a desire to inflict more pain, but he restrains himself from following that impulse.

"Get on your feet," Anselmo says, brushing off some of the dust that is plastered to his skin with sweat. The bitch hit him in the eyes as she landed, enough to cause them to feel the squeeze.

Enough to get him to drop Reed Treston.

It's a primal fury that fills Anselmo, and he knows it well. He takes a breath, looking down to see his bronzed chest inflate with the intake, then deflate as he lets it out. He swipes at the white cobblestone dust that remains matted in his chest hair, but it does little good.

"It hurts, *Capo*," Lorenzo moans, like a little girl.

Anselmo stoops down and surveys the boy. Then he slaps him in the face, drawing a look of shock. "You whine like a child," Anselmo says. "Collect yourself and be a man. Have your balls not dropped yet?"

"No, *Capo*," Lorenzo says, causing Anselmo to raise his eyebrow. "I mean yes. They have."

Anselmo nods. "Then act like it. Get on your feet."

Lorenzo does, though it takes a few minutes. Anselmo watches impassively. This is a good lesson for the boy. Anselmo feels a curious mixture of fury and coldness run through him. He has no pity for the lad who has dragged him into this situation, only scorn and a righteous satisfaction at the thought of whatever pains he might be feeling. Lorenzo sniffles, and Anselmo resists the urge to slap him again.

"How do we find them now?" Lorenzo grunts.

"The Treston boy arrived at our location in less than a minute," Anselmo says, thinking it over. "Less than a minute after you—*idiot*—sent Diana out the window." He spits this out, compiling a list of all the boy's failures. "He was close by."

Lorenzo thinks this over, and Anselmo can see the wheels turning. "We can—we can do a search. A, uhm … a search of several blocks. I have a person who can look at the residential records for that area, perhaps ah—compare—"

Anselmo shakes his head at the lad. "There is stupidity, and then there is you. We have friends in Rome, now, yes?"

Lorenzo blinks. "You mean Don George—"

"Yes," Anselmo cuts him off. "He has his connections within the Carabinieri. A man goes flying over the rooftops, do you think someone might have seen that?" He narrows his eyes at the moron, Lorenzo. "Do you think that once the Carabinieri have investigated all of this, they might have some idea from whence he came?"

Lorenzo swallows, visibly, heavily, and nods. He reaches in his jacket pocket and pulls out his phone. Anselmo watches, waiting to see if he follows the matter to its logical conclusion. The boy dials the phone, and then speaks:

"Don George? It is Lorenzo Benedetti. *Sì, sì.* I am in Rome, and I have need of your assistance … your friends within the Carabinieri …"

35.

Reed

We cross the rooftops for miles. I recognize the Via Nazionale, and we sweep along it on the south side of the road to the Piazza della Repubblica, pausing on the rooftop above the plaza. I help Diana along with the wind as needed, but every once in a while she surprises me by parkouring her way up a building face. We keep moving by unspoken agreement; it's a measure of how scared she is by what just happened that we feel no compulsion to stop running until we're miles from the incident.

When we reach the end of the roof, we stop. It's nothing but empty air in front of us, all the way down to some church building below. She gives me a look like a cornered cat, just for a second, and then it passes and she looks almost human. "Do you know who that was?"

"The guy with a skin of iron?" I ask. "Not a clue."

"His name is Anselmo Serafini," she says, clearly thinking me the idiot for not being aware of this. "He's a *capo* from Firenze."

I do the translating in my head. "Mob boss from Florence." She gives me a subtle, slightly disgusted nod, like it's a concession for having to speak in my language. "He's running with a rough crowd."

She snorts. "Lorenzo and Fintan? There are worse."

"There's always someone badder," I say, throwing out one of my sister's favorite quotes. "Do you know what they're up to?"

"No good," Diana says.

"Other than that?"

"I don't need to know," she says, more than a little defensively. "When I work, I do it for money. This is how it has been for a thousand years. I don't get involved in these—*squabbles.*" She says the last word as the worst sort of curse, and her face is twisted with rage.

"You saved my life in my hotel room," I say, not considering that this might enflame her further. It doesn't. Yay.

She does, however, close her eyes and look even more disgusted. She lowers her voice. "I felt some residual string of loyalty to my brother—Janus—and through him, to you. It was foolish. It was against my better judgment. It was—perhaps just the smallest bit—influenced by my long association with Giuseppe." She opens her eyes, and I see a weariness on her face. "Now even he is gone."

"Times change," I say, not really sure what else to say. I didn't even know Janus had a sister. It's not like we were ever close, though.

She makes a low note of disgust and uses her hand to sweep and indicate the church-like building before us. "This I know. Those used to be the Diocletian baths. Now it is the Basilica de Santa Maria or some such shit, one of countless." She points over my head back down the Via Nazionale. "Over there is the Pantheon, yes? You have heard of this thing?" She spits her contempt. "These were our places, and they have been changed—disassembled—co-opted into the symbols of Christianity. You need not lecture me about 'change,'" she says with barely restrained fury. "I am familiar with change; more familiar than you, upstart."

"I'm guessing pretty much everyone is an upstart after you've lived a few thousand years," I quip, but I take some of the sting out of it by softening my voice. "Or a whippersnapper." Maybe not with that.

She seems to take no offense. "The thing I have learned over my years is that everyone has their problems. You have problems. Anselmo has problems." She gestures to the people passing on the sidewalk below. "Every one of them has problems, surely." She stands upon the edge of the building, and it looks like she's going to drop. "I don't want your problems. I don't want to be involved."

"You're doing a really lousy job of staying uninvolved," I say.

"This only proves my point," she says. "Had I stayed away from Giuseppe, had I let you go to your fate, I would have no problem now." She looks sullen. "I need to leave this town, go into the hills for a while."

She has answers, dammit. Answers I need. And she's about to walk away. "I need help," I say, like that's some kind of compelling argument to a woman who wants zero entanglements. If ever I've met a commitment-phobe, this is her.

"This does not concern me," she says, stone-faced.

"People are going to die," I say.

She frowns. "How do you know?"

"When guys like Anselmo are running the show, people always die," I say, shaking my head. "It's highly unlikely that this preemptive bid to kill us is going to culminate in a philanthropic exercise. They're looking to squelch information and kill powerful people that might get in their way." I extend my hands out, palm-up. "Explain to me how that ends in anything other than a dastardly plan."

"I don't know," she says, shaking her head.

"You said this Anselmo is a *capo*," I say. "Do you see him up to anything other than criminal mischief?"

Her eyes flash. "No."

I give her a moment to marinate in that thought while I change tacks. "What is he?"

"An Achilles," she says, loosening slightly. "His skin is invulnerable to attack."

"Except his heel?" I suggest hopefully.

She shakes her head. "That is a myth, propagated because the real Achilles was tripped in battle and then piled upon by ten strong metas who eventually managed to break his neck." She gives me a look that can only be described as warning. "I would not suggest trying that. He is far stronger than you and will separate your head from your shoulders with his bare hands."

"Can't damage him physically," I say. "Got it. How'd you get him to let me go?"

She hesitates. "His eyes are slightly weaker than the rest of his body. I landed my fingers," she holds up her forefinger and middle, "in his eyes and it staggered him for a moment, purely by protective instinct. It is unlikely it did him any actual harm. I did the same when I threw the rubble in his eyes. He can be blinded, temporarily."

"Still, good to know," I say, mulling on that one. "He's not completely invulnerable."

She dropped the middle finger and wagged her index at me. "But you have nowhere to take the attack after that; there is no follow-up move save to run." She stiffens again. "Which I would suggest you do." She stands there, almost limp, and sighs. "Whatever he is up to, you cannot stop him by yourself."

"I can call in some pretty compelling help, you know," I say with a smile.

"Then I would suggest you do so," she says without a smile and starts to drop over the side of the building, "because if you attempt to take him on alone …" She doesn't even finish, she just shakes her head and disappears over the side. I don't hear her land, but I can hear the faint sounds of someone climbing down the building at speed, making her retreat as I stand there and ponder my next move.

36.

It's a short walk after they get the call from Don George. Anselmo leads the way up the stairs, into the darkened hallway of a three-story building that has a lovely gelato shop on the first floor. Anselmo ponders having some, but decides to go straight to the sweeter promise first, climbing the stairs in the building's residence.

The whole place smells faintly sweet; a perfume of some sort, he thinks. Jasmine? He cannot name the different scents, and has little care for any of them in truth, much preferring the skin and the pleasures offered by the lovely creatures who apply them. He makes his footsteps quiet as he can, listening to Lorenzo shuffle along behind him. The boy is still hurting, but he makes no sound. The grimaces on his face are unmanly, but that is an issue for another time.

Anselmo puts his head against the door, standing outside an apartment for the second time this day. He listens and hears a television blaring inside, and waits until he hears something else.

A soft, feminine cough.

Without another thought, Anselmo smashes the door, knocking it off its hinges. He stands there, bare-chested, staring across an open living room at a woman upon the couch. She is beautiful, classically good looking with sharp

135

features and long, dark hair. He experiences a moment of doubt, wonders if he is in the right place.

Then he sees a planter upon the balcony, knocked asunder as if blown by a particularly strong breeze, and he smiles. *"Buongiorno,"* he says and advances into the apartment slowly, knowing that she has nowhere to run.

37.

Reed

"Sienna, where the hell are you?"

My sister is still not answering, which is really damned annoying. I'm swallowing my pride, calling for help, admitting she's bigger and badder than me, and she's unreachable. Seriously unreachable. Her cell goes to voicemail, and I leave a hurried message. Then I call the agency, and her assistant is a preening little asshat to me. I make a note to get him fired when I get home. What a little prick.

I sweep over the rooftops of the Via Nazionale, trying to remember how to get back to the apartment. I make another call while I go.

Father Emmanuel answers in a quiet voice on the third ring. "Hello?"

"Father," I say, "it has been my entire life since my last confession, and I think there are a few things I should probably come clean about." I jump a gap and catch my footing on a lower rooftop, the shock running through my weary body. "First of all, it was me that took the candy off Ms. Hutchen's desk in first grade—"

"I can't talk right now," hisses Father Emmanuel.

"Hey, listen," I say, "you dragged me into this thing"—sorta true—"you can't just bail now." Absolutely a lie. He's

137

already out of the boat, and I'm trying to pull him back in as he's telling me he'd rather swim.

"Giuseppe is dead," Emmanuel says, "and I have no actual proof of any wrongdoing on the behalf of this Fintan O'Niall. Perhaps I was wrong about him. Perhaps he had a messy encounter with a—" He makes a frustrated noise in the back of his throat. "I am not his priest, and he is not my responsibility."

"Evil thrives when good men do nothing," I say. I wonder if he appreciates the irony of me saying that to a priest.

"I don't know that he is evil," Emmanuel says, and I can feel his frustration through the phone. "He could be misguided, he could be misunderstood, he could be afraid— it is not my task to judge the man."

"Well, he's not exactly out there doing the Lord's work," I say. "Unless—never mind." I filter myself, keeping from making an unnecessarily nasty Old Testament joke. It's low-hanging fruit in any case.

"I am sorry about Giuseppe," Emmanuel says, "and I'm sorry about whatever you're going through. Truly, my prayers are with you—"

"I don't need your prayers," I say, snapping, "I need your help."

"I cannot help you," he says, and I catch a hint of sadness. "I am a man of peace. Violence is not … it's not what I am supposed to do with my gifts."

"You're not supposed to protect the flock with your gifts?" I ask.

"I'm supposed to turn the other cheek," he says.

"Easy to say when it's only you getting slapped," I fire back. I don't even wait for his response. I just hang up.

I continue on my not-so-merry way. I can still hear sirens in the distance, and I wonder if they're related to the strike gone wrong this morning or just the usual city madness. I don't even know that I care, but I let them fade into the background as I think through what's happened so far.

Diana doesn't want to get involved. Father Emmanuel doesn't want to get involved. They're both metas, and in Diana's case, a really badass one, which means I could use her help, at least. I still don't have the foggiest idea what Lorenzo, Fintan and Anselmo—at least I got his name, now—are up to, other than Mafia-ish things. Gangstas doing gangsta stuff.

What do the Mafia even do? I run my head through a short list—drug-smuggling, extortion, whacking guys. Actually, the whacking probably comes along with the other crimes, sort of an enforcement mechanism. Thievery? I mean, they're all about making money and gathering power, right?

So what the hell is this Anselmo doing that he needs to send his right-hand goon out to snap off Giuseppe? What did Giuseppe—a small timer at best—know that warranted him getting whacked? Was it just that he had some idea of Lorenzo's identity? Because Lorenzo hasn't done such a bang-up job of keeping it secret since the night he first came at me in the alley. Admittedly, it ain't easy to get away with wearing a ski mask in the middle of Rome, even in March, but still …

No, that doesn't quite track. I start to wonder how Sherlock Holmes handled this kind of thing, and I remember a phrase from way back, about the dog that didn't bark being the key to the case.

Where was Fintan today?

If they knew that they were coming after Diana, a pretty strong lady, why wouldn't they bring along a third meta? I mean, that would take some arrogance, wouldn't it? If you're coming after someone like her, you want the whole army arrayed against her. But they didn't have Fintan.

Which suggested to me—as the dog that didn't bark, RUFF RUFF—he was somehow key to this.

But how?

I almost miss my turn, gliding down the avenue and heading south. It's a near thing, but I leap over the rooftop gap to come down squarely on the road in the direction I'm heading. I flare the gusts just in time to keep from breaking my legs, and I settle down on the sidewalk, ignoring the surprised looks of a half dozen people around me.

I weave my way up the street and head into an alley. No one follows, and I circle to the back of the building. At least I think this is the one; Perugini led the way when we came yesterday.

I go up the back stairs down a darkened corridor. I don't remember it being this dark when we arrived; wasn't there an overhead bulb? I catch sight of a switch and flip it. Nothing happens.

I come around the corner toward the apartment doors and find them open, light spilling out into the darkened hallway. There's no sound, not a bit, coming from the apartment. Which is concerning. I get closer, and it's obvious that the door was blown completely off by someone strong. Really strong.

I step inside and it's like a tornado has hit the place. Possibly literally, since I doubt Lorenzo is dead. The chairs are overturned at the table, everything is swept off the granite countertops in the kitchen, there's a mess of broken dishes on the tile floor.

I'm quelling the sense of rising panic as I look for something, anything. A ransom note, fingernail scrawl scratched into the table top, breadcrumbs that indicate the direction they've gone.

Expecting the worst, I kick open the bedroom door, and I'm spared because it's empty. My suitcase is open and has been rifled through. I only have to look for a second to know that one of my suit jackets is gone, and so is a white dress shirt. What the hell?

I cast a look back into the wreckage of the living room and wonder—what have they done with her?

38.

Anselmo

Anselmo stares at the beautiful woman sitting beside him in the back seat of the car, taking in every lovely line. Her eyes flare at the caress of his gaze, and he smiles. She does not return it, but he cares very little. She is a means to several ends, a lovely piece of bait to dangle before the Treston boy. And not too bad to look at, either.

"My dear," he says, "you have a lovely perfume." She wears the more modern style of jeans, sandals, a shirt. She has her handbag clasped before her, as though it is the very key to preserving her life. It blocks his view of her chest, which is such a shame. She does not respond to his compliment except with a slight nod of her head in his direction.

The car stops at a light, and Anselmo muzzles his displeasure at the delays. The train to Firenze will be leaving in twenty minutes, and they have almost the entire Via Nazionale to traverse to get there. He sighs, trying to find his patience. It is much closer now that he has the girl, the means by which to make Treston jump into his waiting jaws.

Lorenzo sits quietly in the front seat with the driver provided by Don George, and they find a companionable silence for a moment. Lorenzo is still hurting, Anselmo can tell, but he is much improved. Doubtless found his balls. The air holds the aroma of not only the perfume but also promise. He has finally shown this boy Lorenzo how to handle these problems. It takes a firm hand, one with strength. He smiles as he looks ahead at the traffic on the Via Nazionale, and considers the future. It is bright, the plan coming to fruition in only a few short days.

His smile becomes a grin, and he looks down at the new shirt and jacket he has stolen from Treston. It's not quite his style, but it will do. It makes Anselmo feel young again, that and the beautiful woman at his side. They're enough to make him feel as though all his problems have blown away in the breeze that makes its way through the slightly lowered window next to his head.

39.

Reed

I'm on the balcony, looking out, panicking—not gonna lie, I am panicking—when the first thought occurs to me:

Where is Isabella's phone?

I pull out mine and start to dial her number, then think the better of it and call someone else instead. "Pick up, pick up," I say as I notice the sun is sinking low in the sky.

"Reed-om!" comes J.J.'s voice at the other end of the line. It's a *Braveheart* reference. In normal times, I would find this amusing.

Not right now. "I need you to track Dr. Perugini's cell phone," I say breathlessly, and there's a pause on the other end of the line.

"Okay," he says, "I can do that." All business. There's a tapping at the keys, and I use the moment of opportunity to blast myself onto the roof of the building. "By the way, I got some details for you on this stuff you asked for—"

"Trace first," I say as my feet land on the rooftop. "Deets later."

"Roger that," he says, pausing for a moment before his next words come back thick with concentration. "Looks like Dr. Perugini is in a car heading down a road ... uhm ... not sure how to pronounce this. Vee-uh Nazz-ee—they named a street after the *Nazis?*"

"Via Nazionale," I say and break into a sprint back the way I came only moments earlier. I launch from the rooftop and keep myself from breaking a leg only by flaring my gust at the last possible second before landing.

40.

Anselmo

"You must come be my guest at my estate for a while," Anselmo says, putting all his charm into it. It's a natural fact that women find power and money appealing, and he has both. This is simply the way things are, a universal truth. He glances at her to find her looking at him cautiously, and he knows it means good things. "It's a lovely place, on a grand hilltop—with a pool." He feels the slight rush of the wind through the crack in the window. "You can sunbathe in a bikini … or nothing at all." He chuckles in delight at his own suggestion. "Though perhaps that is not so appealing on a day such as today."

She looks over at him with thinly slitted eyes, and it is impossible to tell exactly what she is thinking. He assumes it is flattering things; after all, has he not just shown himself to be a man worthy of respect? Has he not just demonstrated both power and restraint? Her enigmatic eyes are a lovely brown, and he finds them alluring. She sees much with them, he knows, perhaps even to the truth of things. She would make a fine mistress, he thinks as he lets his own gaze wander over her. Perhaps she will even get that chance.

The car makes a turn at the Piazza della Repubblica, and Anselmo can see the Termini station just ahead. It is a massive structure, high and tall and wide. An impressive bit

145

of architecture, but plain. The car turns around to let them off, and a man in a suit opens the door. Behind him stands another fellow, this one dressed in expensive, tailored clothing, with red cheeks and slicked-back hair. His age is apparent, though Anselmo has known him as a colleague for most of his life.

"Don Serafini," the man says with a hint of a bow. Respect given is respect returned, and Anselmo steps out of the car and inclines his head to acknowledge and return the gesture.

"Don George," Anselmo says. "Your assistance is appreciated and shall not be forgotten."

"Indeed," Don George says. He is a corpulent man, his belly sticking out from too much pasta and too little exercise. Anselmo imagines him unable to exert himself much at this point, but at least he is able to render assistance and pay due respect. He has connections, he has uses, and even if he lacks the vigor necessary to please a woman that Anselmo considers so important to his own life, Don George still has his purpose. "You have called the meeting, yes?"

"Tomorrow," Anselmo says, taking the hand of the woman and helping her out of the car. She accepts his assistance with all the grace a prisoner should. He extends his elbow and she threads an arm through it on cue, clutching her handbag in her other hand. In a proper dress— something slim and fitted—she would be the perfect consort. "In the noon hour. We shall … reshape the world." He smiles at Don George. "Are you ready?"

Don George bows again, just slightly, all his frame can manage. "But of course, Don Serafini." He is one of the good ones, a loyal one. He has seen the direction of the changing wind and knows that it will blow hard on any who do not change with it. "Can I be of any other assistance to you?"

"My men are waiting on the train," Anselmo says with a shrug. "Your support will be needed at the meeting tomorrow, though, if you are willing to give it. Until then, I have need of your sources in the Carabinieri to keep an eye out for a man named Reed Treston."

"Reed Treston?" Don George asks. He shows a hint of skepticism with the arch of his heavy brows.

"An American," Anselmo says, almost dismissively. "A boy, only." He smiles at the woman. What is her name? He should ask at some point, not that it matters. "Is that not right, my dear?"

"Are you a man, then?" she asks, almost coyly. Anselmo sees Lorenzo step up toward her, hand raised to hit her, but Anselmo halts him with look.

"I am the most manly man you shall ever meet, my dear," Anselmo says with a smile. This is simply true, and he knows it to the core of him. He tugs her along as Don George's men pay their respect and open the door to the Termini station for him. "Perhaps I will show you what I mean when we get home."

41.

Reed

I launch onto the same rooftop I'd been standing on with Diana only an hour or less before. I run the length of it, heading roughly southeast. The slant of the rooftops here is a pain in my ass, but it's not so terrible that I can't compensate. I tear along the long building that runs the southern edge of the square and follow it down the avenue. I can see the Termini station from where I'm standing, a few hundred yards away at most.

Termini station has the most bizarre, wave-like portico thing for buses or taxis out front, so strange looking that I notice it even in my exhausted, adrenaline-fueled frenzy. There's classical architecture mixed with modern, and then there's this.

I'm forced to make an unreasonably long diagonal jump to the next building, and my power gives out about three-quarters of the way through. My exhaustion is catching up to me. My arms are so weary I feel like they're going to fall off. I feel a little nauseous, hungry because I haven't eaten and I've exerted myself so much. I hit the side of the building and slide down, catching myself on a window and clawing through the plaster with aching fingers that refuse to surrender in spite of my deep desire to do so.

I scale the building like Spider-Man, ripping at the superficial facade without care. I make it to the roof and heave myself up. I'm so tired I'm nearly drooling down my own chin. I realize I'm making grunting noises that expel saliva with each movement.

If I have to fight my way through Lorenzo and Anselmo in the shape I'm in, this could be very bad.

I realize that somewhere along the run, I must have hung up on J.J. He had told me they were stopped outside the train station, and I just ... I dunno, put my phone away or something. I don't even remember. I fish it out of my pocket with bloody, plaster covered hands and find it's still on. Uncle Sam is not going to like the overage for this month.

Hahah! I'm just kidding. No one pays attention to that sort of thing except Ariadne.

"Where are they?" I ask as I try to catch my breath.

"Oh, hey," J.J. says, all cool and calm. "I was beginning to think you were dying there. All I could hear was you grunting like a caveman, you know, interspersed with the occasional loud WHOOSH of your powers at work."

"Where—" I start to say again. I'm stooped over, leaning on my own knees, trying to catch my breath. I've got no rescue plan, and I'm charging toward the enemy formation. I R smart, as they say on the internet.

"So, I looked up this stuff you gave me, and I finally got an answer back from the powers that be at the NSA," J.J. says. "This guy, Lorenzo, he's working for someone named Anz-elmo? Sarahfeeny." He mangles Anselmo's name, sort of, but I let him get away with it. "Mobster guy. Big boss or something. The politics of how these organizations work is kind of muddled for us, but apparently we stole a primer on it from Italy's Carabinieri through—"

"I don't care," I say breathlessly. "I've met this Anselmo. I need to know anything you can tell me about him."

"Not a lot," J.J. says. "He's from ... Fire-ends?"

"Good God, it's Firenze!" I say, finally losing it with his lack of ability to pronounce. I don't even know Italian, but I know some phonics. "Florence, J.J.!"

"Okay, so, he's from Florence," J.J. says. "Mea culpa. Wait, is that Italian? Never mind. I've got an address—"

"Save it," I say, and take off at a run again, "give me an update on Perugini's phone position."

"She's in the train station," he says. "Uhh … hold on, the map is focusing in … looks like she's at the seventh platform from the left, and standing still for the moment."

I make a jump across a long roof gap only having to use a little wind to pull it off. "So, probably platform seven."

"Probably," he says, still cool. "So you think the bad guys got the Doc?"

"Pretty sure," I say.

"You think she's all right?"

"I damned well hope so," I say, shoving the phone into my pocket and making another jump. This time I don't have to use my powers at all.

42.

"My estate is really quite impressive," Anselmo says as she sits on the bench before him. They wait on the platform, the doors to the train not yet done disgorging their passengers. The platform number only appeared on the lighted signs around the station moments earlier, but Anselmo already knew. They stand at the far end of the platform, near the front of the train, waiting for the first-class car to open. Lorenzo has already bought the tickets.

"Mmm," the woman says. He has yet to catch her name, but in the scheme of things it's not really important. "Tell me more."

"*Capo*," Lorenzo says, and Anselmo looks over at him. The boy looks irritable, some blister in his shoe, perhaps. He nods his head at the train door, which is now clear of departing passengers.

"My dear, it is time to show you a wondrous ride," Anselmo says with just a hint of suggestion. No need to come on too strong.

"I can hardly contain my excitement," she says, still cool.

Lorenzo takes another step at her, menacingly, but Anselmo holds him back with only a hand. "*Capo*, she—"

Anselmo frowns at Lorenzo. "You read too much into her words. Calm yourself."

Lorenzo's face diffuses none of the anger, but a mask of resolve slips over him that tells Anselmo the argument is over. "Yes, *Capo*." The honorific is something that Anselmo never tires of hearing.

Anselmo extends his arm once more to help her off the bench, and she takes it, stone-faced. "Let us go, my dear," he says, and together they walk toward the train.

43.

Reed

I burst through the doors of Termini station. People are going in every direction with luggage and carts and the other assorted detritus of travel. Some lady comes up to me and asks if I need help. She acts kind of official but she's wearing a yellow t-shirt that tells me she's just some tick here to suck fat tourist blood, so I brush past her without a word.

I make my way through the maze of shops and billboards ahead, dodging past automated kiosks toward the back of the station. I've been here before, and I know where the trains are, somewhere behind the passenger lounges for frequent travelers and the news stands.

It's a sea of color, a pure travel-Europe experience you don't get in the U.S. I stick my hands in my pockets and lower my head when I see the first man in a suit watching the area like he's looking for trouble. He's as obvious as a giant nipple in the middle of someone's forehead, and I steer right to avoid him and almost run into another one.

It takes me a second—and a near-collision with the second of these clowns—to realize that they're just watching the crowd for general threats; they're not looking for me specifically. I can spot them dotted throughout the massive area as I make my way toward the seventh platform. I see a few of them malingering at the end of the giant, pier-like structure that's surrounded by tracks on either side, and I have a moment's doubt that I'll make it through the two sentries without raising some suspicion.

I pull my phone out of my pocket and plaster a smile on. I'll blend in if it kills me. I talk in a whisper and try to slur my words just slightly. I watch the sentries as I pretend to pace toward platform nine. "When does the next train to Florence leave?"

"Uhhh," J.J. says. "Gimme a minute."

I resist the urge to frown. "You haven't looked this up already?"

"Dude," J.J. says, "I am a little busy right now handling my own job in addition to your personal crisis, okay?"

I pause. "Were you looking at cat pictures on the internet again?"

"Forgive me for finding humor in Grumpy Cat, okay?" J.J. says. "I wasn't thinking ahead, I guess. That's on me, I'm sorry." He sounds mildly contrite. "Looking it up now." He pauses for about ten seconds in which I let him work. "Umm, it says it's leaving like … now."

I turn my head and see that, yep, that particular train is in fact leaving right this minute. It's pulling out slowly, and I'm not two platforms away. I swear and pocket the phone again, then sprint for platform eight, which is sidled up on the right side of the train. I run like hell, even though it's not moving very fast. The guys who have been watching platform seven are gone, but there's no way I'm going to make it to that platform in time.

I realize in a moment of utter clarity—and exhaustion—that in my rush to catch Perugini, I bypassed the ticket kiosks. Which was dumb. Because now I'm about to get on a train that I don't have a ticket for. I imagine that scene from *Indiana Jones* and keep running, catching the last car as the platform ends.

I say screw it and jump, using my power to boost me onto the roof of the last car as it chugs down the tracks. All aboard.

44.

I hit the steel roof of the car and make a hell of a noise. The wind is just barely rushing through my hair, the train moving at like five or ten miles an hour as we pull out of the station. I hear shouting behind me and glance back.

Gulp.

There's a guy in a black suit, one of the watchers, and he's caught my one-man stunt show. He's talking urgently into his phone, making hand gestures, and I get the feeling my cover is pretty well blown.

Shit.

I fish out my phone. "Where is she, J.J.?"

"First car," he says, and I wish—hopefully not for the last time—I had earbuds or a Bluetooth. I put the phone away again. How deep is the U.S. in debt? Maybe paying my phone bill will help clear a trillion or so.

I sprint down the train car. It's rocking a little on the tracks, that satisfying thumping sound that rails make. If I was in a seat in one of the cars below, it might actually be soothing enough to put me to sleep. Then again, right now I'm tired enough I could go to sleep on the tracks with a train passing overhead, so ...

We pass aging apartment buildings whose construction is so bland I think for a minute I've entered the old U.S.S.R., save for the fact that they're resplendent in oranges and pinks that wouldn't be out of place in Las Vegas. We wend our way onward as I leap to the next car, and I catch sight of a bevy of flat-topped pines, like a large-scale version of the bonsai that sits on Sienna's desk.

The train shifts with the tracks to go left and picks up speed. I'm forced to drop to one knee as it does so in order to keep from toppling off. I don't have much in the way of grip up here, and I'm thankful we're still in the city and moving relatively slowly.

Then, all of a sudden, somebody mashes the accelerator to the floor, and the train lurches into full throttle. I barely catch myself on the edge as I fall over the side, the tracks flashing past so fast I can't even see the individual wood slats that join them together.

The wind rushes past my face and I cling tightly with four fingers, my back against the steel train car as my legs dangle down the side, and I hope—just hope—I can hold on long enough to get back up top.

45.

Anselmo

"To maximum speed," Anselmo says, shaking his head to ward off an attack of pure fury. "Tell the conductor to do it."

"*Sì, Capo,*" Lorenzo says, and moves back to the front of the compartment. The train is already accelerating past the legal limits allowed on the city tracks, but it is not enough for Anselmo. The call was quite clear; the boy is on top of the train, is trying to insert himself into this one more time.

Anselmo smiles at the woman. Trying to reclaim what he has clearly already lost. "My dear, it would appear your boy is reluctant to allow you to be exposed to the charms of a true man."

Her lips press together in a thin, alluring line. "Oh?"

"*Sì,*" Anselmo says, nodding in resignation. "A man would realize when he is truly outmatched." This causes her eyebrow to arch, a most appealing look upon her.

"*Capo,*" Lorenzo says as he pushes past the cabin attendant to re-enter the compartment. "He is speeding up as quickly as he can. There is a station ahead, however, and—"

"Yes, yes," Anselmo says, waving a hand. "Tell him to speed right through."

Lorenzo hesitates, and Anselmo can see the hint that he wishes to make perhaps another argument. "Yes, *Capo,*" he says instead.

The woman speaks, a soft-hearted inquiry. "What will happen to the train conductor once you have made him do these things?"

Anselmo shrugs. "His livelihood is not my concern."

"And if he fails to do what you ask?" She still wears that expression that hints at nothing.

"That would be a personal tragedy for him," Anselmo says, waiting to see if she shows any sign of horror at the thought. She does not, raising his opinion of her still higher. "You disapprove?"

"My approval is hardly going to change your course, is it?" she asks with a shrug of her own.

Oh, yes, this one is quite impressive. Cold-hearted and pragmatic, such a rare combination with true beauty. "You have the face of an angel," Anselmo says with a grin, "and the mind of an animal, I think." He considers what other attributes she might share with an animal, and feels a thrill of excitement.

46.

Reed

The train blows through a station without even slowing down, passengers scrambling to give it a little distance from the platform as it shoots through at top speed. The tracks are clattering loudly now, and I'm still barely hanging on. A seemingly pointless metal crossbar passes overhead, and I'm suddenly thankful I'm on the side of the train, because it would performed a rapid reduction of my height—by taking me off at the waist.

I study the tracks ahead and decide I'm safe for a moment before I roll hard against my arm and blast a little gust at the ground below. It gives me a boost, just enough to get myself back on the roof of the train car in time for another of those damned crossbars to pass about twelve inches over the top of my nose. I lie flat on my back on the metal car and feel the motion of the train. It's definitely progressing to "bat out of hell" speeds in a hurry, and I suspect that the company that runs the train is no longer in charge of it.

We're out of the city now. A glimpse ahead suggests that my next obstacle is a tunnel. It's coming up fast, but doesn't look to be too low of a clearance. Which is fortunate, because I need to move my ass up to the first car.

I decide crawling forward is the right move, and I start scrambling like I'm climbing a horizontal mountain. The train alters course often enough that going over the side again is a distinct possibility. That's not something I want to risk, especially with a tunnel ahead. Who knows how much room I'll have on each side to keep from getting scraped off like a bug?

The world darkens around me and the staccato rhythm of the tracks increases in volume. I'm in a tunnel, and there's only a faint light for about a second before we burst out the other side into blinding daylight. I blink a few times to clear my vision, and then we're thrust into another tunnel. I curse into the wind, to little effect.

I crawl on through the dark until I reach the edge of the next car. This process is maddeningly slow, but the train has got to be going seventy or eighty miles an hour—whatever that is in kilometers per hour. I pull ahead, foot by foot, and finally decide to risk walking upright when I see someone on the car ahead already doing it.

Uh oh.

Yeah, they've sent thugs after me. I'm sure this isn't the smartest strategy, but then I see the guns and realize I've got pretty much no defense. I crouch, ready for them to open fire, and wonder exactly how the hell I'm gonna get myself out of this mess.

47.

"Go after him yourself," Anselmo says to Lorenzo. The boy does not take it well, exhibiting the first signs of—yes, fear.

"Capo—" he starts to protest.

"Do not *'Capo'* me," Anselmo says, an undercurrent of menace in his voice. "Be a man, and stop playing with yourself. He is up there, and he needs to be dispatched. Should you fail in this basic endeavor, with the aid of our soldiers, then I have to ask myself if you are truly ready to be my lieutenant, my right-hand man as we move into the completion of the plan." The message is clear.

"Sì," Lorenzo says and disappears into the next car without another look back. Good. The boy needs to develop this toughness. Anselmo knows he is just the man to teach him.

"Now, where were we?" Anselmo asks the woman. He feels slightly rude for interrupting their conversation, but like a good woman, she has waited patiently while the men discuss important business.

She tilts the eyebrow again, clearly a favored expression, and Anselmo enjoys the look it puts upon her face. "You were telling me all about your estate," she says.

"Ah, yes," Anselmo says, and hears the thump of footsteps on the top of a train car somewhere behind them. He frowns and hopes for Lorenzo's sake that he does not fail this time.

162

48.

Reed

They go for the hail of bullets, and I go over the side. It's easier than trying to soak up gunfire with my head, and I manage to catch a jutting window frame a few feet off the ground. It's not fun, hanging there, but it beats the hell out of hitting the ground or getting sucked under the train to be turned into Italian sausage.

I hang there for a minute, pondering my options. Looking forward, looking back, I realize I can keep crawling my way forward using the lip of the train window for a handhold. Worst comes to worst, if I fall I can probably save myself from splattering on the ground.

Probably.

I let my hopes rest on that thinnest of possibilities, and I start inching my way forward. I realize that there are guys with guns just above me somewhere, and they will probably look over the side soon-ish. I've got one solution for that problem, and it requires haste, so I scoot along as fast as my weary fingers allow.

When the first head pops cautiously over the side of the train, followed by the barrel of a gun, I'm ready and lucky, because he does it just above me. I drop to holding the window with one hand, and throw up the other while unleashing a gust. I catch a scream in the air and look

163

through the train in time to see the guy fly off the other side. Better luck next ride, pal.

I expect what happens next, but it doesn't make it any more fun. I swing forward about four feet, just before someone blindly fires a gun over the side of the train. I see nothing but a hand and a pistol, so naturally I blast it with a gust. I see the gun go flying, which is enough for me to call that one a win.

The train rattles and shifts as the tracks turn to the right. I hurry up, reaching the end of the windows, and I peek my head over and look up the train, then down. One guy fumbling for a gun behind me, two more suited thugs ahead, fully armed. I sigh and try to figure out what the hell to do next.

49.

I'm hanging on the edge here, and my options are up or down. I could go back but not forward, which is a shame because forward is the direction I want to go. I remember that Doctor Perugini came into this thinking it was a vacation, and that gives me a strangely inappropriate case of the giggles as I hang, suspended by the tips of my fingers, about seven feet from hitting the ground.

I try to think about what Alpha Male would do in this situation, but then I realize that Beta Male would not have even jumped on this train to begin with. He'd be curled up with a good book back at the apartment, sitting in the wreckage, hoping his sister would return his call. While that would certainly be safer than what I'm presently doing, it wouldn't be nearly as scenic. I think this as I pass over rolling hills that look almost golden. If they were green I could almost believe we were in Wisconsin. The buildings are a dead giveaway, though, their red tile roofs, and square, blocky villa construction.

We pass into a tunnel without warning and I feel the concrete wall inches from my back. Which is sweating, big surprise. Any second now I could get shot at by the guys who are working their way down the train. It's probably too much to hope for that any of them have been splattered by the tunnel, right?

As soon as we're out of the dark, I hurl myself back onto the top of the train, using my powers to blast back to my feet. The guys with guns are only a car length away, and they're scrambling to their feet. They're wobbly, though. This is my chance, though it's still a long shot.

Then I see Lorenzo coming up fast from behind them, and my long shot gets even longer.

I sprint down the car, hoping I don't lose my footing as I go. The lead guy comes up, unbalanced, tipping his pistol up to get a shot—

I throw a hard gust and it feels like I'm trying to push concrete off my hands, I'm so tired. Wind comes out, though, in spite of my certain belief that I'm going to dry fire, and it causes the guy to pinwheel his arms, eyes wide. His balance is compromised just enough for me to knock him aside as I pass, and he goes tumbling from the train with a scream that's comical, if a little short.

Man, that sounds cold. It's like I'm becoming Sienna.

The next guy snaps off a shot, and I dodge my body sideways, hoping that by presenting him a side profile he'll at least have a harder target. It works on the first two shots, and then he has to steady himself because of his precarious firing position. I throw a gust at him that feels like I'm seriously reaching into my arms and ripping the veins out, but it knocks him backward. He slams into the car and his gun goes bouncing over the side, and that's enough for me for the moment.

I'm just about ready to call this a victory when Lorenzo comes down for a landing and blasts me with a full-force gust. It hurls me back, slamming me against the top of the metal car, but I manage to keep from falling off. He looks pissed, and I don't imagine he's going to offer me a helping hand.

It'd be nice, but I'm not counting on it.

"You imbecile!" he says, voice nearly lost on the wind. He's about twenty feet away thanks to his neat little attack as he descended, blowing me back. "You think you can oppose us? As though we are the pathetic little metas just manifesting that you are used to tracking down?" He sends a gust my way that hits me hard, even at twenty feet, tilting me backward and almost knocking me off the train. "You are nothing compared to me. I don't know why Hera always favored you; you are weak."

I blink, my head aching a little from the slam against the car I've just endured. "I dunno, man, maybe it's your personality?"

He rips another gust at me, and I dodge off the side of the train, a move I'm becoming sadly good at. My fingers find the window ledge and I swing forward, then fire a downward gust that gives me a surprising lift, considering it's mostly dispelled by our forward motion. I spring back onto the roof of the train; Lorenzo is only ten feet away.

"She gave you everything!" he shouts and blasts at me. I throw up enough of a gust to cancel most of it out and duck under the rest because he aims high. I'm ready for his next move, and he does as expected—goes low to try and rectify that error. He's got it in his mind to blast me the hell off this train, and if he does, I know I'm not going to be able to get back on.

I leap as he fires, with the aid of my own gust. It's like nails in the forearms this time, and I'm not talking the kind Isabella might deploy if she got feisty; more the kind Father Emmanuel's Lord and Savior got staked to a cross with. It effing hurts, but it doesn't stop me from landing nearly on top of him.

Lorenzo reaches out and grabs me by the shirt, clearly aiming to take this fight up close and personal, and I'm damned sure ready for it. I punch him in the face and he rocks back, throwing a counter of his own that catches me across the jaw. "Keep your mommy issues to yourself, okay, Oedipus?" I manage to spit out in spite of the pain.

He snaps out of my punch like it's nothing and slams into me roughly, taking control of the situation. We hit the roof of the train and I fight to get him off of me, forgetting there's not a ton of room for rolling around.

Whoops.

I feel the train drop away and we're in mid-air, free falling toward the ground below. I'm on top and he's got hold of me tight with one arm. I can see the ground racing toward us, and I let go of him to throw out my arms to keep from slamming into the dirt and grass at killer speed. I summon a gust with all I've got left. The agony is astounding, pain up my arms all the way to the shoulders this time, but I keep myself from slamming into the ground.

Unfortunately, dipshit Lorenzo hangs on for the ride. And then he does something really stupid, presumably out of panic.

He blasts out with a gust of his own using a hand he's got wrapped around me.

If it had hit me, it would have thrown me into the air and him into the ground, which would have been a beautiful—if ironic—end to our little battle. Unfortunately, it goes past me and hits the ground, sending the two of us into a horizontal spin.

Right toward the train.

But it doesn't send us into the side of the train. Oh no. That'd be too easy. It sends us right at the tracks.

I can see the wheels slicing past at high speed. A couple cars have shot past in the moment since we've fallen off, and we're nearing the back of the train. I watch those metal wheels spinning, almost in slow motion, like my brain can sense death is coming.

We're heading straight for them.

I don't even have time to scream before they pass and we dive right under the train. I can feel the carriage going by about a half inch above my head. Wheels streak past, lightning fast, and I'm only controlling my panic barely.

We're still moving, and I'm pretty sure that we'll be bisected any second now. I imagine derailing the train with my head, getting split in half because the guy who's clinging to me is too stupid to know when to quit.

And then we pass under the train unharmed, and I flare the gusts again, this time sending that shattering pain into my biceps while sending us five feet into the air.

I can feel the world drifting around us as Lorenzo takes stock of the situation. It's on his face as we're hovering there, suspended in the air a few feet from the train. His fear is almost a tangible thing, and I know in that moment that he's fully aware of how close to death we both just came.

And then his face crumples into a fury and he puts a hand directly against my chest and fires a gust.

His move drives us apart at high velocity, ripping me from him at furious speed.

I fly through the air until I crash into something—glass, heavy, with shattering sounds that fill my ears. I tumble down, falling over a table, landing facedown on carpeting, and it takes me a moment of disorientation to realize I'm *inside* the train.

People are staring at me. There's shattered glass in my skin, not that I can tell over the throbbing, screaming pain in my arms and shoulders. I see eyes, countless eyes, fixed on me in shock. I think I've crashed their tea party or something, and I'm just sitting in the middle of an aisle, rolling in the foot or so of space between chairs.

It's a rude shock, getting heaved through a glass window, and I'm just about over it and ready to try standing when someone comes flying in to land at my feet. He does it right, sideways through the narrow window, exhibiting a kind of flight control I wouldn't have believed possible from an Aeolus without seeing it.

Alpha Male is definitely not Alpha Aeolus. Which is good, because that's an alliterative nightmare.

"She gave you everything!" Lorenzo says again.

"God, are you still on about that?" I ask, rolling to a sitting position as I pluck a shard of glass out of my arm. Blood wells up in the wound. "We just went under a fricking train and barely survived. Take a moment and—"

He throws his hands in a sideways motion like he's summoning Tony Stark's armor to him, but I know that's not it. The wind launches me from the floor and I feel the pain as I smash through the window on the other side. The glass shatters as I go through shoulder first, and I feel weightless, once more, as I plummet to the ground.

50.

"You seem like a man who has careful control of himself and all around him," she says. The flattery is all the sweeter for being the truth.

Anselmo cannot help but smile more broadly. This is a very astute and observant woman, to have picked up on this so quickly. "It has often been said," he agrees. Cordial conversation is a mark of civility and class—and this woman? She is among the classiest he has met.

She leans in a little closer, toward the aisle that separates them. "To have set things up in such a manner, to conceal your means and motive … it is impressive." She shrugs slightly, as though it is a compliment hard given, and he revels in it all the same.

"There is an element of planning," he says, "of fastidiousness. To orchestrate great things, one must be great." He is not one for false humility; why should he be? "The old gods, they had flair. They could move openly, show their greatness to all. Impose fear where needed. Hiding like dogs?" He waves his hand. "This is the challenge of a secret society like … well, you know. Our kind—metahumans—we were fools to ever accept that we should hide ourselves." He inclines his head in thought. "And the same is true of La

Cosa Nostra, 'Ndrangheta, and the others. It takes a strong man to walk tall in the face of his enemies."

She nods, and he can tell she understands. "You are such a man, then." She plays a little coy for a moment. "But if it is as you say, then you mean to … walk tall in the face of those who oppose you?"

He smiles. "*Sì*. I do."

She blinks, bats her eyelashes. "But how would you do such a thing? There are so many who would stand against you …"

He feels the thrill, the excitement. Months of planning, months of work, of considering possibilities and trying to find the way to bring them to fruition. "They are of little consequence."

She cocks her head shrewdly. He loves the look in her eyes. "How …?"

He smiles and tells her—just a hint, really. It is enough to cause her beautiful eyes to widen, and very much worth it.

51.

I almost hit the ground before I spin enough to blast a gust off the dirt just in time. I throw everything I have left into it for the millionth time, and my chest hurts all the way through my lungs this time.

The gust is good enough to propel me about six feet up, then I start to drop. I throw up a hand and catch the edge of a window again. I hang there, getting my bearings for about half a second.

I'm on the last car of the train.

Again.

I sigh at the utter lack of progress. Two steps forward, one step back would feel like a prize-winning performance compared to this. All I've done since Lorenzo has showed up is lose ground, and I've got pretty much none left to lose.

I'm resigned to slinging myself back up onto the roof of the train to try again when a guy appears above me with a gun, and I remember I left one more of these goons back here to deal with. Aw, hell. I thought I at least knocked his gun away.

I go to throw air at him and nothing happens. It's almost as embarrassing as the time when I was a teenager and my car sputtered and died on a date, right in front of the girl's house after I'd picked her up.

173

Almost.

He fires, and I sling myself to the side, channeling my inner Spider-Man and hurling myself up onto the car faster than he can bring his gun around. I'm lucky it's a pistol because he's at least halfway through the magazine on gut instinct before I get up on the carriage.

He swings it around, and I try to throw wind again. A short blast ruffles his hair and that's it. Which would be fine if I was just trying to be affectionate with the son I don't have, but unfortunately I'm trying to knock over a guy who's about to shoot me.

He's four feet away, has his gun in hand, and he's drawing a bead on me. I'm exhausted, my powers are depleted, and I have pretty much of nothing left to give.

So I kick him in the kneecap just as he fires, and I swear I can feel the wind as the bullet passes my cheek.

He looks angry, not agonized, because my clumsy kick is not enough to shatter his patella—total bummer, I know— and he's bringing his gun around so that I can look straight down the barrel when the first piece of good news I've had in quite awhile comes to my attention.

The slide of his gun is back and locked. Hallelujah. He's as empty as me after Dr. Perugini – never mind.

I am all over him like a Doberman on a fresh steak. I knock his ass over and pummel him into unconsciousness in about five seconds. If I were fully awake, I might be enjoying the sound of his skull rattling against the top of the carriage. As it is, I'm overjoyed when his eyes roll back in his head, because I don't really want to beat a man to death on top of a speeding express train to Florence today. Or any day. Or anywhere, ever.

I stagger to my feet with a sense of rough satisfaction that I've spared this asshole, and then I feel my heart sink within as I see what's standing in front of me.

Lorenzo.

Again.

And still—shit, even still—he looks mad enough to chew through the steel skin of the train with his own teeth. And I'm standing there, in front of him, completely exhausted, without anything left to give.

52.

"Dude," I say, "aren't you tired of this yet?" I know he's not by the look in his eyes. Lorenzo wants to kill me. He's been trying since he first ran into me. This would be obvious to anyone watching, really, but I'm so exhausted I just want the fight to be over.

He doesn't say anything, just screams in fury (technically, that's not *saying* anything) and comes at me. I don't know if he caught my windless act with the flunky, but he doesn't bother to hit me with his powers. He just comes at me all raging bull and slams hard into me. I punch him twice in the head and it does nothing. He shakes it off like he's Taylor Swift and lifts me into the air over his head. It's a precarious position, and I get the feeling of danger as I tower above the ground—

And then he throws me over the back of the train.

I realize as I drift toward the ground that he's seriously out of his gourd with rage. Apparently my tight relationship with Hera was more of a point of contention in Alpha than I ever knew. I throw my arms back as I fall, and kick my legs beneath me. I reach deep one last time for my power and find it, and this time it feels like a heart attack, like someone rips through my chest cavity with a buzz saw as I blast wind out of my hands and my feet, knocking my shoes clear off in the gust.

The wind kicks me back up to the back of the carriage where Lorenzo is standing, stunned. He may not be as exhausted as I am, but his mind is clearly going, since throwing an Aeolus over the back of a train is probably not the most effective means of killing one of us.

I catch him with an extremely weak kick as I land, and he staggers back with a grunt. I follow up with an uppercut to the face that staggers him. "She wasn't even your mom," I say as I smack him. I go low and work the gut with a couple of solid hits that have him on the ropes. You know, if a train had ropes. Something occurs to me. "She wasn't actually your mom, was she?"

His gaze hardens and he gets even more royally pissed. I can't decide if he's raw because I'm kicking his ass or because she actually was his mother, but either way I hesitate for a second (stupidly), and he catches his furious second wind. He comes at me like I said something about his mother (jury's still out on that one), and he nails me under my guard, right in the groin. It's a cheap shot, and it's full of meta power, and it sends me to my knees.

His anger is boiling over by this point, and maybe that's what saves my life. Rather than engage in reasoned debate, or cold, calculated revenge, he kicks me while I'm down, right in the ribs, and sends me over the side of the train for the last time.

I'm in agony, and I'm falling. I throw out my hands and produce just a small burst of wind as I land, enough to defray some of the momentum and force of the seventy-plus mile-an-hour impact. I roll through tall, yellow grass, countless rocks that feel like boulders pounding into my legs, my ribs and everything else.

I come to a rest staring into a blue sky overhead. It's pretty, I reflect, but it seems so very distant. I stare into it, and the clouds seem particularly white. They glow, they brighten, they fill the sky. I feel my eyes dragged shut by gravity, but the brightness lingers. I let it take over the world around me, dissolving everything into it, and I slip away into blissful unconsciousness.

53.

The woman is still quiet and contemplative when Lorenzo re-enters the car. He looks a bit scuffed up, with blood running from an open wound on his eyebrow, and his suit torn in several places. He looks like a man, though, a blood bubble in one nostril. Anselmo can tell by his bearing that he has faced his problems and has triumphed, and that counts for much.

"Done," Lorenzo says, pouring himself into the seat behind the woman. Anselmo tilts himself to look at the boy, who looks as though he is about to pass out.

"He is dead, then?" Anselmo asks.

"He is off the train," Lorenzo pronounces. "He was lying unmoving in the grass after landing."

Anselmo ponders this for a moment, and finds he is not even angry. "Call the house. Have them send two cars with men. Tell them approximately where he landed, and have them search." He points a finger at Lorenzo. "Tell them to shoot first. Bring rifles."

Lorenzo nods, and pulls out his phone, making a call as quickly as his fingers can dial.

Anselmo turns to look at the woman, and she appears … stricken. "It is okay, my dear," he says, soothing her. "It will

178

be over swiftly. He is likely suffering, and should be put out of his misery."

Like a dog, Anselmo does not add, purely out of sensitivity.

54.

Reed

Pharell's "Happy" fills the air around me, but it's tinny and feels like it's playing at a distance. My eyes are nearly impossible to pry open, and I wish the song would just carry me away on the notes.

It fades and quiets, then starts again, and it feels like it's dragging me physically somewhere.

I open my eyes to find that the sky is still blue. My body aches, a thousand pains registering their outrage through screaming nerve endings.

I move a hand gingerly, trying to localize the sound of the song as it fills the air for a third time. I realize it's coming from my pants pocket and I dip my fingers in, rustling until I finally come up with my phone.

It's J.J. calling. I press the damned green button and let my arm fall to hold the phone against my ear. "What?" I ask, and I sound bad even to myself.

"Dude, you've been unmoving next to the train tracks for like twenty minutes," J.J. says, skipping his usual cheerful greeting. "Are you okay?"

I sit up, slowly, taking inventory of all my miseries. There are so many. "Not really."

"Gotta get going, pal," J.J. says. "You need to walk about five minutes north. I've got a cab on the way for you."

"I just wanna lie here and die," I say and mean it.

"High likelihood that'll happen for real if you don't get going," J.J. says. "I've got two cars moving out of Serafini's compound. Thermal shows they're loaded with guys—with guns—and they're heading your way."

"Awwwghhh," I moan, leaning forward.

"They've got Dr. Perugini, man," J.J. says, and I suddenly remember why I was on that train to begin with. "You gotta make like a cow and mooooove, man."

"Sounds more like I've had a laxative if I'm doing that much moving," I mutter in protest as I manage to get myself into a squat. Standing up is going to be a slow process.

"Haha, like diarrhea," J.J. says, the master of subtlety. "Seriously, though, you need to go. Cab's gonna be there in like five minutes."

"I'm going," I say, getting to my feet and shuffling along the tracks. A really dismal thought occurs to me. "What the hell am I gonna do now?"

"What heroes do," J.J. says, like it's obvious. "Rescue the girl, pee in the bad guy's cornflakes. You got this, you're a natural white hat, dude."

If I had been wearing any hat at all, it would have been crushed in the last fall from the train. I hold up a palm as I walk and try to stir the wind. It's faint, but a little comes, along with a whole lotta pain. "Owwww." I cringe and keep walking. "Man, I don't know if I have anything left. I assume Anselmo has guards at his compound, and even if not, he's still got himself and his iron skin plus Lorenzo, the guy who just threw me from a moving train."

"At least he didn't throw your momma from a train," J.J. says with some amusement. This is just what he's like, all the time. He waits for me to get the joke, and when I don't respond, he says, "You know, like the movie, '*Throw Momma*—'"

"I got it," I assure him, stumbling along. There's a road ahead, and it's not too far off, running almost parallel to the tracks. Exhaustion rolls over me in waves. "But as you like to say, 'Seriously, dude—'" I feel so much frustration welling inside, I don't quite know where to go with it all. "I have no idea what to do. I can't fight them both like this." My feet are dragging as I walk. "I can't fight anything right now."

"Just get in the cab and rest up, bro," he says, and I see movement on the horizon. Sure enough, it's a cab, and it's rolling toward me. "We'll figure something out on the way."

I make it the last hundred yards to the cab like a car rolling along the shoulder on fumes. I lean my head back against the soft interior as the cabby spews out an address at me. "*Si, si*," I say, assuming J.J. gave it to him. He starts the meter and turns the car around.

I watch the horizon for about a minute before I feel my phone slip out of my grasp. I find myself staring at the car's ceiling, the upholstery hanging off in little bubbles here and there, gravity gradually pulling it down. I feel gravity working on me, too, and I pass out in the back of the cab as we rumble along a back road somewhere in central Italy. I have no clue what I'm going to do next but I'm pretty positive I'm screwed in every quantifiable way except the one I wanted to be—the one which would involve a certain doctor whom I have no idea how to save.

55.

He is off the train almost before it has come to a halt, Lorenzo in front of him and the woman at his side, his iron grip on her elbow. "I will show you my palace, darling," he promises her as he steers her through the station.

One of his men is waiting in a car just outside and they pile in. The car is moving almost before Lorenzo is in.

"Have you been to Firenze before?" he asks the woman. He stares at her, starting low and surveying up, again. It is flattering to her, surely, that he should pay such attention to her curves. They are magnificent, perfect in all the right ways.

"*Sì*," she says, but her voice has faded. She is put off by the thought of her friend's death, clearly. Anselmo knows that this is a phase that is certain to pass as her soft heart comes to the realization that she has traded up in the world. Still, it is natural that she should feel a moment's conflict. Now he realizes it is down to him to make her aware of how greatly she will benefit from this change.

"Tomorrow I will take you onto the Ponte Vecchio and buy you something gold," he says. "Have you ever been shopping upon the bridge before?"

She blinks at him. "Once. Many years ago."

"There are charms and rings," he says, "so lovely and so many. None could add to your beauty, of course, but perhaps they could assuage that sense of grief you feel." He smiles. "Have you ever wanted something lovely and expensive, my dear? Because now it could be within your reach. A hundred thousand euros?" He snaps his finger. "Is nothing. You could be drenched with gold tomorrow, diamonds studding the beauteous jewelry draping your … lovely body."

"Do not forget your meeting tomorrow, *Capo*," Lorenzo says, a warning.

"It would be hard to forget," Anselmo says, all breezy charm. He would not miss it for the world, not even for this lovely piece. "We will be back in plenty of time."

She falls into silence and he lets her, staring out on the street as they cross the river on the way to his villa. It is an easy silence, and he fills it with the occasional study of her form. He does so over and over, in a repeating pattern, to flatter her as they ride. She seems not to notice, and this is fine for now.

The pull through the gate and under the portico, and he is quickly out of the car and offering her a hand. She takes it without word, and they enter his abode.

She observes it all in with a practiced eye. The air is scented with a lovely pasta. The chef is clearly at work, informed of the master of the house's return. He steers her, hand gripping her elbow, through the house and onto the back patio.

It is a lovely pool deck, though the pool itself is covered over for the winter with the plastic bubble covering that keeps the leaves and dirt and melting snow from making it filthy. But it is surrounded by trees that give it shade in summer, and the view is magnificent. He takes a breath, a peaceful breath, feels the relaxation flow into him, and snaps his fingers.

The servant girl comes over hesitantly, like a dog that has been whipped. "*Sì?*"

"Brandy for two," Anselmo says. "A cigar." He glances at the woman. "Would you like something to eat, my dear?"

"No, thank you," she says, the epitome of class. Her dark, straight hair sways over her shoulders as she takes it all in.

"What is this?" The voice is high pitched and furious, outraged all out of proportion to the situation. Anselmo turns to see Elena—lovely Elena, his mistress—stalking toward him. She has never shown this particular stripe of anger before, and he raises an eyebrow. "Who is she?" Elena asks, whiplash voice echoing over the patio as she arrives just as the servant girl flees.

Anselmo turns his eyes to the new woman. "What is your name, my dear?"

"Isabella," the woman says. "Isabella Perugini."

"What a lovely name," Anselmo coos. He turns to look at Elena. "Isabella Perugini. Have you heard a more lovely name?"

"You lech!" Elena says, almost hissing. This causes Anselmo's blood to pause, to run cold. "You dirty old man. You bring a new woman here, *in front of me*, without so much as caring—"

Anselmo stares down the steep hill ahead, down to Firenze in all its glory below. This is his home, this is his domain, his place. He listens for a moment more, takes all that he can take, and then he feels a strange snap in his head, like a switch being clicked. He backhands Elena, casually, but with some strength, a little rage bleeding through. It catches her on the cheek and snaps her head back. Her eyes go wide then her face slackens, and she falls onto the bubble covering of the pool and sinks in.

Anselmo puckers his lips together, twisting them. He is parched, thirsty. He knows her neck is broken, that she is done. "Where is our brandy?" he asks, smiling at his new woman—Isabella—as the old one lazily sinks to the bottom of the pool, never to rise on her own again.

56.

Reed

I awaken to the cab driver shouting at me in Italian. I blink my eyes open to fading daylight and a tall hill, with a driveway that stretches up past a gate in the distance. The driver has done me a favor, because there are guys with guns just barely visible up the way, shuffling around a gatehouse. They're not looking at me, and for this I'm thankful.

I quickly pay him via credit card. I manage, despite my bad Italian, to make one last request and exit the cab to dart into the cover of trees that leads up to the wall of a palatial estate. It's not exactly a hollowed out volcano or an undersea lair, but as far as villainous strongholds go, it's not bad.

I slip along the wall and out of sight of the gatehouse, unobserved. I wonder about security cameras, but I realize I can't really afford to second guess myself, at least not at the moment. I've got a fraction of an idea how to do this based on what J.J. told me about Anselmo's estate, and if I don't move quickly, it's guaranteed to fail.

I'm over the wall in three shakes, slipping through thick underbrush that probably takes a gardener hours per day to maintain and make pretty. And it is pretty; professional landscaping of the sort you'd expect from a hilltop mansion.

I can see the house in the distance, and the guard detail looks blessedly light. Presumably a good portion of his guys are still out combing the railroad tracks for my corpse, which is all the better for me, because I'd sure hate to be completely outnumbered and outgunned.

Oh, wait. I still am.

Guys with guns are a major motif around the place. Another guy with a rifle on his back saunters past me.

I seize him by the back of the neck and choke him out. Not dead, just out.

I slip the rifle off his back and futz with it a little. I'm not fond of guns like Sienna is, but I can fumble my way through using one when needed. I figure out where the safety is, make sure a round is in the chamber, and then start moving around the side of the house.

It's a big, sprawling place, a *casa* of the sort that the provincial governors probably used to have. I jump onto the red tile roof of the house and scamper up behind the roofline as I hear voices out back. I peek out and see exactly what I expected: an amazing, tremendous view of a sweeping hillside that leads down into Florence proper, and ...

And a pool deck with Anselmo, Lorenzo and Isabella sitting out and looking across the splendor of the valley below.

It takes me a second to realize there's a body in the pool. It's not moving, and everyone seems to be ignoring it except Isabella, whose furtive eyes keep darting back to it every few seconds. I can't see much in the shape, just a faint outline wrapped up in that bubbly stuff they use to cover a pool.

I put the curious questions about who it is and why they ended up in the drink out of my mind and start planning my move.

57.

Anselmo

"You see, my dear," Anselmo says, "my father, he was killed by a member of the Sacra Corona Unita." Anselmo feels his lips smack together as he tells the story, and stops to slake his thirst with a sip of brandy. "This man, he was a fool, for he let me live. Mercy, he said." Anselmo smiles at the memory. "Even before I manifested, as a boy of fourteen, I became a man that very night. I beat him to death after darkness fell." He raises a hand to show her. "His wife, she screamed in the night as the blood flecked across her face. She could have become an enemy, so I killed her, too." He swings the hand again, his grin wide. "Enemies, it does not pay to leave them alive. Ever." He shrugs. "This is the cost of mercy, you see? Always it comes back to haunt you, so a man—a real man, he shows no mercy in this. Dispenses with his enemies—man, woman, their boys, and even girls nowadays. Is necessary to ensure your power, your survival." He tastes the brandy again, swirls it around. "A real man dispatches his enemies fearlessly, never allowing the possibility that they will come back to him later—"

Gunshots ring out in the night, and Anselmo leaps to his feet, dropping the glass of brandy. He is dimly aware of it shattering against the concrete patio, splattering against his socks and trouser leg. He spins toward the house, toward the direction of the shots, and sees Lorenzo fall. Bloody stains appear upon his chest, and the boy sags, falling to the ground.

"What the—" Anselmo barely gets out before he catches sight of Treston upon the rooftop, a rifle in his hands. The boy tosses it aside and jumps, at him, gliding across the pool toward Anselmo. But Anselmo is ready, the smile already upon his face at the thought of what is to come. He will kill Treston, oh yes, show Isabella that he is a real man, and then he will have her—

He feels the strong hands push him from behind – the force of a shove coming from that damned woman – but he is improperly balanced to do anything about it. He falls forward, into the pool, the splash followed by the deafening rush of his heartbeat. Anselmo flails as he tangles in the covering of the pool. It wraps around him, trapping his limbs, trapping his torso. It fills his vision, everywhere, and he fights it, twists—

And finds himself face to face with Elena's dead eyes.

Anselmo screams in fury, bubbles rushing before his eyes, and feels his feet touch the bottom of the pool at last. He puts everything into his legs and jumps, ripping the cover out of the pool as he breaks out of the surface, limbs still wrapped in the covering, and lands, hard, on the concrete decking.

He lies there, gasping, fearful, dripping water out of his mouth and his nose as the sound of heavy footfalls fills the air around him. He hears the cries of *"Capo! Capo!"* but it takes him a moment to gather his wits and respond.

58.

Reed

"Sorry," I say as I glide down the hill, Isabella Perugini's arms wrapped around me. "I would have waited a couple more minutes, but I felt compelled to strike while the irony of his bullshit about wiping out his enemies was still heavy in the air." I push my power to the straining point and beyond, and I don't even care. My arms are past complaining at this point, my bare feet bearing the brunt of the channeling force. Either I've broken through to a new level of using my powers or I'm going to be dead tomorrow.

Isabella rests her head against my chest as we slip down the hill behind Anselmo Serafini's estate like a high-speed ski run, and I realize that if I die tomorrow, it was totally worth it for this moment.

I steer us around the trees, avoiding the obstacles most likely to cause a skull fracture, and finally catch sight of a road ahead.

"What now?" Isabella asks. "He'll have the train stations watched." She sounds worried.

"Probably the airports, too," I say. "At least within minutes."

She lifts her head off my chest to look at me, and the wind rushes by around us as I take us down the last hundred feet or so and feel the bare soles of my feet touch the sidewalk next to the road. "What do we do?"

There's a squeal of tires and my cabby comes to a stop a few feet away from the curb. "We take a cab," I say, feeling a sense of relief that this one little thing has gone right for me.

She clutches my hand tight as I open the door for her and let her in first. I slide into the car next to her and feel her lean her head against me, warmly, as the cab driver floors it. Back to Rome, away from here. The sirens fill the night air as we make our escape from Florence.

59.

Anselmo

Anselmo sits in his chair, clothes dripping as he stares out across the once-magnificent view. It was magnificent only moments earlier. Sitting here, with Lorenzo and Isabella, it had seemed the grandest thing he could imagine. He puckers his wet lips, feels beads of water roll down his skin.

He feels his face contract with hatred. To be so unmanned in his own home—

He swallows the anger, and it is a bitter taste. "Treston," he says, and it is the vilest curse he can imagine. He lets his eyes drift to Lorenzo, who bleeds quietly upon the concrete.

"Capo." This quiet breath comes from Niccolo, one of his lieutenants. Anselmo feels his furious gaze slide over the man, watches him flinch before it. "The Carabinieri, they will be here—"

"Tell them to fuck off," Anselmo says, letting his eyes drift back to the horizon, to where Treston made his escape, taking Isabella—that traitorous bitch—with him. "I pay them to stay away, so tell them to stay away."

"Si, Capo," Niccolo says and disappears back toward the house.

"And Niccolo?" Anselmo says, feeling the water drip off his body. His shoes are sodden, wet. He looks down and sees that he is still wearing the shirt he took from Treston's suitcase back in Rome. To the victor the spoils.

"*Sì?*"

"Find that servant girl, and have her bring me a drink," Anselmo says. There is a low moan, and his eyes shift to Lorenzo once more. "Drag Lorenzo inside and have a doctor take the bullets out." He waves a hand. "Put men at the airport and train station. Find them."

"Which should I do first, *Capo*?" Niccolo asks, the fool.

"The drink, idiot," Anselmo says, without a moment's pause. "The girl. Then deal with the airports and train station, and finally … this." He waves his hand again at Lorenzo's body as the boy moves his leg in pain.

Anselmo shakes his head, dark plots rolling through his mind, and he continues to stare out at the impressive vista. Night begins to fall around him, and he has needs, emotions, disappointments to make up for. He barely hears the girl as she brings him wine.

No one fails to hear her, though, possibly not even down in Florence.

60.

Reed

"Picciotti," Perugini says as we step out of the cab in Rome. I have no idea what it means, and I don't know whether she's referring to the cab driver or not, though I suspect by the way she rubs her own shoulders, arms crossed over her body, that she's not. The cab driver looks at her out the window, pure outrage on his face. "Not you," she says, answering my question for me, and he speeds off like he didn't hear her apology.

"What?" I ask, trying to maintain a sensitive distance. She looks disgusted, and I don't want to step into that.

"He told me," she says, shaking her head, "that he was up to something."

"Did he tell you what?" I take a step closer, my desire to know what Anselmo is planning overruling my desire to give her space.

"Not exactly," she says and starts down the avenue. We're on the Via Nazionale, though I'm not sure where to go, so I just follow her for now. She's blowing off steam, getting her aggravation out of her system at being kidnapped by Anselmo, and I'm quite content to let her. "But he gave me a powerful hint."

"What was it?" I ask.

"He said that he's going to make Giovanni Falcone look like the work of little boys," she says, not turning to face me, taking each step as though the mere act of walking is enough to drain the poison from her system.

"I ... I have no idea who that is," I say, utterly mystified.

"He was a prosecutor," she says, turning back to give me a look. If I thought she was inscrutable before, all that is gone now. Her eyebrows are down at a forty-five degree angle, her lips are pressed tight together when she's not talking, a line of stress that doesn't give a hint she's ever been happy in her life. "The Sicilian Mafia killed him with a bomb. They blew up his car."

"So he's gonna kill someone," I say. "With a bomb?"

She shakes her head. "He did not get specific. He is mad with power, thinks he is a god or something."

I tilt my head as I think it over. "He kinda is. He's got invulnerable skin, can't be cut, can't be hurt with bullets or swords or fists." I clench my jaw. "And he's sitting at the head of a crime family of some sort."

She gets a flash of wariness at this. "He has a meeting planned. Something big. Tomorrow."

"Big?" I ask. "Like what? And who's he meeting with?"

"Other *picciotti*, probably," she says and spits on the sidewalk. "He is up to something. A nasty little schemer."

"Okay, so maybe he's meeting with other mobsters," I say, my mind racing, trying to figure things out. "Or maybe somebody else? Someone related to this kill he's planning?"

"I don't know," she says, shaking her head. "He is a pig, a lech, a violent man who has no recognition of others or his own limits." She shudders slightly, and it stops her in the middle of the sidewalk. "He thought I was interested in him, the fool!"

I freeze. "But ... you're not, right?" She gives me a narrow-eyed glare, and I feel like I should take a step back. "Uh, right. Of course not."

"He killed his woman in front of me," she says, and it's the closest I've seen to her being truly vulnerable. "Hit her so hard it broke her neck. She fell back into the pool and sank to the bottom." She brings a hand up and covers her eyes. "I knew she was dead, and I had to stand there, act like nothing happened, to maintain the charade. I should have been checking her, trying to resuscitate on the chance it was just a bad head injury." She shakes her head, like she's trying to get the image out of her skull. "He just ... killed her, right there." She doesn't even tear up, just stands there, looking utterly stricken.

I reach out first, I think, but she quickly pulls tight to me as soon as I do. She squeezes me like it's going to get the hatred out, like she can hug it out of me. I don't mind, and I damned sure don't complain, even if it's a little tight. I can take it.

She's almost got it out of her system, I think, when my phone rings. I pull it out of my pocket and press it to my ear, still looking her in the eyes. They're a little moist, but she's doing better than I would have in her shoes. "Hello?" I ask the open line.

"Dude, you made it back to Rome!" J.J. says with a clear sense of relief.

"Safe and sound," I say, and then a thought occurs to me. "Though I don't know what I'm going to do now that I'm here."

"I've got that covered for you, bro," J.J. says. "The agency is in full mobilization to try and help you out."

"What?" I ask. "How'd that happen?"

"I talked to Ariadne," he says, and I can hear the smile in his voice. "She retasked everything—analysis units, Homeland Security liaisons, everything. The American embassy printed you a new set of passports with cover names on them, and I've got a CIA courier on his way to your position now to drop them off. He'll be there in two minutes. You'll also have new credit cards, some cash, new burner phones and a few other toys that the station there could spare."

I stand there, stunned, but not quite speechless. "Thank you, J.J."

"We're behind you one hundred and ninety percent, bro," he says. "I'm sure Sienna would be, too, if she were here."

I nod, even though he can't see me, and feel a little choked up. "Where is she?"

"Northern Canuckistan," he says. It takes me a second to realize he means Canada. "She went up there on a State Department thing, trying to help out our neighbors to the north with a potential meta issue. Pretty far out of contact at the moment. We've got messages in for her, though. You need her help when she gets back?"

I swallow that last vestige of pride. "I need all the help I can get."

"We'll do what we can," he says. "Ariadne is working all the angles, but no promises."

Ariadne. I've always gotten along well with her. Probably because in spite of anything else, I've always believed she has Sienna's best interests at heart. Few do. Still, this is a huge thing, retasking a domestic U.S. agency's resources to something a lone guy is doing in a foreign country. Even if it's me, and I'm facing something as nasty as Anselmo.

"So, bro," J.J.'s voice comes back again, "what now?"

I think about what I've just told him, about needing all the help I can get, and a thought occurs to me. "I need to go back to the scene of the crime," I say, and raise my hand to try and flag a cab. I don't want to be walking around Rome, not right now.

"Courier is almost there," J.J. says. A black car pulls up in front of me and a guy pops out of the passenger side with a brown paper package. He nods at me, hands it over without a word, then steps back into the car. As it drives off, I'm left without any impression of him whatsoever; he's a true grey man.

"Thank you, J.J.," I say and flag a cab as it goes past. It slides to the curb, and I open the door for Perugini and follow her in, telling the driver where we're going.

"No problem, man," he says, and I'm about to tear open the package when he stops me. "Don't open that where people can see you. There's stuff in there you'll want to take a look at in private."

I frown. "What is it?"

"Just a little something extra," he says, and the glee is unmistakable. "After all, you can't be James Bond without the gadgets." He pauses, and thinks it over for a second. "Unless you're Daniel Craig, I guess. But, still ... hopefully it's something that'll help you out if you're gonna fight these guys."

61.

There is blood all over the concrete, and Anselmo still does not care. He stares down at Firenze—his town, his home. He takes in the larger part of the view in a widening sweep.

This is his land, his country.

"Capo?" Niccolo's soft voice asks permission to interrupt his thoughts. Anselmo's thoughts are all dark and clouded in any case, like the night that falls around him, obscuring in the shadows what he has done.

"What?" Anselmo says. He looks at the wine glass clenched in his hand. It is empty, and his fingers drip with blood.

"Our men at the train station have seen nothing," Niccolo says. "Nothing at the airport, either. No reservations for Americans fitting this Treston's description." He pauses, and Anselmo can hear him licking his lips. "We have also canvassed the hotels in the area, and ... nothing. No one has seen them. They are not in Firenze."

Anselmo clenches his fist and hears the glass shatter in his grasp. It tinkles and cracks as the fragments fall from between his fingers. "They have eluded us, you mean. Escaped." He turns his head slowly to look at Niccolo. "Made a fool of me."

199

"No, *Capo*," Niccolo says just a little too quickly to be reassuring. "No one is thinking of you as a fool."

"Yes, they are," Anselmo says, and the tinge of red in the sunset catches his eye. "They are all of them thinking me a fool. Every one of them is in town, every one of them will hear." He looks over his house, knows there are men within that gossip as women. "The men will talk, the other *capos* will hear."

Niccolo looks at the house, the wheels turning in his mind. "*Capo* … are you thinking …?"

"Of killing them all?" Anselmo grins. "I am thinking of it. Is there a reason why I should not?"

Niccolo swallows heavily. "That is … a great many bodies to dispose of …"

"It is a great many lackeys to replace," Anselmo says, and he feels himself grow more bitter at the thought. Good help is hard to find, and killing all his help—while immediately satisfying—would be more annoying in the long run. He looks down at the shattered glass, and realizes that it proves his point perfectly. Who will bring him wine when all the others are dead? "Bring me a brandy, Niccolo," he says instead, and sits back down upon the chair, ignoring the glass, the blood, the bodies that all lie within a few feet of him.

"*Si, Capo,*" Niccolo says, and beats a hasty retreat. "I will … bring you an update when there is something new to tell—"

"Keep your updates," Anselmo says, waving him off coldly. "Dispose of this trash and scrub the concrete clean. We have a meeting to consider. Call the other *capos*; get them over here right now."

"Right now?" Niccolo asks, as though he is deaf.

"Now," Anselmo says, not deigning to explain his thinking. "At this very moment. Then make certain Lorenzo is tended to; there are other plans coming to fruition that will require his assistance." He swings his head around to look at

Niccolo, who now stands on the other side of the pool from him. He doesn't quite quake, but there is a certain weakness evident in his knees. The boy would collapse right now were he not trying to portray his strength. "Now get me my brandy and begin calling the *capos*."

Anselmo looks back to the darkening horizon and considers Treston again. He looks down at his stolen shirt, his symbol of triumph. It is stained with red, and the jacket is torn in several places. He imagines Treston still wearing it, his girlish screams, the thought of his hands around that boy's throat, and it soothes him. The moment will come, and this time—this time—he will not hesitate. Mercy is for the weak, after all.

And Anselmo has no mercy left for anyone.

62.

We get out of the cab at the end of the alley next to Giuseppe's shop and hike in quickly. The cab driver takes off after I've paid, clearly not willing to wait around. I imagine the crime scene tape might have something to do with his reluctance; who wants to be an accessory to breaking and entering, after all? Especially for less than twenty euros.

I walk down the alleyway, ignoring the yellow tape and steering around bloodstains. Isabella stays at my side as we navigate through, eventually coming to the sealed door of the shop. It's got a metal shutter down the front to prevent stealing, but I rip it open in about two seconds. There's a stack of newspapers bundled out front; apparently the paper company did not get the memo about this being a crime scene. Either that, or circulation is so low that they're desperate to sell to anyone they can. I step around the stack and enter Giuseppe's shop.

The place is still a mess, and I linger in the darkness of the entryway for a moment longer than necessary. Isabella hesitates, and I catch her reluctance. "Why don't you wait here?" I ask. "Keep an eye out, let me know if anyone comes this way?"

"Sure," she says, and sits down at one of the café tables across from the shattered deli display. The sandwiches inside are moldering, the *funghi* clearly growing a fungus. I leave her with that and step toward the back of the shop, treading slowly into Giuseppe's office. I'm not sure what to expect when I get inside, but it's not this.

The whole place is empty. Gone. Boxed up and taken, nothing left but the desk, the cot and the lamps. Every personal item, every scrap of paper, even his damned Rolodex is all gone. I can't decide whether the police were exceptionally thorough or whether Lorenzo had people come through and clean the dead man out.

I stare at what's left; even the desk drawers are pulled out to display empty bottoms. I gingerly pick up the phone and hear a dial tone. Using my knuckle so as not to leave fingerprints, I dial J.J.'s number and wait for him to pick up. "Hello?" he asks.

"J.J., I need the call history for this phone," I say.

"Uh, okay," he says. "I'm on it. Give me five minutes."

I hang up and step out of the office to see the bathroom door open opposite his. Realizing I need to take a leak, I step across the hall and do my business. It smells in here. Bad. Astute person that I am, I'm halfway done when I notice the sign over the toilet. It asks me to leave this bathroom as I'd like to find it, but since I'm fresh out of scourging fire to clean it properly, I just take a deep breath and hurry.

My phone rings as I step back out, and I answer it as I pass back toward Giuseppe's office. I catch a glimpse of Isabella, who is wandering around at the front of the store, looking things over. I step into the empty office, and J.J. starts talking before I even greet him.

"Okay, I've got the records for the phone," he says. "No incoming calls in the last few days, but there was a flurry of them on the night of the—"

"Just send me the numbers, okay?" I ask. There's nothing I can do with them right this second anyway. I hear a beep on my phone that signals a new text message.

"That's the basics of the last day of calls," he says. "Only a handful of numbers, so it should be a quick sift."

"Thanks, J.J.," I say and hang up. I look around the near-empty room, at the vast emptiness. Giuseppe's life was carted out in hours, maybe less. An entire existence wiped clean in no time. I didn't know the guy that well, but it feels like he deserves more than this. Some acknowledgment, some hint that there was purpose behind his passing.

Something that would mean he didn't die in vain.

"Reed!" I hear Isabella call, and I'm out the door of the office in seconds. I come around the corner to see her standing at the entry to the shop, staring at the ground.

"What?" I ask, hurrying toward her. She doesn't sound normal. She sounds a little rattled, like there's a reason she's calling me.

"Anselmo has a man still in the Vatican, yes?" she asks, even though I think she knows the answer.

"Yeah," I say, "Fintan O'Niall." I reach her shoulder and stare down with her at a newspaper. The headline is in Italian, and I have no clue what it says. "Why?"

She tears her eyes away from it, looking as stricken as I've ever seen her—way more upset than when I helped rescue her from the clutches of a murderous gangster. She points at the newspaper. "Prime Minister to meet with Pope at Vatican the day after tomorrow," she says, and I don't even need a pen to connect the dots on that one. I get a sick feeling in the pit of my stomach, one followed by a sense of desperation, and I stare at the headline in hopes that somehow—just somehow—it doesn't mean what she and I both think it means.

63.

We check into a hotel under our new names. Coincidentally, we're playing a married couple, which suits me just fine. Isabella is still a little distant, but that's to be expected, even as we settle in on the bed, her to her thoughts, and me to deciphering the phone numbers J.J. has sent me.

I recognize one of them right off as Father Emmanuel's. I know Giuseppe talked to him before he died, so this is not a huge shock. When I pop onto the hotel wifi, I get a half dozen emails from the agency, all manner of stuff from J.J. and others. I read it all at a skim—profile on Anselmo, a note from Ariadne that she's reached out through the State Department to inform the Italians of some dealings going on in their country. The reply is attached, and it's not a happy one. Basically a form letter telling us to keep our metahuman problems to ourselves, signed by a low-level functionary. I send her a quick note asking for clarification, already basically knowing what this means.

We're on our own over here. Big shock.

Of course, if I had some evidence that their Prime Minister is about to be assassinated, it's possible the response would be different. As it is, I've got Dr. Perugini's word and a thin thread of suspicion that the two of us have wrangled into a working theory.

Although, based on what Isabella has told me, certain corrupt elements in the Italian government would probably sell us out to Anselmo in about half a heartbeat. So maybe it's just as well we're going it alone.

I skim J.J.'s next email, which is a slightly deeper evaluation of those phone numbers Giuseppe called before he died. Five of them are to guys whose names are absolutely unknown to me, and it's a safe bet that one of them was what got him killed.

The last is to a cell phone registered in Milan to a Diana Cristina Amatore.

I think about her, not daring to show her face, and wish Anselmo was operating under the same fear. Then my mind flashes to Father Emmanuel, petrified by the thought that he's doing the wrong thing but afraid to expose himself to—I dunno, criticism, ostracism, being wrong? Something.

Then again, after everything I've been through in the last couple days, I can't say I blame him. Whatever Anselmo is up to, he's got an A-team backing his plays. He's the invincible man, Lorenzo is like my dark mirror, only stronger, and Fintan is some sort of super-powered, undercover badass. Between the three of them, they can throw some pretty good hurt.

Add in Anselmo's mobster flunkies, and I'm staring down a threat that could crush me like a fly, rip my lungs out and stake them to a wall. Not that I think they would do that, but—actually, Anselmo would totally do that.

And Sienna is not available. The most powerful fricking meta in the world, she's on my team, she's my sister, and I can't reach her. She's the weight that could tip the scales.

Uh, never mind. Weight metaphors are not good for use with women. She's the power that could balance things out, turn this fight into something a lot more trivial. But there's no guarantee she's going to get my message before Anselmo's scheme comes to fruition. I've got like thirty-six hours. Assuming she got it right now and hopped a plane from Canada, she's still nine or ten hours away. That leaves twenty-six hours. An hour from the airport leaves twenty-five. A day, at best.

I know in my heart that I can't wait on Sienna.

I stare at my phone, at that list of numbers, and I wonder how the hell I'm supposed to take on more flunkies than I can count, in addition to three metas, each of whom could probably clean my clock on their own. I feel so far over my head that I might as well be at the bottom of the Marianas Trench. Even J.J.'s gift isn't going to keep me from getting pulled apart by the mafiosi.

I sigh as my eyes drift over that name again. Diana Cristina Amatore. Father Emmanuel is listed as Moses Ngari on the phone registration.

I glance across the bed at the sole member of my team, and she catches my eye. She gives me an encouraging smile, and I stare at the numbers again before highlighting one. My phone prompts me, asking me if I want to call it, and I hit yes.

It rings, and on the fifth buzz, a female voice answers cautiously. *"Pronto,"* she says.

"Diana, it's Reed," I say, and wait to see if she hangs up.

She doesn't, but she makes a noise of deep disgust. "What do you want now?"

"I figured out what Anselmo is up to," I say, faking confidence in my tone. "He's going to kill the Prime Minister."

"Idiot," she hisses, "this is an open line, anyone could be listening! I'm hanging up—"

"He wants to be a god, doesn't he?" I ask, and she falls silent. "He wants to be like you and yours were, bring back the good old days, but with him in charge?" I'm playing a hunch here and hoping it's right, just based on the little I know of the guy. It's one hundred percent supposition, but hey, when you're dealing with an egomaniacal lunatic like Anselmo, assuming he wants some sort of throne upon which he can sit while everyone kisses his feet and pays homage, is probably not a bad bet. "He's gonna kill his way to it, put himself in charge." I catch a horrified glance from Isabella as she locks her eyes on mine, and I figure maybe I've got it.

Diana is silent for a moment. "Sure," she says, wearily, "that sounds like him. But what can you do to stop him?" This comes out resigned, like I'm complaining about the weather. It's hopeless, she tells me without telling me.

"What I can do to stop him is fricking stop him," I say and wonder if that makes any sense. "And unless you really love the thought of your homeland falling right into that pig's grasping, lecherous fingers, you'll at least meet me to talk about what we can do together."

"You are a fool," she snaps, but she still doesn't hang up. "How many does he have? Metas, I mean," she adds.

"Himself and the other two we've already faced," I say. "Plus as many mobsters as he can muster. But we've got a wild card to play."

She holds for a moment before biting the bait I've laid out, and I'm almost afraid she's going to let it pass. "When and where should I meet you?" she asks, and I pump my fist in silent triumph because now at least I've got a few ounces of hope.

64.

It's after dark when I show up to the café down the street from St. Peter's Basilica with Dr. Perugini in tow. Father Emmanuel is already waiting for us, his head down. I had to coerce and cajole to get him to come out and talk with us, but it's worth the guilt as I sit down across from him at the table and Isabella takes the seat at my side.

"Shall we begin?" Emmanuel asks me in that thick accent of his, but I shake my head. "Why not?"

"We're waiting for our plus one," I say, catching movement out of the corner of my eye as Diana, wearing a touristy ball cap pulled down to cover her face slides into the seat next to him. "And here she is."

"Who is this?" Diana asks, her voice a low hiss. There's one other patron in the café, and he's way toward the back and looks about seventy-five. The young man working behind the counter is fully absorbed in cleaning an oven, his back turned to us.

"Father Emmanuel, the goddess Diana," I say, smiling tightly at the thought of the blasphemy I was tossing out. "Diana, Father Emmanuel." They look at each other with great wariness but shake hands reluctantly. Diana looks disgusted and Emmanuel looks curious. Then they turn their attention to me, and I'm compelled to speak.

"Anselmo Serafini is planning to kill the Prime Minister of Italy the day after tomorrow, either before, during or after his visit with the Pope." I look straight at Father Emmanuel. "That's why Fintan O'Niall is still hiding in the Vatican."

Father Emmanuel can't even disguise his look of horror. "You have to warn them, immediately," he says in a hushed voice two notes from runaway panic.

"The Italian government isn't going to believe a word of it if it comes from me," I say, shaking my head. "Do any of you have connections that might allow for a warning?" I look at Diana, but she has her head bowed, the bill of her cap keeping me from seeing her eyes. "Anyone? Anyone? Bueller?"

"No," Diana says sharply. "But in our conversation before you promised that Anselmo was up to more than petty assassinations. Killing the Prime Minister of Italy is hardly enough to grant him apotheosis as you suggested."

"It's all about fear," Isabella says, leaning in to take part in the conversation for the first time. "Think back to Giovanni Falcone. This Prime Minister has been talking about organized crime and a crackdown on a very high level for a while, not taking any action. But if three metahumans were to jump out tomorrow and kill him, put the fear into people that anyone can be killed at any time—"

"Then it will be exactly like any other time dealing with the Cosa Nostra or 'Ndrangheta or Camorra," Diana says with a shrug of her shoulders. "This is always a threat. Falcone knew it before he was killed, and everyone knows it now. How is this different?" She looks across the table at us. "Other than a bigger target, this is—I don't mean to be cold enough to say it is not bad, but it is an affair of state, not the end of Italy."

I'm out of straws to grasp at. "I don't know," I say. "I don't know what his next move is after that, but you're right. Killing a man who hasn't even made much of a threat to him is not going to be the end of whatever Anselmo has planned. There's more. There has to be more, and I don't know what it is." I put my palms flat on the table. "But you know the man, and you know he's not some amateur who's going to sit back and coast. He's got ambition, some intent to do real harm. He's talking pretty grandiose, and I'd bet he's intending to back that talk up."

"But how?" Father Emmanuel says, listening intently. "If he is this … corrupt and horrible man that you say he is, then surely he would not commit to such a monumentally dangerous course of action without something to back it up. Surely he would fear reprisal. Surely he would fear … some response?"

I think about that for a second. "He thinks he's invincible," I realize slowly.

Diana makes a low sound in her throat. "He is."

"Could a bomb blow him up?" I ask, focusing intently on her.

"No," she says with a shake of her head. "Perhaps a nuclear one, or the sort that burns extremely hot—perhaps—but not a conventional one, no. His skin is immune to the fragments, no matter how hard they are propelled."

"He doesn't care about anyone," I say. "Not a soul. He cares about himself and power, and he's making a play to aggrandize one and seize the other." I sigh and shrug my shoulders. "I don't know how, I'm sorry. But it's happening. I know in my gut that he's going big, not going home."

"Perhaps we've been thinking about this all wrong," Isabella says, her voice quiet. She glances sideways at me then looks at the others. "Anselmo is a corrupter of people, yes?"

"One of the worst," Diana agrees.

"But he's hardly the only one," Isabella says. "The other *familias*—Sacra Corona Unita, 'Ndrangheta, La Cosa Nostra—every last one of them has people in different places, has different parts of the country as their territories …" She falls silent.

"Yeah?" I ask, prompting her, and her eyes widen.

"The meeting," she says. "He has a meeting tomorrow—"

Something clicks into place, something telling. The head of a crime syndicate doesn't just have a meeting, like it's another day in a boardroom.

"He wouldn't treat it like it's this important—not if it's with his underlings," Isabella says, spelling it out for me. "He made it sound important, and that means that whoever he is meeting with *is* important—to him, at least."

Diana leans back in her chair, and I can see her eyes. She's gotten there, figured it out, and I can see that there's some little hint of concern buried underneath all the effort at concealing it. "He's going to unite them. He's going to bring them all together."

Isabella nods slowly. "And when he does, he will own every corrupt politician that they own. And with that much power, that much authority concentrated while everyone else argues and bickers at the fall of the Prime Minister—"

"They find themselves in control of Italy itself," Diana says, and her voice is a deathly whisper.

65.

"Thank you all for joining me early," he says, and he walks around the pool deck. The house lights are shining, Firenze is glittering below, and around his long table sit more mafiosi than have been assembled together in a long, long time. Don George sits to the right of his empty chair at the head of the table, his place firmly established. There is unease among them, Anselmo can feel it, a strong scent of fear that is driven by the knowledge—the suspicion—of what he is about to ask of them. "I apologize for summoning you this evening rather than waiting until the appointed hour tomorrow, but ... unfortunately, events have necessitated that we hurry things along."

"Hurry what things along?" This from Vicenzo, the head of one of the smaller families of the south. An upstart, a fool. Anselmo knows he wants the purpose spelled out, to have it clearly stated so that he can register his fear, spit his insults, and leave.

But he has no idea what Anselmo is planning.

"Things," Anselmo says, with a mysterious smile. The hour is dark, and that darkness is hiding the bloodstains upon the concrete. It would not matter if it did not, however, because the truth is likely already known to at least some of them. "Important things."

"You play word games with us, Don Serafini," Vicenzo says abruptly. Anselmo calculates he is seconds away from standing, from storming out in an insulted huff.

"I tease," Anselmo says, smoothing it over. There is a ripple of amusement down the table, and Vicenzo blushes. "Sit, sit, and I will explain everything." He takes long steps behind each of the men, behind their seats. There are only a dozen or so. He knows each of their names, but knows each of their territories better still. "Do you not all weary of the constant worry about the Carabinieri? Wondering if you have paid the right people, if you will get word before they take one of your drug houses? Before they crash one of your construction rackets? Before some do-gooding politician with more righteousness than brains intends to make his name by exposing your attempts to barter for government contracts?"

"Does a Carabinieri fuck a pig he's left alone with?" Vicenzo says with a wide grin, prompting a laugh that ripples down the table.

Anselmo laughs, too. "Very clever. But if you are laughing, you know the truth of these things. There was a day when we could operate freely, when our kind had the reins of power, and no one disputed it. No prosecutor would dare to harass us, no Prime Minister would call us by name, and no president would breathe a word against us."

"There was also a day when we would kneel to a king instead of elect a Prime Minister," Vicenzo says. "I doubt we are going to go back to that." This prompts another laugh down the table.

"Why not?" Anselmo says, this time stopping the laughter cold. He waits, feels the unease settle over the table. "Why not?"

"Because the people would oppose it," Vicenzo says, as though he is speaking to a fool.

"And the people are the power, yes?" Anselmo smiles.

"Yes," Vicenzo says. "They are."

"No," Anselmo says, "they are not. They perhaps think they are, but it is an illusion." He grips the back of a chair and swings his other around in a gesture. "The power belongs to those whom the people fear. If we make them fear us, then we rule them."

"And we get our heads cut off when the power swings the other way," Vicenzo says, shaking his head. "What is this foolishness you speak?"

"The world has changed," Anselmo says, taking the slow walk toward the end of the table. "The world has changed and most people have not noticed. The governments of the world pay lip service to this idea of change, of metahumans, but that is all. They pretend that the low numbers will spare them, even as they plot to hoard their help for themselves. But the balance of power has shifted, my friends, and I think it is time to drive that point home for our own purposes."

Vicenzo has the look of a man bewildered by an idiot. "Let us assume for a moment that you are right," he says. "We have all read about these people, these wondrous people. But you are a fool if you think they can stand against the Carabinieri, or the army—"

Anselmo pulls a pistol out of his jacket and the table falls silent. He slides it down the table and it comes to rest perfectly in front of Vicenzo. "The Carabinieri bring guns and bullets. The army brings more of the same."

"And these things will kill these metahumans you speak of," Vicenzo says, nodding at the pistol in front of him. "They will kill them dead, even if you assembled an army of these powerful men—"

· "Perhaps some," Anselmo says, and he wears a muted smile of his own. "But not all." He nods at the pistol. "Shoot me, Vicenzo."

Vicenzo's smile is plastic, cold, disbelieving. "You are a fool, Anselmo."

"Perhaps that as well," Anselmo says, grinning. "But shoot me anyway. In the face, in the head, in the chest if your gentle, womanly heart prefers—" There is a round of nervous laughter around the table.

Vicenzo needs little provocation. He pulls the pistol and jerks the trigger. His aim is true, and Anselmo feels a slap to the right breast. He shrugs it off, no more than a light shove. Vicenzo fires again, then again, then again.

Anselmo rips the buttons off his new shirt, pulls open the front and displays his bronzed chest. "Care to try again?" he asks, taunting Vicenzo.

Five shots are his answer, and not one of them does anything but hit him and fall onto the concrete.

Anselmo holds his hands open, catching the last of the bullets as it falls. He holds it up, flat-headed at the tip from impact. "Between all of us, we have paid more in bribes than this country is worth. We pay to grease the wheels. We pay to keep ourselves hidden, to keep ourselves from troubles, to allow the rackets and extortion to continue as unimpeded by the system as we can manage." He walks the length of the table, then turns back to look at all of them. "I am sick of working around their system. I want to own the system, to make it work for me." He holds up the bullet. "And the way to that goal is power. To seize it, to make it ours, to work the levers for our own profit."

"How do you do that?" Vicenzo's calm defiance is all gone now. His mouth hangs slightly open, and when Anselmo's eyes fall upon him, the man is cowed enough to avert his eyes.

"Fear," Anselmo says, and he knows he has them all now by the balls. "We make them fear us, and then run them in the direction of our choosing." He squeezes his hand closed, as though he is placing it around a neck. "We seize the power, corrupt what we must, and take control of the rest." He pushes his hands together so tightly that a fly could not survive between them. "We kill the old, we crush all who oppose us—make them fear us—and then we take it all for ourselves."

66.

Reed

"Look," I say into the silence that has fallen after Diana and Isabella's grim pronouncements, "I realize we're no Avengers, but maybe we can do some good."

"What does this have to do with Diana Rigg?" Diana asks, her face a mask of confusion.

"Who is Diana Rigg?" I ask. She gives me a furious look, like I've just insulted her.

"I am sympathetic to your concerns," Father Emmanuel says, "but I just don't see what the three of us can do against these men. Even discounting their powers, just thinking of how many followers with guns they have …" He shrugs. "It seems like to much for us to handle."

"Maybe it is," I say quickly. "Maybe it is. And maybe I'm the last person who ought to be putting this together. I mean, I'm no Captain America—"

"I don't understand. You are from America, yes?" Diana asks, looking at me, brow furrowed.

"Okay, so, you didn't see the *Avengers* movie," I say, and let my gaze slide to Father Emmanuel. "Did you—?" I cut myself off midway through the question. "Of course not. Never mind."

Father Emmanuel looks a little insulted. "I saw it in Mombasa. It was very enjoyable. I like tales of good versus evil."

"Huh," I say. "That'll teach me to assume." I search for my angle of reasoning again and get back on track. "I know this looks impossible. And I know that the idea of the three of us—" Isabella coughs, and I can see her ire out of the corner of my eye without even turning, "four of us," I amend without missing a beat, "are—on paper, anyway—out of our league. Outmatched." I look from Father Emmanuel to Diana. "I've been fighting those kinds of fights for a little while now, though, and Anselmo is a piker compared to the last guy I went up against who was threatening conquest."

"That your sister went up against, you mean," Diana says. She leans in and lowers her voice. "I don't mean to offend you, but your little winds are nothing compared to the power of an unleashed succubus. If she were here, I could see this being a fight. But with you, me and a priest?" She shakes her head and turns to Emmanuel. "Can you even fight?"

He thinks about this for a second. "I can fight. I will not kill, though. That is where I draw the line. There is a difference between protecting God's flock and committing murder."

"Yes," she says acidly, "and it's exactly that difference that will get you killed in a fight with these men." She slides back from the table, ready to leave.

"Wait," I say, and she does. "Like I said, I know we're up against … a lot."

"And we don't even know their plan," she adds.

"And we don't know their plan," I agree. "But I think we all know that their plan, carried out, means the worst kind of change." I look her in the eye, and I don't spare the gravitas, trying desperately to convey the seriousness of the situation. "No one else is going to stop Anselmo if we don't. Do you believe that?"

She looks at me and sighs. "I believe that. But I do not believe we can stop them."

"I believe we have the obligation to at least try," I say, not looking away from her. "But if you want to just walk away and let the consequences fall wherever they may … I understand that. And I guess I can respect your desire to live more than to make a stand." I nod at her. "I wish you the best of luck, but for me—I can't stand the sting of thinking myself a coward, which is exactly what I'd think every day if I walked away from this without at least trying to stop Anselmo."

The lines across her brow soften. "You would hold your manhood cheap if you didn't fight."

I raise an eyebrow at her. "Uh … not quite how I'd put it, but … yeah. I guess."

"It's from Shakespeare," Father Emmanuel says. "The St. Crispin's Day speech." He nods once, sharply. "I don't know if we can stop them, but I am with you to at least try. I don't think I could consider myself a good man if I didn't at least try."

"I am with you," Isabella says, and I can see by the look in her eyes that she is.

"We are all of us fools," Diana says quietly, staring down at the table with that thousand yard stare. "I should have died at the end of the last age of our kind; I have seen too much change." She looks back up at me, straight in the eye. "If Anselmo wants to harken us back to the old world with him at our head, like that bastard Zeus, then I will do my utmost to help you stop him." She sighed. "Even if it means joining my fate to all of yours." She looks up. "Where do we start?"

67.

"So how does this go down?" I ask as the four of us walk along the Via della Conciliazione, the road that stretches between the Vatican and the Castel Sant'Angelo. I can see St. Peter's down the way. I'm spitballing, trying to figure this thing out before it hits us all like a runaway bad metaphor. There's quiet in the night air, a sense of foreboding that hangs over this little corner of the city.

"If they truly mean to assassinate the premier," Diana says, pensive, "they could hit him anywhere along the path, from here to his residence."

I chew on that for a second. "Let's assume he's going high profile. That means somewhere in here, right?"

"There will be a full ceremony as he meets the Pope," Father Emmanuel says helpfully. "This is a formal meeting of heads of state, since this is a new Prime Minister."

"Any chance the Pope's guards will take this threat seriously if you bring it to them?" I ask. I'm grasping at straws here.

"I suppose it is possible," Emmanuel says with a shrug of his shoulders. "I don't know how they'll respond, but I can try."

"And you're willing to do that now?" I ask. "Even if it means speaking up?"

He almost bows his head. "I cannot live with myself if I do not. I will try."

"Well, that's something," I say as we keep going. A few cafés are open here and there, but not many. I glance behind us, and realize that somewhere back there is the Castel Sant'Angelo, that mighty drum of a fortress, though it's hidden behind the buildings from here. "So we've got a long avenue here …"

"Which will be shut down by the Carabinieri for a special occasion such as this," Dr. Perugini chimes in. She's moving along at a brisk clip with the rest of us. The air is a little chill now that the sun is down. "It will be closed to vehicle traffic for a papal event."

"So the premier comes driving up for his formal occasion," I say, musing my way through it as we approach St. Peter's Square. The basilica is lit up ahead of us. "Fintan's involved for a reason, so maybe they snuff him right as he's arriving?"

"Makes sense," Diana says, and she's got a tight expression, green eyes looking surprisingly lively. "There will be plenty of cameras present for that, and Anselmo is cracked enough to want it seen."

"So how do we stop them?" I ask, thinking it through as I speak. "Maybe a zone defense, or man-to-man—"

"This is English you are speaking?" Diana looks at me with a sharp frown.

"Sorry," I say. "We take them one-on-one."

"Bad odds against Anselmo," Diana says.

"I think I can handle him," I say. She cocks an eyebrow at me questioningly. "I got a toy from home that should take care of him in a pinch. Which leaves us with Lorenzo and Fintan."

"What is Fintan?" Father Emmanuel asks.

"Firbolg," I say. "They get into this kind of battle fury, kind of an adrenaline-fueled rage that makes them really hard to stop. They can do a lot of damage like that—smash cars to pieces, shred people—it's pretty messy."

"Are they invulnerable?" Emmanuel asks.

"No," I say, "but they can take a lot more punishment when they're in the fury. It's like they don't know that they're taking damage."

"I can handle him," Father Emmanuel says, nodding with a certainty I find oddly comforting. "And he is my task in any case."

I think about questioning this, but let it drop. "Okay. The priest has got the rage-roidal monster, and I've got Anselmo." I swivel my head took at Diana, who seems focused on the basilica. "You think you can handle Lorenzo and his mighty hurricanes?"

She doesn't say anything at first, staring straight ahead. "I remember when this was the Circus of Nero." She waves a hand toward the basilica and the massive obelisk in the center of St. Peter's Square. "That used to sit in the middle of the Circus, and was moved—I don't even remember when." She looks disgusted. "Change. Everything changes, always, and I watch as it does." She looks at me, and I see something stirring behind those eyes, some sense of rage that's looking for an outlet. "I will handle your Aeolus problem for you."

I stare back at her. "He's been pretty good at dodging your arrows so far. You sure you're up for it?"

I see the first hints of a cold satisfaction take root in those emerald irises of hers. "Yes. Though I think perhaps it's come to the point where I will change with the times as well." She stalks away from us without another word, down the street toward the Castel, and does not even look back.

"Uh, okay?" I say to her retreating back. "We'll see you here, morning after tomorrow, bright and early and—" She gives me a wave to signal her concord, and that's about it. She dodges down a side street and is gone a moment later.

"What do you think she meant by that?" Father Emmanuel asks.

"Hell if I know," I say without thinking, and I catch a disappointed look from the priest. "Uh, sorry. What are you going to do?"

"Use the power that God has given me," he says. He bows his head to me, then heads off toward the Vatican without another word.

"Everybody's gotta be all vague and mysterious," I say to Dr. Perugini, who is the only one left with me. She's standing at my side, and I feel her fingers interlace with mine. It feels … good. "Not sure how well this team-up is going to go," I confess, and as I look at her I can see the reservations that she immediately puts aside.

"It will go fine," she says, soothing.

I speak without thinking, just looking for reassurance. "Really?" I breathe out an aura of hope.

She half-shrugs, and the uncertainty breaks through. "It kind of has to," she says, and leads me back down the Via della Conciliazione to catch a cab back to our hotel. As we walk in silence, I come to the conclusion that she's pretty much right.

68.

Anselmo

Lorenzo comes hobbling out of the house around midnight. Anselmo is still staring out across the view below. He never tires of it, not really. It is a perpetual reminder of the power he wields, and that is nothing if not exciting to him.

"*Capo,*" Lorenzo says. The boy is favoring his arm. He wears a pained expression, one suitable for a whipped dog, perhaps.

Anselmo acknowledges him with a lifted drink and little else, and the boy comes to stand beside him. The table is now empty, the others long since gone back to their hotels or their homes. There will come an hour for revelry, and it is soon.

But not just yet.

"Capo ..." Lorenzo begins, and Anselmo can tell merely by the hesitation that what will follow is certain to be something weak. "Do you ever ..." The boy halts himself, and starts again, elsewhere. "The hour draws near."

"*Sì,*" Anselmo allows. It is only a little over a day from the fulfillment of the plan, now. Years of effort and planning, drawing to their conclusion.

"Do you ever ..." Lorenzo begins again, "... doubt?" Anselmo gives him a look, and he hastens to explain. "The plan, I mean? Whether we should take these steps, whether they might be too drastic or—"

"Doubts are for girls," Anselmo says, dismissing him with utter finality. "Reach down between your legs and let me know if a bullet took your balls from you."

Lorenzo blanches. "But, *Capo*, this plan … it is … bold—"

"We are men," Anselmo says, contemptuous. "Men see what they want and take it. The cup of life is ours to drink from, and you want—what? Water instead of wine? You labor under the delusion that things are meant to be asked for, oh so sweetly, 'May I please …?' *Fah!*" Anselmo swipes broadly and spills some of his wine. "Men are not men anymore. They are so polite and cultured, with their perfect hair and nails, like a woman. Well," he leans close to Lorenzo, "I am a man. I have been a man my whole life. And tomorrow, I will take what I want, and become a god in the process. You know what a god does?" Anselmo cracks a smile, and lets it fade as the seriousness of the thought falls over him. "Whatever the hell he wants." He tosses the wine glass over the edge, hears it fall and shatter somewhere below, some kind of poignant marker that puts the punctuation on his point for him, and he turns away, leaving Lorenzo standing there alone. "Reach down deep, boy. Find your balls. Join me in godhood, and we'll take whatever we want from this life—from this country—together."

69.

Reed

The last day goes pretty damned quickly. I don't like to think of it as the last day, but it kind of is. It passes in alternating patches of frenzied speed and boredom, usually linked to whatever activity I'm in the middle of at the time. Isabella and I end up having sex several times throughout the day, which—holy hell, is more fun than I remembered, but the moments between are long stretches of awkward silence, especially during meals, which are the only times we leave the hotel. We chew in silence, and it's terribly uncomfortable. She's back to being an enigma, a face I can't read, especially by the end of the day.

When we come back from dinner, the pensive silence turns even more uncomfortable. I'm thinking about this whole thing, about what I'm going to have to do tomorrow. How I'm going to have to face off against a maniacal killer whose agenda is pretty crazy. He wants to take over a country, for crying out loud.

We go about the business of getting ready for bed, and I find myself in the strangest circumstances since I helped take on Sovereign six months ago. Maybe stranger, because I'm in charge this time. I fixate on the strangest little details. I set the alarm on my phone, and make sure it's charged. I floss and brush my teeth, like it's super important to my performance tomorrow to have good dental hygiene.

Then I lie in bed and watch TV with Isabella, the evening news playing like there's not a thing wrong in the world.

I'm watching the newscaster, who wears these really big, rounded glasses that seem to be in fashion here in Italy, and as I'm watching her speak a language I still can't decipher to save my life, I realize that if Anselmo gets his way, she'll be quaking in fear tomorrow. Her and however many Italian citizens there are. Because that's the kind of big honking douchebag Anselmo is.

It gives me a moment's pause to think that standing up to assholes like Anselmo is almost a family tradition for me. My sister did it. My dad did it, and it cost him his life.

Dad.

Isabella finally breaks the silence, and it's almost painful. "You don't want me to come with you."

I've seen *The Return of the King*, and I know what happens when you tell a strong-minded woman not to head out to battle. "I would never tell you not to," I say, "but this is going to be a really nasty meta fight."

"Anselmo could rip my arm off with the thought I give for tearing a wing off a fly," she says, and there's a sense of resignation when it comes out. I realize she's been fighting herself over this all day. "If I had the strength of Diana, I would be there. But as it is, if he saw me, he would come for me, and you would be distracted, I think."

I nod. "I think so, yes."

"I will stay here," she says, "until after it has happened, and then I will help with triage."

"A sound plan," I agree because it's totally logical and reasonable.

She lowers her voice a little. "Do you want me to tell you that I love you?"

This catches me a little off guard. "Do you?"

She shakes her head. "No. But if you need reassurance … I could."

"Heh," I chuckle, but it's mirthless. "I don't need you to say it if it's not true. This thing we've been doing, it's … fun. I know you think you've been using me, but … I don't feel that way. It's not love, but it's been …" I flail about for a word, and she interrupts.

"Lust?"

"Well, there is that," I agree. "But I don't really know you yet, so there's not a possibility for anything more. We've worked together for a while, but I mean … I don't even know your middle name. Me loving you at this point would be like me filling in the blanks of your personality and history with whatever answers I want. Lots of people do that, they assume the best, but, uh … I'm not like that. I know what we're doing here." I take her hand. "I don't need you to tell me you love me. Just being here … it's … enough." And it is.

She seems to understand and leans her head against my shoulder. She falls asleep like that a short time later, and I stare at the walls until after midnight, when I give up and get dressed quietly. I know there's no chance of me finding rest now, not in the last few hours I have before this powder keg gets lit up. I get my stuff and get ready to leave, watching her sleep the whole time.

The truth is, if I had died on the day before I met Sienna Nealon, there would not be a single person left alive who would remember my name to even mourn me. Everyone I know, from Sienna to Isabella, came to me because I met my sister. The embers of my past life are gone—family, friends, everything that was mine before it all scattered to the damned wind.

Love? Well.

There's a first time for everything, I guess.

I realize I'm ready to go. The clock reads a little after four. There's not even a hint of dawn from outside the curtains, but I can't stand sitting here, antsy, any longer. I consider stirring the wind, just slightly, to ruffle Isabella's hair as I leave, but it reminds me of my dad's farewell, all those years ago, and I stop myself just in time.

I close the door silently and go off to meet my destiny.

70.

I find Diana loitering at the end of the Via della Conciliazione, looking about as nondescript as an angry woman hanging out on a Roman street can, I guess. She's missing her signature golf bag, bound up instead in a hoodie, which gives her kind of an *Assassin's Creed* vibe. It fits.

She acknowledges me with little more than a look as I slide into place by her. The hour is early, damned early, like five in the morning or so. There's no sunlight yet in the sky, and the chill in the air is not like the Rome of summer I'm familiar with.

"Couldn't sleep?" she asks without looking at me.

"No," I say. "Can't imagine why."

"I can never sleep before a battle," she says, shaking her head. "Never, even after all these years." She glances over at me. "The night after a battle though; then I sleep like the dead."

"Hm," I say, "I guess I haven't really been in enough classic battles to know what that's like."

"But you've fought," she says.

"With Sovereign and Omega," I say. "Sneak attacks almost all the time. Strike and feint, hit and run. Guerilla tactics, no one wanting to stick their neck out and go big and public with it. Except for Sovereign, of course. He went big. But it always felt like we were moving too fast to have a night of preparation before one of those fights. We were just always moving."

"I think it is called operational tempo," she says, though the words sound strange coming from her. "He did move quickly. Wiped out so many of our kind, so very fast."

"But you escaped," I say.

"I have been a survivor for longer than most," she says, narrow eyes flicking about underneath the hood. "I survived Zeus's reign of terror when so many—including my parents—did not. I survived the time of transition when we interred the gods into a place of myth and legend. I have survived much, and I was not going to be finished by some scheming half-wit incubus refugee's attempt to kill us all in revenge for perceived wrongs."

I frown, glancing at her. "Wait ... did you know Sovereign?" She looks at me with contempt. "You knew him."

"My brother knew him better," she says. "But I knew him, yes."

"Huh," I say, a little surprised. "You don't seem much like the socializing type."

She regards me impassively for a moment. "This fight is not like what you did with Sovereign. If Anselmo takes Italy—assuming he can even pull it off—that doesn't change your life at all. Why are you fighting this battle?"

I can't help but give her a frown. "How can you even ask me that? People are going to die if I—if we—don't stop Anselmo."

"People die," she says, "it is their signature and trademark. It is what they are born to do, the common fate that none of us can escape."

"But not today," I say. "They don't have to die today."

She nods almost reluctantly then nods at the end of the street near St. Peter's Square. "I am going to start patrolling between here and the basilica. You should stay at this end of the street and keep watch."

I give that a half second's thought. "Okay. Seems reasonable. If anything happens, I'll dial you up."

"Good," she says and hesitates. Then she looks me in the eyes, and I get a full dose of garden green. "You are a good man, Reed Treston. Your father, Jonathan Traeger—he was a good man as well. You are like him in that regard." And then she just stalks off down the street, head down.

She gets about a hundred feet away before I manage to get my wits about me. "Wait," I call after her, "what?"

71.

For the next few hours, Diana pulls an elliptical orbit up one side of the Via della Conciliazione and down the other, neatly avoiding me by about a hundred yards each time. I consider intercepting her, but even I know that hashing out something as distracting as how she might or might not have known my father would probably be best saved for later.

But not too much later.

At about seven, my phone buzzes, the vibration function shaking me out of a stupor. I fish it out of my pocket to see that it's J.J. I answer.

"All aboard the Reed-ing Railroad," he says as I answer, "next stop, Boardwalk and Park Place, cha-ching." I kinda get what he's going for with that one, but he's struggling with the most tenuous connections at this point. I guess it's hard to constantly come up with something new to make a pun out of my name.

"Isn't it like half past the middle of the damned night there, J.J.?" I ask, staring down the street as Diana makes another lap. She's changing her pattern and path as she goes. Crowds are starting to gather, and the Carabinieri shows up to block the street about an hour before go time. They ignore me, and her for good measure. I doubt it's as much a commentary on their policing skills as it is the seriousness of their threat consideration. Or maybe it's both. Either way, they're pretty disinterested in what's going on here, which benefits us.

"Burning the midnight oil, yes, indeed," J.J. says. "I know you're going to need help, and I'm here for you, buddy. Tireless, sleepless, whatever. I am your fearless Q, ready to crack some codes and hack some ... well, whatever needs hacking, man. I am with you in spirit. And by spirit, I mean digitally, because I'm looking at you on a surveillance cam on the Vaya ... della ... concilia—whatever." He gives up.

"Conciliazione," I finish for him. "Like conciliation. But with a -zione at the end."

"Mad linguistics, my friend," he says. "You're practically like a native-born Italian. But seriously, though, I'm looking right at you. You're dressed to rumble in a polo and jeans? I like your confidence. Because nothing says you're down to fight like showing up in casual."

I lean against the wall awkwardly, suddenly self-conscious about being watched. "I, uh ... do you have eyes on Diana?"

"Is she the power walker in the hoodie doing laps down the street?" he asks. "Because if so, I have a lot more than eyes for her."

"Don't let her hear you say that," I say, "or you're likely to lose the eyes and all else."

"The sensitive kind," he says. "Err ... about her looks ... you know, that doesn't sound right either. She's touchy. Err, not like touching ... aw, forget it."

"I know what you mean," I say. "She's quick to anger."

"Yes!" he says. "You speak my language, brother from another mother."

"Mmm," I say. "You see any signs of the bad guys of our piece?"

"Nothing on facial recognition, and I'm scanning the whole area," he says. "Or would that be *recognizione*?"

"This bad guy," I say, sorting a thread out of my thoughts. "Anselmo. He's a ..." I labor for an appropriate descriptor. "He's a real sonofabitch."

"Oh yeah?" J.J. asks. "What'd he do to piss in your Kool-aid?"

"Just has one of those personalities," I say. "Let me put it this way—clearly, he was the inspiration behind Tom Jones' song for *Thunderball*."

"Ooh," J.J. says. "That's bad."

I grunt. "Tell me about it."

There's a moment's pause. "How you feeling there, champ?"

I feel the skeptical frown crease my brow in the early morning cool. "Gee, coach, I dunno. I guess I'm about ready to go in to the big game." I let every word drip with irony.

"Seriously, man," J.J. says. "I know you've been through a few rodeos by now, but maybe this one's a little different since Sienna is on the sidelines." He pauses, and I can hear his tone soften. "Just lettin' you know I'm here for you, man. In whatever way you need."

I stay silent for a handful of moments. "It is different," I say. "You're right. It's all on me this time, and it kind of is my first rodeo. At least the first one I've been in charge of." I shake my head as I survey the avenue. "I don't want to do this, man. I don't want to go toe to toe with Anselmo, that crazy bastard. I don't want to think about Diana or Father Emmanuel getting killed while trying to fight this off." I shiver under my coat and know it has nothing to do with the weather. "I don't know how Sienna does this, keeps putting her jaw out there for people to take aim at it over and over." I think about Gail Roth and that interview, how my sister got picked apart by the news afterward. "This is not my scene."

"Then why are you there?" J.J. asks.

I laugh. Something about the situation seems totally absurd. "Because no one else is gonna show."

"They're following your lead this time, bro," he says.

I thrust my hands deeper in my pockets. "I'm feeling a little like Dorothy here—I just want to go home."

"You've faced off with some of the nastiest metas in the world, dude," J.J. says. "You sure aren't lacking for courage."

"I feel like I am," I say. "I feel like a coward for questioning everything—every angle, every action."

"I think that just makes you a leader."

His words resonate through me, and I think about all the times Sienna has put herself on the line without looking like she put any thought into it. If I compare myself, bravery-wise, to my sister, I look like a chicken. She's fearless guts, endless courage, so much brass it puts every man on earth to shame.

I'm not her. I'm scared witless right now. Not so much for myself—maybe a little bit—but for what happens if I fail. What happens if my little fledgling team of near-strangers fails here.

"You gonna make it, man?" J.J. asks. "Do I need to find, like, an inspirational video from YouTube and link it to you?"

I laugh again, sincerely this time. He really does want to help, and this guy—this geeky dude who speaks my language—he makes me feel braver just talking to me. "I think I got it now, pal. Thanks." I settle against the wall. "Let me know when you get something."

"Prime Minister's motorcade is about a half mile away," J.J. says. "They're moving at a decent clip, should be at your position in about two minutes. I mean, I'm estimating, but—"

"That's fine," I say, "just keep me apprised." I wave an arm at Diana as she makes the circuit back in my direction, and she crosses the street toward me. She moves at a steady pace, and she takes less than a minute to reach me.

"The Pope has a processional coming out now," she says. "Father Emmanuel is with them."

"Nice eagle eyes," I say, and I see a glimmer in the green. "Is your power—"

"Precision muscle control," she says abruptly, and I see her face become masklike.

"Oh," I say, nodding. "Okay, then."

"And before you ask, because you men always do," she says, cocking her head slightly at me, nearly completely inscrutable, "yes, it does extend to all muscles."

I blink, and she turns away. "That was … uh … informative."

"Did she just say what I think she said?" J.J.'s voice blares in my ear. He sounds like a hungry dog panting over the line.

"Not now," I cut him off. "Anything to report?"

"Sorry," he says, "I didn't catch that. I was too busy thinking about—"

"J.J.!" I snap. "Head in the game." There's a hard wind that blows down the Via della Conciliazione, and it prickles the hairs on the back of my neck.

"I got nothing on the Via," he says. "The software is running on every camera I can scoop access to, but unfortunately, I'm working with limited server resources, so I've only got about six square blocks worth of camera feeds running at the moment. I could try and get broader access to some NSA servers, but it would take—"

"Do it," I say.

"Dude," he says, almost pleading, "you didn't let me finish telling you what it would take to make it happen. Rocha. I'm going to have to talk to Rocha."

"You talk to Rocha every day," I say.

"I email with him whenever possible," he says. "Man's a dragon. A man-dragon. He breathes fire and smoke, leaving the charred bones of lost souls outside his cubicle in broken mounds—"

"Spare me the epic fantasy imagery," I say, "and do it."

"I'm gonna have to wake him up. Wake the dragon. Dude. The things I do for you—"

"Thanks, J.J.," I say.

"Whoa," he says, before he can even finish his thought. "Um. Hooboy. Okay, so I got good news and bad—"

I frown, turning to look at Diana, who is lingering nearby, clearly listening to my conversation even as she scans the Via della Conciliazione. "Good news first," I say.

"I'm not gonna have to wake the dragon."

I feel my eyes roll with exasperation. "Seriously? This is not—"

"And the bad," he steamrolls me, which J.J. never does. "I've got your boy Lorenzo as well as Anselmo, like an 80% match. No, 90%. Oh, and there's Fintan. But—and this is the bad news—"

I start to reach for Diana, but she's already tensed, listening to every word, waiting for the axe to fall.

"—they're in St. Peter's Square," J.J. says. "About a hundred yards from the Pope, and holding position."

My head turns involuntarily, swiveling the long blocks to the basilica, far down the way. It's at least a minute's run, at meta speed. I see movement out of the corner of my eye as the Prime Minister's motorcade passes, and I suddenly realize that we've made a terrible, terrible mistake in assuming we could even come close to guessing what Anselmo has planned.

72.

Anselmo

The moment is arriving, and Anselmo is utterly prepared. The Prime Minister's motorcade is coming into sight even now, and the Pope is standing only feet away.

Yes, this is about to be a great day. A day of destiny.

Anselmo looks neither right nor left at his lackeys, but straight ahead. Into his future. "Remember what you must do," he says, his words carrying more than a hint of what will happen to them should they fail. "Do not fail me now. Soon, these countries will be ours, and this fortress will be our capital, the place from which we will repel any attempt to take back what we have won."

The car approaches, slowly, taking its sweet time, like it is out for a Sunday drive through a countryside village. Anselmo can wait, though. Soon enough, it will arrive here, at its final destination.

73.

It's only in the last moments before it all goes down that I realize, rather suddenly, how deeply I've underestimated Anselmo. I've been operating from the assumption all along that he's a grandiose but sane gangster, looking to corrupt the institutions of man by trying to take over a country. With a meta behind it, especially one with his sort of invincibility, it almost seems possible. They send an army after Anselmo, he shrugs off their bombs and bullets and personally kills every one of the men that come after him. It seems almost like he could do it, if he acted intelligently, chose the battlefields himself, and had enough of the country's movers and shakers on his side. Fear and intimidation, as well as the established institutions, these would be his allies. A judicious use of force, intelligent application of terror—I mean, it's kind of low odds, but I can see the possibility that someone could pull it off.

But here's where I underestimate Anselmo, and where I finally realize what it takes to be a Bond villain—you've got to be out of your damned mind.

There's no way Anselmo's scheme—even if it worked, which is a mighty big if—will go unanswered by the rest of the world. The EU is about as likely to let Italy fall off the map unanswered, dropped under the heel of some meta dictator, as I am to just blithely chop off my own arm. But he's standing near the Pope for a reason, and I've finally realized in this moment why he's chosen to do this at this time, at this location.

He's going to kill the Pope as well, and try and take over the Vatican as part of his campaign. Like the place is just some country that you can roll over and not some deeply significant spiritual nation state with ties to more governments than you can count. Arguably, what he is planning to do to the Vatican might produce more international outrage than a simple attempt at takeover by force of Italy.

Either way, it's breathtaking in its scope, and it's in this moment that I realize that Anselmo is completely effing nuts. It's like his version of a big dog pissing all over the place to mark his territory, without any regard for how he's going to defend it from a legion of wolves. It's every bit as much about intimidating the lesser mammals—and I think we're all lesser mammals to him—as it is about killing the Prime Minister and the Pope. This is public. This is visual. It's about as high profile as you can get. Anselmo is spraying his impotent little hose everywhere, and I, for one, am not impressed.

Unfortunately, in the short term, my team and I are all the response that there is for what he's about to do, and so I'm sprinting down the Via della Conciliazione while all this is rushing through my head. I shoot past the Prime Minister's car at meta speed, only a few dozen yards behind Diana (she's fast, I remember as she takes a lead). I can hear hastily applied brakes behind us as we book it down the Via, and I hope that the Prime Minister's security detail takes this blatant meta activity as a hint to get the hell out of Dodge.

Then I see movement ahead, a frenzied level of activity as something happens near the Pope's security detail. The sound of gunfire fills the air, sharp and terrifying, and the crowd falls into screams all up and down the Via della Conciliazione as whatever insanity Anselmo has planned starts in earnest.

74.

Anselmo

He can see the Treston boy running up the Via toward St. Peter's Square, and it fills his throat with a raw, scratching hate. Anselmo wishes he could breathe fire, but there's a deeper, sicker pleasure he feels at the sight of the lad. The fool is charging into death, into confrontation, into a three-on-one battle that will see him forced to watch as Anselmo's brilliance is shoved into his face once more, and he is forced to—

Anselmo catches a blast of water like a hydrant turned loose, right into his face. He loses his footing, feels the square collide with his back, a dim hint of where the concrete has struck him. He blinks the water out of his eyes, feels it coursing out of his nose, is sputtering and gasping in surprise.

"Capo," Lorenzo says from above him, reaching a hand down to help him up. Fintan lies to his left, shaking it off, the ground around them wet from whatever has just happened.

As Anselmo takes Lorenzo's hand, he sees another blast of water come his way, dispelled by Lorenzo with his wind. It comes from a priest—an African priest, of all things! With Swiss guards, machine guns at the ready, advancing slowly behind him. The Pope is gone, long gone, already hustled off across the square by bodyguards whose step is quick enough to suggest they are not all of them human.

He looks down the Via again, and this time he sees the Premier—that pig—his motorcade already moving in reverse back toward the Castle Sant'Angelo. The timing has gone wrong.

Everything has gone wrong. Because of—

"Your mother was a whore," Anselmo breathes to the priest. "Your Virgin Mary was—"

A blast of water as thick as the spray from a fire hose makes hard contact with Lorenzo's shield of air, and there is a dispersal that turns the air damp from the force. They are evenly matched, turning loose what they have, this priest with his water against Lorenzo's air, and the stalemate is a distraction from everything Anselmo intends—

His gaze alights once more upon the fleeing motorcade, and he shakes Lorenzo by the shoulder, turning his attention back to what matters. "Forget the priest," he whispers. "We have more urgent matters to attend to." He spins his head to look at Fintan, who is now back on his feet, drooling water. "Keep this fool occupied," he says and sprints toward the Via della Conciliazione without so much as a look back. He shoves Lorenzo in front of him as the first shots from the Swiss Guards ring out, and he can feel the bullets upon his skin as others might feel the touch of a thrown pebble as he runs to catch the Italian Prime Minister's motorcade and fulfill at least one part of his plan. The pope, after all, will remain in his fortress, and can be dealt with later. But this?

This can still be done, very publicly—and very painfully.

75.

Reed

I shout ahead to Diana as I see Anselmo and Lorenzo coming our way. "You might want to get out your bow or whatever you've got hidden up your sleeve for this!"

"I use a bow when I want to be quiet," Diana says. Her hands fall into the pockets of her hoodie and come out bearing dual Micro-Uzis. "No need to be quiet now." She swoops ahead the last hundred feet and starts firing at Lorenzo, who barely gets his hands up in time. I see at least two bullets skim through his wind barrier and draw blood, but he manages to divert them into grazing wounds.

I see Anselmo charging ahead like a runaway bull, ignoring Diana and hauling ass with his full attention focused on the motorcade, and I suspect he's not going to so much as pause to swat me if I stand in his way. He's plowing over the few people from the crowd who are running in front of him, and it's not pretty. A few of them die immediately, others get injured pretty critically, and I know that somehow I need to stop this metaphorical running of the bull.

I halt in the middle of the avenue, dig in, and prepare myself. The sound of Diana's guns ripping off shot after shot, is hard to ignore, but I focus. I see Anselmo charging me down, not even really cognizant of the fact that I'm in his path, and I know for a fact if he keeps going that I'm going to end up exactly like everyone else he's callously run over in pursuit of his overarching goals. This dude does not give a shit about anyone but himself, and the rest of us are simply objects to be moved, used or ignored as he goes about his life.

I, for one, am not going to be moved for this ignorant lump. I sure as hell am not going to be used by his pathetic, inhuman ass.

And I'm a meta with the power of wind on my side, so the likelihood he's going to be able to ignore me is low, especially given what I'm planning.

I tap my power, channel it up from deep within, and start a vortex about ten feet ahead of him. It starts small, like these things do, just the drift of winds spinning. It gathers power as I add to it, though, thin threads of wind spun together. It gyrates as it grows, until it spins in a full circle, more force applied as it knocks aside the crowd and becomes a funnel cloud with no top.

When he's five feet away, I give it a little more kick, pouring all my power into it. I feel that ripping sensation down my arms even earlier this time, like I've run through all my reserves in record time. This isn't like making my own body hover, after all.

This is starting a tornado out of thin air.

The pain spreads into my chest and I scream in outrage and exertion as I give it a little something extra and Anselmo runs into it without stopping. I see him in the funnel, and his feet lift off the ground. His face dissolves into shock, and I watch him drift up to the top of the cone, legs ripped from beneath him oh-so-rudely.

"Got you, you son of a bitch," I whisper as I watch him drift twenty feet into the air, arms pinwheeling comically as he rolls helplessly in the midst of my—if I may say so— rather impressive feat of wind engineering. I doubt even Lorenzo has ever done something quite as cool as this.

And, I reflect as I let out a ragged breath, there's probably a reason for that. It hurts. A lot.

The vortex continues, though, standing tall in place, a perfect prison tower for Anselmo as he spins round and round. He looks kinda dizzy after the twentieth—or was it thirtieth? So hard to keep count—time around.

I am just thinking that a few more dozen go-arounds and the idiot will pass out, problem solved, when shit goes awry.

An off-center gust from outside the funnel disrupts the spin just enough—thanks, Lorenzo— that Anselmo tips a few degrees too far. Three spins later, he falls over the top and out. I'm on one knee, and cursing the luck as he lands on his head on the street and stands right back up, teetering wildly as he spins like he's still caught in the funnel.

He chucks in the street, and I fight the temptation to laugh. I'm glad I did a second later because he has a look of pure rage on his face—well, rage and a little nausea—as he continues to wobble, what looks like wine discoloring his chin. It's clear that I've done a number on his inner ear, but when his eyes alight on me, I still fear for my life for a moment, because he steadies enough that I know he's still a perfect killing machine even in his current condition.

Then his eyes slip past me and land on something else, and I chance a look back for long enough to know that the motorcade is still there, still in sight, in front of the Castel Sant'Angelo, and when I turn back he's already blasting past, ignoring me, the perennial dog that's focused on chasing his car to the exclusion of everything else.

And I sit there, exhausted, leaning on one leg for support, wondering how the hell I'm going to catch him before he kills the Prime Minister of Italy.

76.

Anselmo

He ignores the Treston boy, as satisfying as it would be to splatter his face along the Via della Conciliazione. It would be a short-term gain, a mindless revenge, the pursuit of a silly vendetta when the larger point is there to be won.

A whole damned war about to be won.

He sees the motorcade, mired in the crowds, snared in the running and panicking people. Here, the sheep have seen their shepherd coming toward them with his stick in hand, and they feel the fear, knowing that the crook will descend upon their backs. They bleat and run, but they cannot outrun their fear. Anselmo feels the thrill as he runs down the street, the car in front of him a target waiting to be smashed to pieces, that arrogant Premier and his empty promises of reform and putting the halt to people like Anselmo just seconds away from being exposed as nothing but hot air.

Anselmo reaches the end of the Via della Conciliazione, sees the Castel Sant'Angelo springing up to his left like the imposing fortress that it is. Here it stands, a foundation thousands of years old, improved upon by those who came later. It is like Italy, he thinks, and he is going to be the one that makes sure that his country stands timeless as the Castel. He will stand atop his nation, like the statue of the Archangel that is on the roof of the Castel.

An improvised Carabinieri barricade screeches into place in front of him, two of their pathetic little cars, as though they could block his passage. Anselmo hears laughter and realizes it is his own. He reaches their pitiful blockage and seizes hold of one of them, lifting it into the air, and he swings it around once before letting it loose like a hammer of old. It arcs through the air toward the motorcade, now trying to turn in the shadow of the Castel Sant'Angelo, at the end of their road. He watches as his throw falls closer and closer to home …

77.

Reed

I see the car fly as I'm about twenty paces behind Anselmo. He lets it go and it feels like it's moving in slow motion toward its target, a perfect toss that's going to catch the Prime Minister's motorcade before it can execute a three-point turn at the end of the Via della Conciliazione. It's trapped against the pedestrian-only walkway in front of the Castel Sant'Angelo, and Anselmo's toss is heading straight toward the Premier's limo, squarely in the middle of the two chase cars that comprise the motorcade.

And I feel almost powerless to stop it.

But I'm not. Not powerless.

I surge past Anselmo as he stands there, probably feeling an overwhelming sense of satisfaction for what he's just done. I sweep his legs as I pass. Invincible skin be damned, his ass goes down like a sack of potatoes. Gravity is a master even most metas have to obey, and Anselmo is no exception to this rule.

I keep running, though, and reach my hands out, far, far ahead. Farther than I've ever reached with my power before. It hurts like jagged glass, like cuts rolled in lemon juice, like fires in the veins, but I draw deep. Icepick to the heart, flames breathed into the lungs, acid sucked into my guts.

I start a vortex over the Prime Minister's car. It's weak compared to the one I just imprisoned Anselmo with. But it's what I've got.

Even as the thrown Carabinieri car begins to arc downward, I feel the stirrings. The winds begin to spin, to swirl, to howl. I need seconds, really, enough time for the motorcade—and specifically the limo—to get the hell going.

The Carabinieri car enters my tiny funnel at the top and wavers. Its downward path slows, it wobbles, spins—

And holds.

The funnel is churning, spinning madly in place. The car rolls in a hard circle, like a gyroscope, defying the downward pull of gravity. It stays there for a second, then two, then three, then five. The Prime Minister's limousine roars into gear, streaks off out of sight behind a building, chase cars in pursuit—

And the Carabinieri car comes down to earth as my vortex fades. It's not a gentle landing, but it's a survivable one for the occupants of the car, which is more than I can say for what Anselmo had planned.

I feel the last of my power drain out of me and I hit my knees, utterly exhausted. I feel a faint sense of triumph, because the Premier has escaped. The Pope has escaped. I've just taken a big damned loogie and hocked it right into the eye of—

Oops.

I feel the bull charge slam into my side and I go flying end over end down the Via della Conciliazione. My head tries to keep from entering conciliation with my ass as I roll. I feel my shoulder dislocate, and I finally come to an abrupt stop against the Carabinieri car I just saved. It takes me a minute to realize this, though, because I am beat all to hell.

"You little prick!" Anselmo says, his face alight with rage as he comes into view. I barely feel it as his hand wraps around my neck and lifts me into the air. His dark skin is nearly purple with anger now, and I feel the world go hazy as he squeezes tighter, the world around me darkening as he finally makes killing me his number one priority.

78.

I throw fingers at Anselmo's face and he doesn't even blink. I force power through them and blast him in the eyes with air, and he blanches just a little. It's kinda like that glaucoma test, the puff of air to the eyes, and it's uncomfortable at best.

Anselmo is not impressed, and it's obvious by the way he throws me again.

This time I'm slightly more in control of my flight path, and in spite of agonizing pains of all kinds, I manage to turn his rage-filled, unthinkingly hasty move into an advantage. I control the currents carefully, not exerting too much power, and gradually spin myself around as I come down for a relatively soft landing about a hundred yards away from him. It's a finesse move, something I wouldn't have been able to pull off at the top of my game a week ago. Now I'm doing it when I feel like I've exhausted everything in me.

If nothing else, Anselmo and Lorenzo have shown me exactly how much power I haven't tapped.

I keep my injured shoulder at the most comfortable angle I can find as I stare down the empty stone sidewalk that separates me from where Anselmo stands, still on the street. The space in front of the Castel is closed to traffic, and everyone around has fled, so I'm left staring at him with nothing but empty air separating us. "That all you got, old man?"

"I *am* a man," he shouts back, and he starts toward me with a purpose, walking with a fury that is evident in the way he maintains his stride. "You are a little boy, and you insult me, constantly—you are like a woman with—"

"Blah blah blah," I say, holding my ground. I start to tune him out, because it's always the same with him. It's pretty clear what he values and what he doesn't, and listening to him on a ramble is like taking a dose of misogynist toxin and pouring it in my ear. Pointless. Besides, I need him to get close. I've got one last card to play, and it's a doozy, but it won't work if all I do is circle around him.

At the same time, I doubt he's so feeble-minded he'll just assume he can catch me easily without being a little suspicious. Although I can hope.

"Do you know what I have done?" he shouts to me. He's about fifty yards away and closing. I'm holding myself at an awkward angle due to this injury, and I start to wonder how injured I can make myself look. I need to draw him in, but I need to keep a hand free. Since I only have one that's fully mobile and it's obvious to anyone with eyes to see me, this is going to be complicated.

"Other than totally failed in your objectives and embarrassed yourself in front of the whole world?" My sister is a master taunter, but I like to think I can throw some ego-bruising jibes when the occasion calls for it. "Demonstrated your basic lack of competence to everyone on the planet with access to cable news or the internet?"

He reddens noticeably, and since he's a pretty dark-complexioned fellow, this probably says worrying things about his blood pressure. He swears, something really bad, in Italian. *"Brutto figlio di puttana bastardo!"* I'm passingly familiar with the phrase, but it doesn't translate super well. He spins off in a rant as he comes at me, the only word of which I recognize is "mama."

He takes a wide honking swing at me. It's got a lot of power and it comes fast, but he telegraphs it a little too much, and I shoot into the air with a gust-aided jump before he connects. I hover above him as he stares up, apoplectic. "Hi," I say.

"I was to rule them all!" he screams at me in impotent fury. "'One ring to rule them all,' I have heard them say in your language!"

I frown down at him and wonder what the hell he's talking about. For all I know his brain has slipped off into la la land, quoting the *Lord of the Rings* at random and in a completely inapplicable situation. "Dude," I say, "what the hell are you talking about?"

"'Ndrangheta," he says, staring up at me like a cat waiting for a bird to land. "Cosa Nostra. Sacra Corona Unita. Camorra. Mala de Brenta. I will bind them all in the darkness, and they will be mine—"

Something he says rings (ha ha) a bell for me. His delusional nature is just sad at this point. "You think the whole country's organized crime is going to follow you after they just watched you fail this big on television?" I stare down, and he seems pathetic from here. "Man, your intellectual wine glass is empty. You have lost your mind, however you would say it in Italian." I'm still hovering over him, and I feel zero compunction to come down. My arms ache, but manageably.

"You are a fool and a boy!" he shouts, and starts looking around, presumably for something to throw at me. There's a vendor stand not far from where I'm hovering that looks promising, and I know that getting hit by that will pretty much be the sort of thing I won't be able to recover from, so I let one of my gusts sputter out.

I fall three feet and barely catch myself, letting my other gust sputter quickly. Anselmo watches me with a hungry look on his face. My injured shoulder lets me know that it hates me.

I'm now one good leap from Anselmo getting me, and he knows it. I feign trying to get away, letting the very real strain of my powers play across my face, and he does exactly what you'd expect a predator to do in this situation.

He jumps into the air and grabs me by the leg, dragging me back to the earth.

I cushion the landing as he tries to smash me into the ground with all his strength. He's trying with all his might to tug me down as soon as he gets his feet back on the ground, like a mule trying to drag a wagon. It's almost comical to watch from above, but I don't fight it too hard. He reaches up and snakes a hand around my neck and pulls me to him. I feel the force, the pain, the boa constrictor squeeze that tells me he's done playing and just wants me finished.

He drags me down to look in my eyes, and he knows with everything in him that he has me. The satisfaction drips off him like sweat in the cool morning air, and his smile grows wider as he prepares to end my life.

79.

"Do you expect me to talk, Poop-flinger?" I ask, finally coining my own little name for his cro-mag-style ape behavior.

He blinks at me, maybe astonished that I'm bothering to talk crap to him when he's so sure I'm about to get smothered.

I just stare back and let him drag me closer, my hand firmly behind my back until the last possible second, my James Bond gadget ready in hand. I rip it out and squint my eyes as shut as they can get before I trip the trigger. The world goes blazing white even through my lids, and his screams are so loud they probably just woke every corpse in the Vatican Necropolis. Or maybe Emperor Hadrian, if he'd still been in his old tomb behind me.

The light fades, and I blink the stars out of my vision as I open my eyes. Anselmo has let loose of me because he's figured out a more pressing need for his hands, and that's to scratch at his own eyelids as if doing it long enough will somehow restore his sight. Good luck, pal.

A string of Italian swear words rips through the air around me, and I maintain a healthy distance between myself and the Italian Stallion's ass (another nickname for him, these things are coming to me like crazy now) as he staggers about blindly. "What the—!" he screams in pain again. "What have

255

you done to me?" he asks once he finds his power of cogent speech again.

"Overwhelmed your optic nerves, probably," I say coolly then creep around behind him. I cut his legs out from underneath him and he hits the ground and begins rolling about wildly. I take a few steps back and let him, not really sure what to do now. "You know how they say you shouldn't look directly into the sun? I sort of delivered a bottled version of that experience directly to your retinas. Time to bind you in darkness, I think."

I stare down at the small light that fills the center of my palm. I'm not sure how James Bond it is, but it's a pretty cool little device overall. Pretty well guaranteed to blind a human being, but a meta? Well, we'll heal from it eventually.

I make a move to restrain him with the cuffs I have on the other side of my belt, but he's flailing madly. He's strong, too, strong enough that it'd cause me plenty of pain to tangle with him. I keep my distance and circle like he's a dog on the end of a chain, looking for an opening.

He blinks at me, and I realize that he's seeing me. He blinks again, those bleary eyes still focused on me, and the thought *Oh, shit* fills my mind yet again. How can he heal this damned fast?

Right. Top of the power scale. Seriously, though? Why couldn't I have been facing off with something on the low end of the power scale, like a meta with the power to slightly alter the curvature of light? Something useless.

He strikes out at me, and the sound of gunshots fills the air. I see a few hit him in the face, doing little more than distracting him. He turns his head to look, and so do I. Diana is sitting in the branches of a nearby tree, one of her Uzis pointed down at him.

I stare up at her. "Lorenzo?" I ask.

"He's experiencing some crippling pains in his arms and legs at the moment," she says and fires off another burst that hits Anselmo unerringly in the face.

He actually growls at her like the dog he is. "You think the two of you can stop me, with your little flashlight," he spits at me, "and your little cap gun? I am invincible. I am a god!"

Because of the way he's got his back to the river Tiber, Diana and I see it and he doesn't. He's ranting again, stomping, and behind him, a steady funnel of water is rising out of the river, guided by hands I can't even see. It's a column of water, thousands of gallons, and it stretches skyward like a temple of old rising over the city. It makes it to a height of almost a hundred feet before it tips and comes for him, perfectly steered to land on his head and swirl around him like it's constrained by some sort of aquarium.

I see him thrashing inside the makeshift prison as the water surrounds him. Anselmo claws at his throat, proving that even invincible, egomaniacal would-be gods have weaknesses.

I see Father Emmanuel striding forward, his hands raised high, fury and satisfaction etched on his features. "I baptize you with water," he says, "but the one who follows me will baptize you with the Holy Spirit."

Anselmo fights his way through the water, and it's a sight to behold. He breaks through the wall and staggers to the ground, vomiting forth water and bile as he does so. I silently congratulate myself on making him vomit before the priest even got here. Diana shoots him again for good measure, but I'm not sure he notices.

I make a move to cuff him, but he dodges me and staggers back toward the Castel. "You think you going to take me?" he asks. He thumps his chest, but he's walking backward, retreating the whole time. "You think you are man enough to stop me?"

"I think I already did," I say, and I keep coming. He's backing up furiously, his eyes floating from me to Diana to Father Emmanuel as we all advance on him. I feel like I could go about one round with a declawed elderly cat at the moment, but I won't let him know that. "Put your hands on your head and get on the ground like a good boy."

He screams fury at me and runs, but not in the direction I expect. He turns tail and sprints along the empty stones in front of the Castel Sant'Angelo.

"Shit," I say, and run after him, but I'm lagging right out of the gate. He hauls ass past the enormous jutting turret of the Castel and along the wall. Diana and Emmanuel are right with me, which makes me turn my head to look at Diana. She should be way out in front. She's hesitating, and I can't say I blame her. She's playing like she's part of a team, for once. "He's gonna get away," I say, Captain Obvious to the end.

He turns south in front of the Castel, then stops, doing a comical dance as he considers which way to go. I realize he's probably agonizing over the decision to cross the bridge if he goes south over the Tiber, because it will pretty much put him at Father Emmanuel's mercy. He goes east instead, sprinting along the siege wall that protects the Castel.

We lose time steering around the other turret, and by the time we clear it, he's almost a dot in the distance. He stops a car and throws somebody out, and he's gone in a squeal of tires. I curse and pull out my phone. J.J. is already there.

"Dude, you kicked his ass!" J.J. says. "Good job, way to go!"

"Not good enough," I say, and my breathing is ragged. "He's on the run. He's gonna get away."

"Relax, bro," J.J. says. "Like you said, you got him on the run."

"I have to finish this," I say, staring as I realize I am completely out of ways to beat this bastard. My entire body hurts, and I've just watched my culprit disappear. This is why Sienna kills her bad guys, I swear. I sag, falling to my knees, unable to stand any longer.

"It's gonna be okay," J.J. says, and there's sound on the earphone behind him that I can't make out, low voices. "It's all gonna be okay now." I can hear sirens blaring in the distance now, coming closer, but somehow, I just don't know how what he's saying can logically be right.

"Reed!" Dr. Perugini comes sprinting across the stones to my side. She drops to a knee and runs her fingers over my face, and I realize for the first time I'm bleeding. "Are you all right?"

"I'm fine," I say, "but the bad guy got away."

"Only one of them," Father Emmanuel says, looking down at me. "Fintan is restrained."

"So is Lorenzo," Diana says, though she doesn't look that happy about it. I know she wishes he were dead.

"And that leaves Anselmo," I say, staring at the corner he disappeared around. I feel Isabella's hands searching me for wounds, looking for injuries, but the only thing that matters is that the bad guy—my bad guy—got away.

80.

My back is sweating as the train rattles along, rolling through the Italian countryside. It's a few hours after the battle of Rome (it's my dramatic name for what happened; leave it be) and Isabella is at my side in the first-class car. The Italians appear to like it just a little hot, and the leather is sticking to me. The cabin attendant is moving around, bustling to the next compartment, and when he leaves, I lean over to her to say something.

"What?" she asks before I can.

"I was just thinking about what you said earlier," I say. "About how you'd tell me you loved me if—"

"You were going into battle," she says.

"Well, yes," I say. "But I had said that I know you think you're using me—"

She frowns. "Yes, yes. All this was said." I get the sense she's not comfortable with emotional discussions all of a sudden. Which is kinda funny.

"So I finally figured out how to describe what we've got going on here," I say, with a little hint of pride. I found the adjective. That's gotta be worth something, right? She looks at me with that one eyebrow cocked up in the air, like she can't decide if she's going to have to call me an idiot or not. "It's not love. It's convenience." I deliver it like it's a solemn proclamation of brilliance.

She stares at me for a moment, inscrutable, then shrugs. "That sounds about right."

I blink a little. "Uh. Good." That wasn't quite the answer I was hoping for. I was kind of hoping she'd refute it, say that, no, it's something new with rich possibilities for—

"You are making that face," she says, not looking at me, eyes on the magazine I just realize is in her lap as she waves a hand vaguely at me. In my defense, she is across the aisle, and I've been trying to compose this clever verbal trap to get her to admit to—well, something. Anything.

"You were a hell of a lot more than convenient to me," I say, exasperation leaking out. "You were ..." And I realize that I've played this wrong, and I go coy. Coy and smiling. "... Awesome. You were awesome. And hot." She looks up at me, and I see the irritation. Now she's hot in more ways than one. "Very hot?" I ask, playing like I'm trying to appease her. "Very hot and awesome?" I pretend to think for a second more. "Which also describes how it felt—"

"Oh, enough," she says, making an exasperated noise of her own as she tosses down her magazine. "Sometimes you are too expressive."

"Like how Muppet Yoda was actually more expressive than CGI Yoda," I say, nodding.

"This is not the most attractive side of you," she says, shaking her head. "No, not like a yodeler." I don't correct her, because this is not the moment to instruct the gorgeous Italian on SF/F geek blasphemy. "You are a little like a girl in this."

"Hey," I say, frowning. "If I'm a little more expressive, is that such a bad thing? I mean, I could be all buttoned up and one-hundred-percent testosterone-fueled battering ram like Anselmo, if you'd prefer—"

"Uck," she says. "Fine, convenience. Have it your way." She gestures in a way that stirs her lustrous black hair, and she picks up her magazine again. Another hilltop Italian village drifts by the window, and I have to wonder how many of those this country has. The answer? At least one more.

We make it through three more tunnels before she turns to me again. "Can you not just be happy with ... whatever this is for now?" Like we didn't just leave the conversation in the middle.

"I want more," I say, and I see her flinch a little, her lips pursing, dark eyes studying the magazine even though I know she's not reading it any more. "Because I kinda know you now. I know enough to know ... I want more of you, Isabella."

She gives me a slightly harried look and puts the magazine aside. "I will ... think about it," she says. And for now, that's enough for me.

81.

Anselmo stares out over the countryside, stroking his face and taking slugs of brandy. It runs hot, like his blood, and his mind swirls with anger and thoughts of his revenge.

The bottle is empty, and he tosses it over the ledge with a fury. He ignores the body of Niccolo, splattered upon the concrete where he left it. Others are scattered around the house where he found them. One of them betrayed him, surely. Niccolo brought him the messages from the others, filled with insults. Even Don George had sent one. So polite, yet the most insulting of all of them. Anselmo takes up another bottle and swigs directly from it. This one is wine, and he will finish it soon. He will drink the day away, lick his wounds as a man does, and then, tomorrow—

Treston will pay. Oh, yes. Anselmo will see him bleed, the little shit. Him, his little bitch, his little friends—Diana and the priest. Anselmo will see them all dead, them and the other *capos*, starting with Don George.

In the silence of the house, Anselmo hears a footstep. But this is impossible; the house is empty. He swivels, and drops the bottle.

He needs no time to lick his wounds.

The revenge can begin now.

263

"Hi, there, Anselmo," Treston says, smirking, standing at the edge of his pool. "You and I ... we've got unfinished business."

82.

Reed

I stare at him, his back to that marvelous vista of Florence at night. The sun is going down, and the sky is lit all orange, fiery hues turning it magnificent colors. Anselmo looks pissed, and I'm hardly surprised. He's an easy guy to read, after all, pretty much a one-track/one-emotion mind.

"Unfinished … business?" Anselmo manages to slur out. There are enough shattered bottles around him to tell me he's more than three sheets to the wind. "You have ruined … everything … in my business." He gestures to one of the nearest corpses. "There is only one response to this insult."

"Insecure dick wagging?" I ask helpfully. He stares in disbelief. "Just a guess, based on your responses up to this point. I mean, guy," I wave a hand up and down to encompass the whole of him, "you really put the Italia in genitalia, if you know what I mean—"

He bellows and charges at me, and a shock of water from the pool hits him a moment later, knocking him back and drenching him. A half dozen staccato shots pop him in the face as well and he staggers toward the edge of the patio, toward the edge. He blinks away the surprise and looks back. "You think this will kill me, this fall?"

"I doubt it," I say, not budging.

He waves a finger at Father Emmanuel. "You think this ... Poseidon? You think he can stop me?"

"He could probably drown you if he had to, yeah," I say. "But he won't." I glance back at Father Emmanuel, who gives me a nod of deference. "He's not that kind of guy."

"No," Anselmo agrees, still staggered. "Because you cannot stop me. Because you are weak. You are not even a man." He waves at my genitalia this time, then grabs his own. "You have nothing. I said it before, and I will say it again: I am invincible. I am a god—urk!"

It's at this moment that what I've been stalling for arrives, a streak out of the sky that smashes into him, seizing him by the back of the neck and slamming him into the concrete. I'm just a non-god, non-invincible guy, but it looks like it hurts to me.

"Hi, invincible," says the lady who's on his back like a bullrider, clenching an iron grip on his neck. "I'm Sienna, and I'm about to change your name to vincible." She squeezes him tighter, and I see him blanch with the pain. "Also, if you piss me off, I'll change your voice for you, *capische*?" She looks at me a little self-consciously. "They say that in Italy, right?"

I almost faint from exhaustion and the relief of seeing her arrive and take matters in hand. One hand, actually. "Took you long enough to get here."

"Hey," she says, a little crossly, "I fly plane-free all the way across the Atlantic for this level of gratitude? I'm cold, you know." She slams Anselmo's head into the concrete decking, and it makes an impression. I can see his eyes rolling as her power works on him. "Also, Yellowknife, Canada, to Minneapolis? Not a warm flight, either. Next time you have an emergency, do it in Aruba or something, will you?" She slams him down again, and I can tell by her demeanor she knows he's unconscious.

She stands up and stretches, dropping the annoyed act. "How you holding up, brother?"

I stare at Anselmo's unconscious body, then back to Diana, who looks jaded, and Emmanuel, who just looks relieved. "Fine now," I say, and I mean it. "Just fine."

83.

The plane meets us in Florence for the prisoner transfer a few hours later. All our orders come through Ariadne via the U.S. State Department. The Italian authorities are being extremely cagey, apparently not wanting anything to do with me or, by extension, us. Which is fine by me, since answering questions from police officers is not exactly something I'm excited about, in Italian or any other language.

Sienna and I take alternating turns guarding the prisoners at Anselmo's house, with the help of Diana and Emmanuel. By the time our plane arrives, we're all pretty exhausted and ready to bind the bastards up with every meta-restraining countermeasure available. We ride in enervated silence in the back of a van, with Carabinieri cars following en masse at a respectful distance. Dr. Perugini drives.

The whole time we're waiting, Isabella plays it ultra-cool with me. It takes me a bit to realize that she's still not happy with my sister. Right. Sometimes I forget that one. I don't know why; she's so damned endearing. They're probably just a little too similar for each other's tastes.

We're straight through the perimeter fence onto a runway where our plane awaits. Apparently they don't even want us passing through security. The plane's a big beast with military coloring that apparently came from one of our airbases over here. I drag Lorenzo out first, his hands completely shattered by someone (Diana) and a good dozen gunshot wounds that have yet to heal still oozing blood. He's chained nice and tight with meta-resistant cuffs, but I'm looking forward to seeing what the prisoner transfer unit has in mind for restraining him. J.J. has assured me that the U.S. Government is well-prepared to deal with meta prisoner transfers of this sort. I have my doubts.

They're proven unfounded. Which, if you think about it, is kind of worrisome.

I secure Lorenzo in an airtight container with atmospheric sensors that are designed to flood the chamber with anesthetizing gas at the slightest change in pressure. As I chain him into the chair, I wonder exactly why the government would have this stuff readily available—and modular—enough to stick on a military aircraft in Italy with minimal notice.

How many units like this must they have around the world?

It looks pretty new, I reflect as I watch a specially trained tech activate the machine. Little computers beep and boop as it powers up, and I stare in at Lorenzo. "Guess it doesn't really matter who she favored now," I say, and he looks up at me with a pissy attitude, "since it had pretty much zero bearing on who won our little struggle for dominance."

"Taunting the prisoners?" Sienna says from behind me. I turn to see her dragging Fintan along with one hand and carrying a still-insensate Anselmo with the other.

"Like you haven't done worse," I say.

"Lies," she says. "I have no prisoners." She wavers a little, but it's all a dramatic act. "Okay, well, lately I do. But in my heyday? No prisoners." She eyes Anselmo. "And if it were up to me, this little gem wouldn't be walking away."

"It's not up to you," I say calmly, and she shuffles toward the little chambers in the back dedicated to Fintan and Anselmo. She raises an eyebrow at me. "We take 'em alive. Government orders, remember?"

"I'll let you make the call because it's your collar, *technically*," she says, and I feel that itch that comes from my little sister oh-so-subtly rubbing it in that I needed her help to bag Anselmo. Apparently, she can be a little passive-aggressive after all.

Fintan and Anselmo are placed in gelatinous—I'm not even freaking kidding—liquid. I watch Fintan go in up to his neck, his face mashed all to hell (I guess Father Emmanuel gave him a serious what for in St. Peter's Square). The gel apparently cancels or suppresses metahuman motion to the point where our strength can't be applied. I watch them both drift for a few minutes, their cuffs still on, and it's interesting to watch. Anselmo goes in his own container, still not quite awake, which is just as well. I think he and I have said all we need to say to each other at this point.

The liquid runs along their jawline, and their toes barely touch the bottom of the container. I see Fintan try and squat down to see what it gets him. It gets him an eyeful of jelly, which, judging by his reaction, burns. He caterwauls for a while, yelling shit in Irish I don't really understand. Just another language I don't get the nuance of. Wait: is Irish a language?

"Prisoners secure," Sienna says, sighing relief. "We're ready for takeoff. You might want to say goodbye to your friends, unless they're coming along." She makes a kind of shooing gesture, another reflection of how excited she is to be in the company of people, and I take the hint to say my goodbyes.

"Diana," I say, as she looks around the plane like a caged animal trying to figure out how to break free. There are some other modules besides the ones we brought for the idiots three, and I get the sense she's going to be a lot happier once she's out of here. "Thanks for all the help."

She's stiff, but she manages a nod. "It was … good to be back in the righteous cause again. It was a good fight." She looks me up and down. "I will sleep well tonight, I think—

and Giuseppe will rest in peace." Then she grabs me by the front of my shirt and kisses me full on, with savagery. I think two things: number one, I hope Isabella doesn't see this. Two: I don't dare return it, I just play dead and hope she leaves eventually.

She does stop after a moment, and she pulls clear of me. "I'm not sure what that has to do with Giuseppe," I say.

The green eyes flash. "Next time, maybe," she says, and I feel like territory that someone just marked, like I've just been doused by the female version of Anselmo.

Bonus thought: Muscle control. Mine is totally dedicated to keeping from peeing myself at the idea of what that woman would do to me in a bedroom. Yikes.

I make my way back to where Father Emmanuel is lingering just next to the rear cargo door. I watch Diana go past him with barely a nod, and he catches my eye.

"Father," I say, and shake his hand when it's proffered. "Thank you."

"Thank you," he says.

I don't need a detailed explanation of what he's thanking me for; I'm kind of afraid to know, actually. "You're welcome," I say instead. "I'm just glad you decided to join us."

"I am just glad that you reminded me that a good man and holy man are not necessarily the same thing," he says. With a last nod, he heads down to the tarmac.

I glance back as I climb down the ramp. Sienna is milling around up near the front of the plane, staring at the crosshatched decking like it looks familiar or something. She's got the prisoners safely under watch, so I don't even feel bad for ducking outside for a minute. I'm even happier she can't watch me at the moment.

I make my way over to Isabella, who's waiting by the van, watching me coolly, her arms crossed in front of her, dark hair blowing lightly in the wind. Her sunglasses are impenetrable, and the fact that she's wearing a skirt in this weather suggests she's at least a little acclimated to Minneapolis at this point. And she looks very good in said skirt, I might add.

"Thanks for waiting," I say as I lean against the van next to her. She doesn't look over at me, still playing it cool.

"I'm going to stay with family over here for a few days," she says, matter-of-factly. "Would you tell Ariadne I'll be back to work next week?"

"I can do that," I say, wondering if she's just going to give me a message and say not a thing more. She hasn't really spoken to me since our conversation on the train, after all. "Have you ... thought about what I said at all?"

She looks sidelong at me, the glasses maybe defraying 20% of what looks like aggravation. "Have you thought about thanking me for coming over here and helping you with your very obvious problems?"

"I've thought about it," I say slyly, "but I'm afraid it'll lose something in the translation." Using my meta speed, I quickly kiss her before she can get her argument out.

It sort of works. She frowns at me. "Did you kiss someone else?"

"No," I say a little darkly, "but Diana tried to cram her tongue down my throat. Unsuccessfully, I might add."

She still frowns. "And then you try and kiss me?"

That gives me pause. "More successfully, I might hope?" Lots of uncertainty.

She narrows her eyes. "You are young." She shakes her head. "This was my concern when we started. I am ... over fifteen years older than you." I sense she's maybe being a little cagey on the actual number; she'd have seen my file and know the specifics in my case.

"Well," I say, "I did just have a woman a little older than you—by several thousand years—try and kiss me with a little more enthusiasm than you exhibited just now, so I would take the lesson of experience there if I were you."

She glares at me, and the glasses, they do nothing to hide it. "You are so very terrible at this. So very terrible."

"I'm … young," I say, and it sounds like a flimsy excuse to me. "I'm … lacking experience."

She looks at me skeptically. "Not that I could tell. Or are you a gifted amateur?"

"Not there," I say hurriedly, "I mean … in relationships. I've been moving around most of my life, since my dad died. Lived with mom for a while, with grandparents, with found family, sort of … but I didn't …" I sort of wave my hands like I can't get it out. "I'm not … experienced like that."

"You are young," she says with a nod, and leans back against the van with me. "And blown on the wind, eh? In this way … maybe we are alike." She looks slightly uncomfortable. "And in relationships, perhaps I am a bit young in experience as well."

I look over at her. "Really?"

She wavers a bit. "Perhaps it is not obvious, but I have an occasionally off-putting personality." I can see her looking at me through the glasses, waiting to see my response.

I don't give her a hint. "Huh. You and I always seem to get along well enough." That much is true.

She seems to be thinking about it for a minute. "It is possible we could try." She looks over at me. "When I get back. Perhaps we could … get to know each other. Slowly."

"I like the sound of that," I say, giving her a smile.

"Do you?" she asks. "Are you ready for a grown-up relationship?" I sense she's testing me, poking at me a little, like the thought of being immature would be enough to sting me. But over the last few days, I've been called "boy" more times than I can count by a pig who thought it was the epitome of insults. Well, other than calling someone a woman.

I just smile at her, my little insecurity all gone. "I'm willing to change," I say, and I mean it.

84.

"So that was Janus's sister?" Sienna asks, letting out a low whistle. She looks exhausted, the bags under her eyes full enough to keep her clothed for a week's vacation. "Why does she look so good when he looks so damned old?"

"I thought older guys looked sexy?" I ask. We're in seats in the front of the cargo plane, rattling along. It's the single roughest damned flight that I've ever been on, and the bathroom is—seriously—a curtained off area at the rear of the plane. It smells worse than the can in Giuseppe's shop. I'm determined to hold it in for the entire trip.

"Ewww," she says, shaking her head. "Janus is just old, not silver-foxy. He's like a dad-type." She hesitates. "Uh … not that I think he looks like Dad." I can tell by the look on her face she's uncomfortable; she never even saw our father, after all; she only has old photos to go by. She leans a little closer, and drops her voice so low that it becomes a conspiratorial whisper. "So … you slept with her?"

I blink. "Uhm …"

She nudges me with her shoulder. "Come on. I know you did."

"Who?" I ask, blinking. "Diana?"

"So," Sienna says, smiling, "how did it feel, sleeping with one of the wonders of the ancient world?"

I'm pretty flabbergasted, and a little relieved she thinks I slept with Diana, because I doubt Isabella would be happy to

274

hear me discussing what happened between the two of us with her worst enemy. I know my reaction is giving something away, but I'm not sure what. "I, uh …"

The overhead speakers fill the cargo hold with a sudden burst of static. "Say again, Florence tower?" I realize a second later it's our captain speaking, but he's not exactly making an in-flight status update. It's a radio transmission in real-time, and the other party clicks on a second later.

"U.S. military flight, please follow your current heading out to the Mediterranean Sea," the voice says, thickly accented. "From there, you must remain over international waters for your entire flight."

"Negative, Florence tower," our pilot says, and I realize he's broadcasting this down here for our benefit. "We're to head—"

"You are not to cross European Union sovereign airspace," the voice says sharply. "You are not welcome here with your current passengers."

"You talking about our prisoners, Florence Tower?" the pilot asks. "Because they are secure—"

"Negative, U.S. military flight," comes the reply, a little slower this time, almost like they're savoring it. "Brussels has issued new regulations—after the incident today in Rome, metahumans will no longer be allowed in the European Union. Do not deviate from your present course. We have fighter escort at—" The speaker clicks off, presumably because our pilot has made his point. It's an elegant one, that's for sure. I wonder if he'd heard the chatter in advance before the tower radioed him.

"Aw, hell," Sienna says, looking over at me, "you broke the whole EU."

A week ago, this sort of thing might have really bothered me. Okay, it still does, at least a little. But maybe not as much as it would have before this. I just sigh, throw up my hands, and shake my head. "Just as well," I say, going the path of sarcasm, "I was never gonna be able to top this trip anyway."

And I turn and look across the cargo bay at the prisoners, and that little sense of insecurity is pretty much all gone. Because the EU or Italy can blame me—and every other meta—as much as they want; these three guys would have made a hell of a lot bigger mess if I hadn't been there to stop them.

"Is that all you've got to say for yourself?" Sienna asks, and I can tell by the snark that she's just playing at this point. She's not blaming me at all. "For shame, you dirty meta with your clearly evil intent."

"Yes," I say, "shame on me, for sticking my nose where it clearly doesn't belong." Anselmo is now awake and kicking in the goo. He's having zero luck, too, and it's almost fun to watch. It's like a souped-up version of Father Emmanuel's water prison for him.

"Good thing we're heading home," Sienna says, and the snark is just flowing, "where everyone loves us and no one ever thinks bad things about us or our kind." She lets that sit for a moment, the loud, ambient noise of the cargo hold rumbling around us. When she speaks again, her voice is a lot smaller. "Do you think ... it'll ever change?" And it's the voice of a child, of insecurity, of someone who wants to be told it'll all get better.

It's the voice of my little sister.

The only family I've got.

"It'll get better," I say, the voice of confidence. "Absolutely." And we settle back for the rest of the flight in peace.

Sienna Nealon Will Return in

RUTHLESS

**Out of the Box
Book Three**

Coming March 31, 2015!

Note From the Author

Okay, so that was Reed's story. It did not come out quite like I thought it would, to be honest. I realized something about him pretty quickly: Reed is a really good second banana, but he didn't have the confidence yet to lead like Sienna developed throughout the Girl in the Box series. But he hides it really well. Next book, we're back to Sienna, though we'll see a little more from Reed in Book #5 (Tormented), where he and his sister will split the narrative duties (for a very good reason, I swear). However, that story won't be in present tense. In fact, I can pretty well promise you I won't be writing in present tense ever again. This was purely for experimental purposes. Also, while Limitless and In the Wind were able to somewhat stand on their own (I might have put a couple little seeds in them for future harvest), Out of the Box #3 will begin a new storyline that will last about four books and culminate in...well, death and destruction, of course. This is one of my books, after all.

I've set a release date for book three. I make no promises about doing this for future installments. If you want to know when future books become available, take sixty seconds and sign up for my NEW RELEASE EMAIL ALERTS by visiting my website at www.robertjcrane.com. Don't let the caps lock scare you; I don't sell your information and I only send out emails when I have a new book out. The reason you should sign up for this is because I don't like to set release dates (it's this whole thing, you can find an answer on my website in the FAQ section), and even if you're following me on Facebook (robertJcrane (Author)) or Twitter (@robertJcrane), it's easy to miss my book announcements because...well, because social media is an imprecise thing.

Come join the Girl in the Box discussion on my website: http://www.robertjcrane.com !

Cheers,
Robert J. Crane

ACKNOWLEDGMENTS

My thanks to these fine folks, without whom this book would not be possible:

Sarah Barbour, Jeff Bryan and Jo Evans – Editorial clean-up crew.

Nicolette Solomita – First reader.

Brian and Jean Elms and Kombe Ngari – For their excellent assistance on developing the character of Father Emmanuel.

Karri Klawiter – Cover by.

Polgarus Studios – Formatting.

The fans – For reading.

My parents, my kids, my wife – For all their help.

About the Author

Robert J. Crane is kind of an a-hole. Still, if you want to contact him:

Website: http://www.robertJcrane.com
Facebook: robertJcrane (Author)
Twitter: @robertJcrane
Email: cyrusdavidon@gmail.com

Other Works by Robert J. Crane

The Sanctuary Series
Epic Fantasy

Defender: The Sanctuary Series, Volume One
Avenger: The Sanctuary Series, Volume Two
Champion: The Sanctuary Series, Volume Three
Crusader: The Sanctuary Series, Volume Four
Sanctuary Tales, Volume One - A Short Story Collection
Thy Father's Shadow: The Sanctuary Series, Volume 4.5
Master: The Sanctuary Series, Volume Five
Fated in Darkness: The Sanctuary Series, Volume 5.5*
    (Coming in 2015!)
Warlord: The Sanctuary Series, Volume Six* (Coming in late
    2015!)

The Girl in the Box
and
Out of the Box
Contemporary Urban Fantasy

Alone: The Girl in the Box, Book 1
Untouched: The Girl in the Box, Book 2
Soulless: The Girl in the Box, Book 3
Family: The Girl in the Box, Book 4
Omega: The Girl in the Box, Book 5
Broken: The Girl in the Box, Book 6
Enemies: The Girl in the Box, Book 7
Legacy: The Girl in the Box, Book 8
Destiny: The Girl in the Box, Book 9
Power: The Girl in the Box, Book 10

Limitless: Out of the Box, Book 1

In the Wind: Out of the Box, Book 2

Ruthless: Out of the Box, Book 3* (Coming March 31, 2015!)

Grounded: Out of the Box, Book 4* (Coming June 2015!)

Tormented: Out of the Box, Book 5* (Coming September 2015!)

Vengeful: Out of the Box, Book 6* (Coming December 2015!)

Southern Watch
Contemporary Urban Fantasy

Called: Southern Watch, Book 1

Depths: Southern Watch, Book 2

Corrupted: Southern Watch, Book 3

Unearthed: Southern Watch, Book 4* (Coming Early 2015!)

* Forthcoming and subject to change

Made in the USA
Middletown, DE
10 December 2018